NO ONE
TO TRUST

Books by
Lynette Eason

NO ONE TO TRUST

A NOVEL

LYNETTE EASON

Revell

a division of Baker Publishing Group
Grand Rapids, Michigan

Published by Revell
a division of Baker Publishing Group
P.O. Box 6287, Grand Rapids, MI 49516-6287
www.revellbooks.com

Printed in the United States of America

Library of Congress Cataloging-in-Publication Data
Eason, Lynette.
    No one to trust : a novel / Lynette Eason.
        p.   cm. — (Hidden identity ; book 1)
    ISBN 978-0-8007-2208-1 (pbk.)
    1. Missing persons—Fiction. 2. Murder—Investigation—Fiction. I. Title.
PS3605.A79N83 2014
813'.6—dc23   2013031326

Lyrics for "Wake" © 2004 Jack Eason, U.R. Worthy Music/ASCAP. Performed by Jupiter Wind. Used by permission. All rights reserved.

14   15   16   17   18   19   20   7   6   5   4   3   2

Dedicated to my fabulous editor, Andrea Doering,
and my super agent, Tamela Hancock Murray
of the Steve Laube Agency.

Thank you for believing in me and my stories!

PROLOGUE

SATURDAY MORNING
8:02 A.M.
NEW YORK CITY

"You killed him!" David Hackett pulled his fingers from the still pulse of the man who lay sprawled on his partner's office floor. Blood pooled beneath the man's head and his empty eyes stared, fixed on the ceiling.

Sam Gilroy slid the gun into the top drawer of his desk and sat down in the leather chair. "It's Saturday. You weren't supposed to be here this morning."

"Well, I am!" He'd heard the gunshot from his office across the hall and burst through the door to find . . . this. A sight his brain was having trouble processing.

Sam spread his hands. "He was going to the building inspector. I couldn't let that happen."

"Going to the inspector about what?" David stepped aside to avoid the blood. This was not happening. It was a bad dream and he was going to wake up any minute.

But no. His partner studied him. "I caught him going through my laptop. He found out about some of the materials we've been using to build with, claimed they were substandard, and said it had to be stopped. I assured him everything was aboveboard, but he was having none of it. Said he had proof and was going to shut us down."

David swallowed hard. He'd just learned about the substandard materials and had been trying to decide what to do about it. One of the reasons he'd come in to the office this morning. Sam usually worked Saturday mornings and David had been planning on confronting the man. Only, he'd gone to his office first. To plan, figure out how to approach Sam. Now a man was dead because of his hesitation. Sickness filled him. "So . . . murder?"

"You have a better idea?" Sam's hands shook when he clasped them in front of him on the desk. David realized his partner wasn't quite as unaffected as he was trying to portray. "Look, you know as well as I do, if we hadn't found cheaper suppliers, this company was going under."

"That's just not true. When I left for my last assignment overseas, we were doing great, had a comfortable profit margin." He'd been gone longer than usual, that particular mission a delicate operation that had gone wrong in so many ways. By the time he'd come home, Sam had made some catastrophic business decisions. David rubbed a hand down his face. "I can't believe this." He paced from one end of the office to the other, careful not to step in the blood staining the wood floor. "Do you know who his father is?"

"I know who he is. Trust me, he won't be a problem. Don't worry about it."

David stared at Sam. "Trust you? Don't worry about it? There's a dead guy on the floor of your office and you're sitting there like you're about to have tea with the queen. What about his family? He's got three kids, Sam."

Sam placed his hands on the desk and leaned forward. "Then he should have kept his nose out of my business." Sam shot him a ferocious frown. "What's wrong with you? It's not like you've never killed anyone."

David flinched and held in his vicious desire to wrap his hands around the man's throat. "I was in the Army, Sam. I didn't kill anyone who wasn't trying to kill me." And he still saw their faces in his dreams. David made an effort to unclench his jaw. "I was protecting our country so people like you could sit in a fancy office and make money hand over fist." He glanced at the man on the floor. "And we'd still be doing that if you'd kept things status quo."

"It's your money too, partner." Sam shot him a sly look. "Or have you gambled it all away in the six months you've been home?"

David had to leave or he was going to do great bodily harm to the man he'd once considered a friend. But he had to know. "What are you going to do with him?"

"Get rid of him. The Hudson River has swallowed its share of evidence over the years. One more piece won't be a big deal."

David sucked in a deep breath. How did Sam sleep at night? David admitted he'd done a lot of rotten things in his life, even things that were borderline illegal. And yes, he'd killed in self-defense, but he'd never murdered anyone. Unsure of his next move, he shook his head and headed for the door. "Just make sure when he's found, it won't come back to bite us."

"Who says he'll ever be found?"

David stared at Sam for a moment, then lowered his gaze to the dead man. "Right."

1

He'd been found, and if he didn't think fast, he was dead.

Computer technician Kyle Abernathy didn't move from his position under the desk as he formulated a plan. His brain moved at light speed and his pulse pounded with the sudden rush of adrenaline.

He never imagined installing a computer would be the thing to save his life. Kyle scooted a little farther under the desk, yet not so far he couldn't see. Satisfied he was hidden from anyone looking in his direction, Kyle plugged in the last cord and watched the man with the square jaw and blond hair stop to question one of the workers in the cubicle across from the bathroom.

Corbin Hayes, one of Alessandro Raimondi's cohorts. Kyle would have recognized him anywhere—even though over a year had passed since he'd last seen the man.

The question was, how had Corbin known where to look for Kyle?

He pulled his cell phone from the back pocket of his pants. Getting out and finding a safe place should be priority. But he wasn't thinking of himself. He was thinking of his wife, Summer. Beautiful, innocent Summer.

The thought of them finding her made him nauseous. Kyle was three hours away from home. He'd planned to drive home early and surprise her, as she wasn't expecting him until tomorrow morning. But he'd finished this job ahead of schedule and was ready to see his wife.

Now she was in danger and he had to get to her and get her away from the threat that was sure to come. If it hadn't already.

He glanced at the touch screen and pressed the numbers that would send the distress signal to his handler, Mike Thomas. Then he rose with caution, his plan to slip out unseen, call Summer to get somewhere safe, meet her there, and wait for Mike to call him.

Kyle gripped the phone and waited to see which way Corbin would go. The man turned right toward the CEO's office. Kyle went left, grateful the CEO had been busy on his phone twenty minutes ago and had motioned for Kyle to come back later.

Only later would never happen for Mr. CEO. It was time for Kyle to disappear again.

The only problem was, Corbin Hayes never traveled alone. Kyle glanced around and saw no sign of anyone else that had Kyle's demise in mind.

That bothered him. Did Corbin have his goons covering all of the doors? Possibly.

He backed toward the exit, knowing he had to chance it. It wouldn't be the first time he'd been in a tight spot and had to fight his way out.

His back touched the stairwell door that led to the parking garage. His mind filtered through questions he had no answers for. Did they know which car was his? Was someone watching it? Had they already planted a bomb on it?

No, they wanted him alive.

For the moment.

If he died too fast, they couldn't torture him.

Or use Summer to get information from him. To find out exactly how much he knew and what he'd told the authorities.

Corbin stepped out of the CEO's office and Kyle had no choice. He backed out the door and spun to face the stairs, ready to defend himself.

Blood rushed through his veins, adrenaline kicking along. The area before him was empty. He took a deep breath.

The door clicked shut behind him. Up or down?

Up led to the roof where he could be trapped.

Down led to the car and escape. Or where Corbin's men could be waiting.

He went down. He had to get to Summer.

Kyle descended the stairs on light feet, senses tuned in to the air around him. Danger pulsed. Fighting instincts surfaced, making his nerves hum. At the bottom, he stopped and took a slow, deep breath. He listened.

Heard nothing. No pounding feet above him. Nothing outside the door.

He pushed the door open and stepped into the parking garage, unclipped his name tag from his shirt pocket, and ditched it in the nearest trash can. Next went any IDs in his wallet. He couldn't afford to have any identification on him should he be caught. The car was registered to a young man who'd died three years ago. When there was nothing on him that could lead anyone back to Summer, Kyle headed for the vehicle. His breath became visible, the temperature was dropping. The middle of November had arrived with a cold front, but his shiver didn't have anything to do with the weather.

Footsteps of people hurrying to their cars on a Thursday afternoon at five o'clock. Kyle didn't bother to relax. Corbin wouldn't let a few people get in his way of kidnapping Kyle in broad daylight.

A woman with a toddler in her arms hurried past him.

A man with a briefcase in one hand and a cell phone attached to his ear stood at the driver's door of a black Lexus.

Kyle's gaze darted, registering faces, expressions, body language. So far, he was in the clear.

He made it to the black Honda, slid behind the wheel, and cranked the vehicle. As he backed from the parking spot and headed out of the garage, his gut hurt. It had been too easy.

Something wasn't right.

He dialed Summer's number and waited. Then realized his phone wasn't working. He tried again as he dodged cars in the left lane while watching the rearview mirror for a tail.

The phone still didn't ring. With a groan of fury, he felt the first stirrings of real fear. They'd jammed his phone, cut off his service, whatever. "How?" he whispered. Had Mike gotten his trouble call? If not, that meant Summer wouldn't even get a warning that danger was heading for her doorstep.

He made a left turn, got a quick flash of silver a second before the car slammed into the passenger side of the Honda. Kyle heard the crunching sound of metal on metal, felt the airbag explosion slam into his face. Blackness threatened. Bolts of pain shot through his head and down his neck.

His heart thudded, not for fear for himself, but for the woman he'd come to love. The woman who'd said, "I can take almost anything, Kyle, but don't ever, ever lie to me. I could never forgive that."

The woman who was about to find out his entire existence—and hers—was a lie.

2

Summer Abernathy opened her eyes to find a gun pointed at her face. A scream formed as she lifted her gaze to a pair of onyx eyes set in the granite face of the man who held the weapon.

"Good morning, sunshine," he said.

Summer choked down the cry as her mind scrambled to find the appropriate response. Her insides froze as her peripheral vision told her he hadn't come alone.

He lifted a brow at her silence. "I'm disappointed. That's all the reaction I get?"

Summer simply looked at him, her vocal cords refusing to cooperate.

He frowned. "Can you speak?"

Somehow she forced the words from her paralyzed throat. "I usually have a little trouble finding words when I wake to strangers in my bedroom and a gun in my face."

Surprise blinked across his face and he barked a short, amused laugh as dark bushy brows pushed up into his hairline. "You're spunky. I think I like that."

"Who are you?"

"That's not important. Where's your husband?"

"My hus—? Kyle?" Only then did she look at his side of the bed. It hadn't been slept in. Her brain fought through quicksand. "I . . . I don't know." These guys were obviously not cops. Which meant they were working for the other side. Summer clenched her jaw. "He's on a . . . a business trip." But he was due home early this morning. In fact he should have slipped into the bed next to her about two hours ago so they could start their long weekend together. They'd had this day planned for two weeks. There was no way he'd miss it if he were physically capable of being by her side.

A desperate fear for the man she loved consumed her.

The phone rang, nearly shattering her nerves. She reached for it, only to stop when the man next to the door stepped forward, his threatening stance clear.

"It might be Kyle."

"Look at the number."

She did and her heart sank. "It's not him." It was her sister, Marlee.

It rang three more times before it went to voice mail.

The man with the weapon spoke. "I need to find your husband. He has something that belongs to my boss, and my boss wants it back." His eyes slid down her in a way that made her skin crawl. She clutched the covers to her chin and glared.

"What does he have?" she asked, trying to hide the terror shivering through her. She did her best to ignore the gun still pointed at her face and raked a hand through her hair. Her mind spun. There were three of them. The one with the gun and two others who stood on either side of her bedroom door. Her heart thudded. "I think you have the wrong house, the wrong person. Kyle would never be mixed up in anything . . . ," she paused and bit her lip, "um, illegal."

The phone rang again. Summer knew it was Marlee. Her sister knew she was home and would keep calling until Summer picked up.

With a curse, the man spun and knocked the phone from the table, then yanked the cord from the wall. He turned to his partner nearest the door. "Disconnect any other phones in the house."

Seeing the instant obedience of the other man, Summer lifted her eyes to the only one who'd spoken. The one with the weapon trained on her.

He leaned forward, the gun moving closer.

Summer refused to shrink away, even as his minty breath brushed her cheek.

"You asked me who I am. My name is Corbin Hayes," he said. "And your husband was very much involved in something illegal." A red flush started at the man's neck and moved up. "Like I said, he stole something from my boss and I'm here to get it back."

The gun lowered and he moved away from her. Summer drew in a breath but didn't feel any relief as she knew he wasn't leaving yet.

He flicked the weapon toward the picture of the two children she kept on her dresser. "Nice-looking kids."

Her heart pounded and she kept silent.

He picked up the picture and pointed the barrel at an older picture of Laura Todd at age ten. "Would be a shame for something to happen to the little ones."

"You leave them alone." The thought of something happening to those children cramped her stomach. They weren't hers, but they were the reason she did what she did, why she fought as hard as she fought to win the cases that were important. As a family court lawyer, she handled some of the most delicate cases that involved precious, innocent lives.

Cases like the one they were involved in.

Hayes handed the gun to his cohort, who in turn passed him a very wicked-looking knife.

Fear glued her tongue to the roof of her mouth.

Hayes turned the knife over and tested the sharpness of the blade with a chewed fingernail. A piece of his nail flaked off. Summer couldn't blink, couldn't move, couldn't fight. She was completely outnumbered.

Lord, help me!

"Grab her hand," Corbin ordered.

"No!" Fighting them would be futile. *Think! Think!* "What do you want? Just tell me!"

Those hard black eyes slid back to hers as the man on her left grabbed her wrist in a brutal grip. The knife settled at the base of her left pinkie. A sob threatened and she choked it back. Were they going to take her finger and let her live? Or were they going to kill her slowly, piece by tiny piece?

Nausea threatened. She held it back by sheer will. "Please . . . ," she whispered, keeping her gaze locked on his. The other brute's grasp on her wrist had just about cut off all feeling in her hand. "I'll do anything."

"Anything?"

"Yes. What do you want?"

The blade pressed. "I want the laptop he stole and the flash drive that goes with it."

"Okay! I'll get them!" A stinging sensation started in her pinkie finger and darted up her arm as a warm, sticky wetness tickled the side of her hand. She wanted to struggle, to scream, to fight. But why waste her energy when she could clearly see the end result? Summer closed her eyes as she waited for the agonizing pain of having a finger cut off.

But it didn't come. Instead, the blade lifted. She opened her eyes and blinked to clear her gaze of the tears that now dripped down her cheeks.

Hayes asked, "Where are they?"

"I don't know." The blade returned and she screamed, "But I'll find them! I'll look everywhere, I . . . I promise."

"You have twelve hours." He glanced at her clock. "I'll be back at 8:36 tonight." His gaze raked her once again and she prepared herself for a fight of another kind.

His fingers touched the base of her throat and Summer swallowed hard but refused to shrink away. She knew he could see her fear, feel the pounding of her heart, beating like the wings of a hummingbird beneath his fingers.

He lifted the necklace Kyle had given her for their one-month anniversary. An ornate silver cross. A sign of their shared faith. Hayes turned it one way, then the next. "Lovely," he murmured. "Such an intricate design." He dropped it and it thudded against her throat, feeling heavy—and defiled. She swallowed.

"You're very beautiful," he whispered.

Nausea churned again. "Get. Away. From. Me."

His lips curled, his eyes glinted with a wicked light, and Summer caught her breath, wondering if he had something even more sinister planned for her. She lifted her jaw.

And then he moved away from her. The man holding her wrist released her. The two silent partners backed toward the door. Summer sat shivering, trembling, clasping her whole hand to her chest.

Hayes, the last to leave, turned suddenly and she nearly shrieked. But he didn't approach her.

"Don't call the police," he said. "If you do, we'll know because we'll be watching you." He held up a finger and waved it at her. "And just for your information, your husband's name isn't Kyle Abernathy, it's David Hackett." He smirked. "Google him."

3

FRIDAY
8:40 A.M.

David groaned and tried to move, but his body wouldn't cooperate. Steady beeping echoed in his ears, aggravating him, exacerbating the pain in his head. Nausea swirled.

"Sir? Are you awake? Can you hear me?"

David wanted to answer but couldn't get the words out.

He might have grunted.

"Are you in pain?"

Yes! What happened? Where was he? Antiseptic, the smell of . . . sterile. Alcohol. A hospital.

"You've been in a car wreck."

Memory returned with the force of a tsunami.

He remembered the flash of silver before the horrific jolt against the seat belt.

And he remembered Corbin Hayes.

Summer!

David struggled against the pain, against whatever held him to the bed. He had to get to Summer.

"Sir, calm down." To someone near the bed, she said, "His heart rate is dangerously elevated."

20

"Let's sedate him for now."

"No . . . please . . ." David heard his low rasp that no one else noticed.

He wanted to weep, but uttered a desperate prayer to the God he'd only known a short time.

As he drifted back toward the black void of nothingness, he prayed for Summer, begging God to keep her safe.

8:45 A.M.

Summer leaped from the bed, raced into the bathroom, and lost what little she had in her stomach. She sank to the bathroom floor and cried until she wondered if she'd ever stop. Finally, she splashed water onto her face.

"Stop crying and think," she muttered. "Think. Now." *God, tell me what to do, please!*

As she cleaned and bandaged her finger, her thoughts swirled. Where was Kyle? Why hadn't he come home? Had someone in their organization found him and the guys who invaded her home just didn't know it? No. They would communicate better than that. Wouldn't they?

And who were *they*?

Her best guess was Mafia, but she wasn't sure. Her experience was family court, not criminal law. But she was smart enough to recognize evil when she saw it.

A shudder rippled up her back.

Members of the Mafia. In her bedroom. Looking for Kyle and threatening her. Could it be?

Maybe. Maybe not. After all, this was South Carolina, not New York or Chicago. She rubbed a hand down her face as she forced her mind to work.

No. Whoever they were, they were lying. They had the wrong

person. Kyle would never do what they'd accused him of. Because if he had, that meant that he'd lied to her and he'd promised he'd never do that. He'd sworn to it.

Still shivering, she stumbled back into the bedroom and snatched the cordless phone from the base. Then remembered she had to plug it back in. It took her four tries, but she finally managed to get her quivering fingers to cooperate. Once she had a dial tone, she pressed 9-1, then stopped. He'd said not to call the cops. He would know.

How?

Would he really know?

What if he had her phone tapped? Could she take the chance?

She slammed the phone down and sat back on the bed to think. Summer looked at the clock. Twenty minutes had passed since she'd experienced her meltdown. Tremors shook her, but they would fade. It was time to push past the terror and focus, to figure out what to do. She found her purse, pulled the cell phone out, and punched in Kyle's phone number. "We're sorry, this number is no longer in service."

A new fear clutched her.

She tried again and got the same message. By the fourth time, she accepted she wasn't going to get through.

As soon as she hung up, the phone rang. She gasped and looked at the caller ID.

Her sister. Summer groaned, dropped the phone on her bed, and let the call go to voice mail once again. She rose to pace the bedroom, her mind spinning. A laptop.

Where would Kyle—or was it David—hide one? No, of course it wasn't David. His name was Kyle. They had the wrong person. Right?

For the first time since they'd left, doubt crept in. He'd said, ". . . your husband's name isn't Kyle Abernathy, it's David Hackett." He knew Kyle's name. He knew he was her husband.

22

Google him.

All right, she would. In a minute.

Summer grabbed her cell phone and found Kyle's work number. She paused. What if *they* could listen in on her cell phone?

She had to chance it. She pressed Send.

"Top Choice Software."

"Stacy, this is Summer. I'm trying to reach Kyle and his work phone has been disconnected. Is he there?" She didn't believe it for a minute, but didn't want to set off any alarms in case *they* were listening.

"Hi, Summer. No, Kyle hasn't been in this morning. Hold on, let me check his schedule." Summer heard rustling, a keyboard clicking. "He's been in Charlotte this week and had today off, remember?"

"Oh, right." Summer pressed for the information she was really after. "What company was he working with in Charlotte? I'll just give them a call and see if he said anything to anyone about staying late." Stacy paused and Summer could almost hear the questions forming in the woman's brain. "We have a little family emergency," Summer said. "And I just need to talk to him."

"Is everything all right?"

Summer grasped hard for patience. Keeping her voice calm, she said, "Everything will be fine. I just need to talk to Kyle."

"Of course." More clicking. "The company he was working with is a new client of ours, a medical supplier, James and Sons Medical. And here's the number." Stacy rattled it off and Summer jotted it down.

"Thanks." She hung up and dialed the Charlotte number.

And got an automated response. "All of our operators are with a customer at this time. If you would like to hold, please stay on the line and someone will be with you momentarily."

She hung up and tried again. And again.

Frustration filled her. One thing was certain. She had very little time to figure out where Kyle would hide a laptop and flash drive.

If Kyle had even hidden them.

Michael Thomas was tempted to toss his cell phone in the nearest trash can. Kyle wasn't answering, his service disconnected. So where was the man? Mike had already driven by the house where David and Summer lived but had seen nothing out of the ordinary. Summer had no idea who Mike was and he wanted to keep it that way. If Kyle was in trouble, he'd contact Mike first, then Summer.

Summer.

A problem in the WITSEC equation as far as he was concerned, but Kyle had been adamant that marrying Summer would throw off those looking for him. They were looking for a single guy, not a married man with a mortgage.

Mike had to admit, it had worked well for the last year. And he couldn't blame Kyle for being attracted to the dark-haired beauty.

But now there was a problem.

Kyle was off the grid, and Mike's neck was on the line if he didn't find him. And besides, Kyle had become more than just a client to keep safe. He had become a friend.

Mike was determined to find him.

And he may have to start with Summer.

4

Olivia Todd stared into the rearview mirror. She curled her fingers around the steering wheel and listened to the praise and worship music pouring from her radio speakers.

She had it turned up, needing the comfort she found in the songs, the reassurance that she wasn't alone, that God really did love her and want the best for her and the girls. Summer had turned her on to the band that now sang about every day being another day to wake from her sleep and raise her hands in praise to him.

She sang along, "'I am tired, I am weak, your hands wake me from my sleep.'"

"I like that song, Mommy," Sandy said. "What's it called?"

"'Wake' by Jupiter Wind. Summer told me about it."

Even while she regretted the day she ever met the man she'd married, the music filled her with hope. It might be a desperate hope, but at least it was something.

Her eyes landed on her two precious girls in the backseat and she sighed. No, she couldn't wish she'd never met Silas Todd, but she could sure wish he were a different type of man than the one who was trying to take her girls away from her. Not because he wanted them, but because he hated her and wanted to hurt her with the deepest possible wound he could think of.

And that meant going through her children straight to her heart. Twelve-year-old Laura already had eyes that were too old and burned with anger. And eight-year-old Sandy was scared of everything. Most especially males. Silas had done that to them. He'd done it to her too, but she'd finally managed to find her backbone when he'd put Sandy in the hospital with a broken rib that had pierced a lung.

Her baby. Her heart. Fighting to breathe, bewildered and confused, hurt by a man who was supposed to protect her, lay his life down for her.

Even now, the conversation she'd overheard between her girls echoed through her mind. She'd gone to get a much-needed cup of coffee. When she returned to the hospital room, the door was cracked open. Low voices reached her ears and she stopped to listen.

"What did I do to make him mad, Laura? Why didn't Mommy stop him? Why didn't she make him stop?"

Olivia flinched at the breathless, gasping words.

"Because Mom's scared of him too. I don't blame her."

"But you tried. You threw a lamp at him."

"That's because I don't care if he hits me, but he's not going to hit you. Ever again." Laura's suppressed rage filtered through the crack in the hospital door as she climbed into the bed next to her sister, who was succumbing to the painkillers. "That's a promise. I'll take one of those big butcher knives in the kitchen and run it right through his heart before I let him touch you again."

Olivia slid to the floor, her legs no longer containing the strength to hold her up. "Oh, sweet Lord, show me where to go." Because it was no longer a matter of what to do, it was now a matter of where she would get the help to leave her abusive and powerful husband.

A powerful husband who had her followed and didn't bother trying to hide it. She couldn't even go to her mother's without him doing his best to intimidate her. She firmed her jaw and her resolve. He was a bully and she and the girls were his victims, but she wasn't going to play by his rules anymore.

A decision which had led her to her present situation.

Olivia turned left, then right. The car behind her did the same.

But that was fine. Tuesday, she and the girls would be free of him. Free to leave the state and disappear. And if the judge ruled otherwise, she was still prepared to run.

Silas Todd would not lay a hand on her or her girls ever again.

She just had to make it to Tuesday and Summer would take care of everything.

Or Olivia would.

One way or another.

5

Summer's phone rang and she snatched it. "Hello?"

"Summer?"

Summer's pulse slowed. "Hi, Olivia." Olivia Todd, her number one client.

"Celeste called. They moved the court date to Tuesday. Are we going to be okay with that?"

Celeste Martin, her paralegal. "Yes, of course. We'll be there. I could argue this case today if I had to. It's no problem." Summer hadn't checked her email this morning. She calculated. Today was Friday. Surely everything with Kyle would be fine by Tuesday. This was all just a horrible misunderstanding.

Wasn't it?

"You promise?" The anxiety and fear Olivia lived with on a daily basis came through loud and clear.

"Yes, I'm ready. We've got the evidence of his affair, dated pictures of him at bars partying when the girls were in his care. All of this will work in our favor for getting you custody." She paused. "And if we have to, even though I don't want to put her through that, we can use Laura's willingness to testify against him."

A shaky sigh slipped through the line. "I can't believe this. It

28

wasn't supposed to be like this, Summer. We were supposed to grow old together and now he's . . . I don't even know who he is anymore," Olivia whispered.

Summer had felt sympathy for her clients before. She'd been angry on their behalf. She'd fought for their rights. Now she felt empathy. Her heart hurt for Olivia. "I know exactly what you mean." Her throat clogged and she cleared it. "But you have to keep the safety of your kids in mind. You're doing the right thing."

"I know."

On impulse, Summer said, "Do you want me to pray with you?"

Silence greeted her question and she bit her lip. She thought Olivia was a Christian, but maybe Summer had made the woman feel uncomfortable. "Of all the things you could do for me, that's the one that counts the most. Yes, please. Let's pray."

So Summer prayed. Prayed for the safety of her client and her two children, prayed for a favorable outcome with the judge on Tuesday, and then added a silent plea for the Lord to reveal the truth to her about her husband and her marriage.

She hung up with Olivia and tried the Charlotte number again. She'd gotten that stupid automated message for the past two hours and she was fast losing patience. *Lord, what do I do?*

The doorbell rang, interrupting her prayer. Fear swept through her. Had Hayes and his crew come back?

No, he wouldn't have bothered with the doorbell. Her tension eased slightly. She moved to look out the window and frowned when she spotted a stranger standing on her front porch. She didn't have time for interruptions. Maybe if she ignored him, he'd go away.

The bell pealed again.

Maybe not.

She opened the door a crack and shivered as a gust of wind blew across her bare arms. "May I help you?"

"Hey, you must be Summer." An engaging grin creased his cheeks and she thought she saw a dimple peeking from the right side. "I'm looking for Kyle, is he around?"

"No, he's not here. Sorry."

Disappointment flashed. "Aw, man. Do you know where he is?"

Her fear returned in spades. So if they couldn't threaten her into telling her where he was, they'd send Mr. Nice Guy? "Why do you want to find him?"

The man held his hands palms up in an "I'm innocent" gesture. "Hey, I'm Mike, an old friend. We used to live in the same neighborhood when Kyle was growing up."

Summer let the door open a little more and crossed her arms. A glance up the street showed two vehicles she'd never seen before parked on the curb. "Really? And where was that?" She heard the hostile tone in her voice, but after her early morning visitors, she wasn't interested in politeness right now. Especially not for some greased-up car salesman twin.

He blinked. "Dayton, Ohio. What's with the third degree?"

She relaxed a fraction. Kyle had told her a little about his childhood and growing up in Dayton. "So how did you track him to Charleston, South Carolina?"

"Track him? I didn't. I'm home visiting family and happened to see him in the parking lot of Home Depot the other day but couldn't catch up to him fast enough before he drove away."

Summer lifted a brow.

"I followed him, trying to find him," Mike said, "but lost him when he went in the Top Choice building. I didn't want to bother him at work so I asked a co-worker where he lived. I've been busy and didn't have a chance until today to get out here and say hey."

Kyle had gone to Home Depot to get a part for the garbage disposal, and he also worked with Top Choice Software. Maybe this guy was legit. However, she wanted to have a word with the co-worker who was giving out her home address. "What's your name again?"

"Mike Thomas."

The man certainly didn't look harmless, but he didn't look dangerous either. Not like her visitors this morning. She shuddered. "Kyle's on a business trip, Mike. I'm sorry you missed him."

And she was worried. He hadn't called and he hadn't come home. She'd called all the hospitals and gotten nothing. But that just meant he wasn't in a hospital near her. "A business trip, huh? When will he be back?"

"Sometime today." She swallowed hard as her fear resurfaced. His eyes narrowed. "What is it?"

"What do you mean?"

"You had a funny look on your face."

"Nothing. Now, if you don't mind, I'm busy. I'll tell Kyle you came by." She glanced again at the unfamiliar vehicles and shut the door. She felt a pang of remorse for her borderline rude behavior, but she was scared and running out of time. She had to find that laptop before those creeps came back. She opened the coat closet and pulled out a fleece hoodie. Slipping it over her head, she walked toward the den.

"Kyle? What's going on?" she whispered to the empty room.

She'd cleaned out the closet, even tapping the walls on the off chance he'd stashed it behind one, and still came up with nothing. Every fifteen minutes, she'd stop to call the Charlotte company.

Finally, the phone rang. She waited for someone to pick up.

After the tenth ring, she slammed the phone down.

And went back to searching. One hour passed. Then two. She stopped to eat a pack of crackers, then went back to her search. Sweat rolled down her face and she cut the heat off. She yanked off the hoodie and kept going.

Summer worked on bedroom number three, cleaning out and tapping. Her knocks echoed around her and she nearly wailed in frustration another hour later when she came up empty-handed.

The only place she hadn't torn apart was the garage.

Summer hurried into the two-car garage and stood staring at the space. Her baby-blue Ford Fusion blocked her view of a lot of the garage. Where to start?

The toolshed in the corner? Maybe. The storage closet that they'd packed full and never bothered with?

Or the area Kyle had built soon after they'd married? She moved to the wooden worktable. Now that she thought about it, Kyle never did spend much time there. She ran shaky fingers over it, felt the sleek treated wood. She tried to think of one occasion when she'd seen Kyle use the table—and couldn't come up with a single time.

He used it as a shelf. She tugged on it. Solidly built, it didn't budge. She examined the sides, knocked on them with her knuckles. Nothing.

Summer dropped to her knees, ran her hands underneath and all the way to the back.

And felt it.

A latch. She flipped it up and a metal box dropped with a clang to the concrete floor.

Stunned that she actually found something, she stared at it for a moment. Then she gathered her wits. Snatching the box to her chest, she hurried back into the house to set her discovery on the kitchen table.

Her breaths came in shaky pants as she reached to open the box. She noticed right off it was too small to hold a laptop, but this was something Kyle had very purposely hidden.

Her fingers touched the latch and she snatched them back. Then forced herself to reach back and flip the latch. She opened the top and sank into the nearest chair, scared to death about what she might find, but too scared not to look.

She reached in and pulled out a stack of papers, a few photos and—a birth certificate that said DAVID RYAN HACKETT. A picture of him in the Army.

Oh goodness, Lord, what's going on?

The shakes set in again. This time they were due to pure un-adulterated fury that overrode the strangling fear that had been her companion since early this morning.

He'd lied to her.

With quick, efficient movements, she emptied the rest of the contents and froze as a small piece of paper no larger than her little finger fell onto the table. It contained ten numbers and the words, "I'm sorry."

She frowned. I'm sorry? Ten numbers? A combination? A code? A checking account number? No. A phone number?

Summer grabbed a legal pad and a pen and started listing the contents of the box. Birth certificate, photos of Kyle and another young man who looked a lot like him. Another picture of Kyle smiling stiffly with a man and a woman. His parents? She picked up the picture and walked into the den. She held it next to the picture Kyle had said was his family. Three sisters and a brother and Kyle. With his smiling parents. The picture she held was nothing like the one on the mantel. So who were they?

She pulled a set of silver dog tags from the box and read the information.

HACKETT
DAVID R.
965-46-9875
A NEG
CHRISTIAN

And then the small piece of paper with the numbers.

Summer snatched her cell phone, and before she could punch in the numbers, it rang. She didn't recognize the number. "Hello?"

"Who was that?"

"What? Who is this?" But she knew.

"I'm surprised you don't recognize my voice."

She did. Terror flashed hot and fierce. "I haven't found them yet. You gave me twelve hours. I'm looking."

"I know. I'm watching you search. Now who was the visitor?"

"A friend of Kyle's. He was looking for him. I told him he was out of town on a business trip."

"Good, because I'd hate to think you were trying to involve the cops in some way."

"I'm not." Chills danced up and down her spine. The nausea from earlier returned and she swallowed hard. Was he really watching? Or simply playing with her? With more bravado than she felt, she took a deep breath. "Now don't bother me again, you're taking up time I need to use looking."

She clicked off the phone and laid her head on the table. "I can't believe I just did that." Whispering the words aloud brought her back to the items in front of her and the reason she needed to find Kyle.

Summer pulled out her phone and punched in the number for the Charlotte business where Kyle had last been seen.

And finally got a person.

Relief rushed through her. "I'm looking for my husband, Kyle Abernathy," Summer said. "He was doing some computer work for your company this past week and I need to get in touch with him."

"I don't know who he is, I'm sorry. If he's a contract person, I would have very little contact with him." She sounded harried and hurried.

"What about the people who hired him? Or who he reported to when he got there?"

"That would have been me. I just pointed him in the direction of the computers with the list of things that need to be done. That's it." Disapproval tinged her tone. "And he was supposed to meet with our CEO before he left. He won't be getting a good referral from us."

"Right. Sorry about that. I'm sure he had a good reason. Could I speak to the head of your company?"

"He's not here right now."

"When will he be back?" Summer tamped down her impatience.

"I'm not sure. There was a bad car wreck right outside our building yesterday and he's at the hospital with Jerry Iles's family. The phone has been ringing off the hook since it happened."

That explained the difficulty reaching them. "What car wreck?"

A long-suffering sigh filtered through the line. "One of our employees was hit by a car coming out of the parking garage. Or he hit him. I'm not really sure what happened. But Jerry was hurt pretty bad."

"What about the other driver?"

"They said he didn't have any ID on him. I haven't heard anything more since they took him to the hospital."

"Which hospital?"

"Trident Health."

"Thanks for your help."

She hung up.

Find Kyle or the laptop? Anger burned in her chest. If that was Kyle in the hospital, then he could just stay there.

Alone. The liar.

As hard as she tried to tell herself to stay tough, she couldn't do it. She'd loved him too long, too much. Against her will, she reached for the phone, her heart overruling her head. Then drew her hand back. If he was in the hospital, then he was being cared for. The best thing she could do for him—for them—was to find that laptop. Right?

Summer offered up a prayer for his safety. "Let him live, Lord," she whispered. "Let him be okay. Bring him home to me." She paused. "Because if he's lied to me, I want to be the one to kill him." Another pause. "Amen."

She looked at the numbers on the piece of paper she still held. Then punched them into her phone.

6

Mike sat in his hotel room/office and stared at the map on the wall. He contemplated whether or not to report in to his boss about David's vanishing act. He looked at his watch. Not yet. Bernard Holcombe, a tall, well-built man who demanded perfection from his marshals, would not be pleased with this new development.

Mike didn't have a mark on his record after seventeen years of service, and he wasn't about to start now.

He jerked as his cell phone rang, grabbing his attention. The unfamiliar number on the display made him frown. He slipped from the room and pressed the phone to his ear. "Mike Thomas."

"Why does my husband have your number hidden in a box?"

Mike froze, then demanded, "Who is this?"

"Summer Abernathy." A pause. "Wait a minute. Mike Thomas? Kyle's friend? The man who just left my house a few hours ago?"

Uh-oh. "Where did you say you got this number?"

"I found it while searching my house."

Mike closed his eyes. There was no way his number should have been written down anywhere. What was Kyle thinking? "We need to talk."

36

"I think you're right."

"I'm on my way back."

"Fine, I'll see you—no! Wait! You can't come here."

"Why not?" Mike heard the thread of fear in her voice. "Is someone there with you?"

"No, but . . . are you a cop?"

"I'm a US Marshal."

Her breath whooshed through the line. "Oh no. Okay, that's not good."

"Why?"

"I can't talk to the cops."

The near hysteria in her voice set off alarm bells for him. "Who's threatening you, Summer?" She went quiet. "Summer? Mrs. Abernathy?"

"I've got to go." She clicked off the phone.

He called her back even as he headed out the door. She knew something. The phone rang three times before she finally picked back up. "Don't call me anymore."

"Please! Don't hang up." He climbed into his vehicle and cranked it, ready to break all the rules in order to find Kyle. "Look, your husband is in the WITSEC program. I'm his handler and he's in serious danger—as are you probably. Now, I need you to talk to me."

He could almost see her indecision as the only sound that came over the line was her hitching breaths. "WITSEC? Witness Protection? Are you kidding me?" Her breaths came through staccato and uneven. "I don't know what to do, I just don't know," she whispered. "They're coming back."

"Who? Who's coming back?" He drove through the streets with his lights flashing but kept his siren off. He would cut the lights before he got to her place since she was worried about the cops for some reason.

"Oh please. I don't want—"

"Mrs. Abernathy! Summer! Talk to me!"

She hung up.

Mike barely restrained himself from throwing his phone across the car. He didn't have time for a temper tantrum. He had to make another call. Swerving around the oblivious driver in front of him, he merged back into the right-hand lane and kept going. Then he punched in his boss's speed dial number. Fury ripped at him. He did not want to make this call.

But he had no choice. He needed help.

Bennie answered on the fourth ring. "What do you need, Mike?"

"I need help and I need it now."

"Tell me."

As fast as he could, Mike filled Bennie in. "And you're just now telling me this?"

Mike winced at the man's bellow. "You can lambaste me later. I need two deputy marshals on standby probably in Charlotte, North Carolina. That's the last place he was seen. When he turns up again, I want immediate coverage on him."

"I'll have them ready."

"And I'll fill out the report. At some point."

"Just get to his wife and make sure she's safe."

Mike hung up and pressed the gas, praying he wasn't going to have to call Bennie back with more bad news.

7

Shaking, heart hammering, Summer set the phone aside and stared at the contents of the box she had spread over her kitchen table. She glanced at the clock. 3:10.

Worry for Kyle . . . David . . . her husband . . . nagged at her. She felt frozen inside as her mind flitted, wondering what she should do. Fear, anger, and a churning desire for answers swirled inside her.

She didn't know a lot right now, but one thing she was sure of. Evidence pointed to the fact that Kyle had lied to her. Lied in a really big, life-changing, soul-shattering way. She scooped everything back into the box and hurried back to the garage to return it to its original place.

Once finished, she bolted into the kitchen, grabbed her purse and car keys.

Then paused. Running? Was that her only option?

"Well, you sure can't stay here." Summer peered out the living room window, her gaze sweeping the street.

A silver-and black Mustang sat against the curb two doors down and across the street. She'd never seen that car before.

They were definitely watching.

"Or it's someone visiting a friend," she muttered. Right.

Either way, her nerves danced. She could leave and see if anyone followed. No, not if. They would follow. One thing for sure, she wasn't going to be here tonight without that laptop. But leave now? Or when the sun went down around 5:30?

Before she could make up her mind, the car from this morning's visit pulled in front of her house. Summer drew in a deep horrified breath. Mike Thomas. A US Marshal.

A cop.

"No, no, no," she breathed. How was she going to get rid of him? Summer opened the door and pointed to his car. "You have to leave, now."

He blinked, then placed a hand on her shoulder and shoved her back into the house hard enough to make her fight to keep her balance.

She whirled on him, fear darting through her. "What do you think you're doing?"

The door shut behind him. "I need to find Kyle and I need your help."

"I don't know where he is." She had an idea, but that didn't mean she had to share with this man who'd already lied to her once today. "Where's your ID?"

He showed her. "Where did you find my number?"

"That doesn't matter right now." She wasn't ready to share what she'd found yet. Not until she'd talked to Kyle. She paced from one end of the foyer to the other. "They gave me until 8:36 tonight to find this laptop and flash drive. Well, I don't know where the stupid things are." She pointed at the door he'd just forced himself through. "You need to leave. Now." Frantic, she paced from the foyer into the den.

He caught up with her. "What laptop? What flash drive?"

She stopped and crossed her arms. "A laptop and flash drive these guys obviously want and think my husband stole." She waved a hand at the mess that was now her house. "I've turned this place upside down and I can't find either of them. If he's hidden them, he didn't hide them here."

"How do you know they want these things?"

"Because they broke into my house and threatened me if I didn't get them and hand them over. And they said no cops, so . . ." Summer dropped onto the couch. She buried her face against her knees and struggled for control.

"Start at the beginning, will you?"

She gave him the short version, then jumped up. "We need to get out of here. They said they'd be back." She glanced at the clock. 3:20. "Actually, I'm pretty sure they're sitting out there. They know you're here."

"So, we'll have the cops here waiting for them when they show up tonight." He pulled out his phone.

Summer paced. "I know that seems like the reasonable thing to do, but if you have the cops here, then they'll know it. They won't show up and I'll look like an idiot. Then if something else happens and I call—" She gulped. "No, I have to figure this out."

"Do you know where Kyle is?"

Did she trust this man? No, but what choice did she have? She couldn't take on those men by herself. She had to let Mike help her. The thought turned her stomach.

He shut his phone. "You said they're watching, that they probably know I'm here."

"They know. They knew you were here earlier and called to ask who you were."

His brow furrowed. "Okay, then we need a plan."

"I can't even think straight."

Mike got on his phone, and while Summer listened in on the one-sided conversation, she couldn't follow the exchange. Something about three or four vehicles and wild-goose chases.

He hung up and looked at her. "They're going to know I'm a cop. If these guys are as powerful as you say they are, they've already traced my car tag and know who I am. You're going to have to come with me. It's the only way to keep you safe."

"The way you kept Kyle safe?" She flung the words at him.

He winced. "Kyle must have done something stupid that led these guys to him. He's been fine for almost a year."

"When's the trial?" she asked.

"What?"

"The trial. That's what you're waiting on, isn't it?"

He studied her, then nodded. "Three weeks."

"Three weeks away and they find him now?" She gave a humorless laugh. "I'm not so sure Kyle's trusting the right people."

His eyes snapped at her and his lips tightened. After a few seconds, he blew a breath out. "You may not be far off the mark." He moved closer. "Now, do you know where he is?"

She met his gaze. "Yes."

"Then they do too."

8

Summer wanted to scream at Mike to hurry up, but he was already going eighty-five, so she figured she'd stay quiet and just pray. They were almost to the turnoff anyway. Mike was talking to someone named Bennie. "Who's on him?" A pause. A sigh of relief. "Chase and Adam . . . yeah . . . yeah, I got it. I promise." They went back and forth for the next few turns, then Mike said, "I'm pulling in now."

She barely waited for the car to stop before she threw the door open and bolted to the hospital information desk. Clutching her purse to her chest, she leaned against the counter, "I'm looking for Kyle Aber—" No, he wouldn't be registered under that name. "—the man who was brought in and had no ID. I believe he's my husband." Or should she just go ahead and ask for David Hackett? Anger simmered. She ignored it. She would be mad later. After she found out if he would live or die.

Armed with the room number and her self-appointed bodyguard, she found the elevator and jammed the button.

"Are you all right?" Mike asked.

She lasered him with a look. "Just peachy. Wouldn't you be if you'd just found out the last year of your life had been a lie?"

At least he had the grace to flush. "Look, Kyle has worked hard to stay alive this past year. He hasn't done anything except what he promised to do."

"He promised to never lie to me. Where does that fit in with him keeping promises?"

"He didn't have a choice, Summer. Can you look at things from his point of view and maybe cut him a little slack?"

Okay, so she would be mad now. So angry she couldn't breathe, she held up her hand. "I'm not talking about this with you anymore."

The elevator opened and she stepped off. Room numbers posted on the wall gave her the direction to Kyle's room. As she approached, she swallowed hard and rubbed her sweaty palms down her jeans. She wanted to turn and run, pretend this wasn't happening, that her husband wasn't a liar.

But he was. And she'd never run from anything in her life. She sure wasn't about to start now.

She turned the corner and came to a halt. Two men stood outside Kyle's room. Fear flashed for a brief moment until she realized Mike was approaching them with an outstretched hand. Fellow marshals, she figured.

Of course. As soon as he knew where Kyle was, he would have called for help.

Her phone rang and she snatched it from her purse. Marlee. She was going to have to find some time to call her sister back or Marlee would be filing a missing person report.

Summer forced herself to be polite to the two other marshals. This wasn't their fault and she wouldn't take her anger out on them. "Hello."

"Mrs. Abernathy." Tall, good-looking with green eyes and military-cut brown hair, the one nearest her held out a hand. "I'm Adam Buchanan, US Deputy Marshal."

She shook his hand. "Nice to meet you, Marshal Buchanan."

So nice I could puke. She clamped her lips together, refusing to let the words out.

"Call me Adam." He gestured to the man next to him. "This is Chase Tollison."

They exchanged greetings. She got to the point. "Is that man in there my husband?"

"Yes ma'am," Adam said.

She took a deep breath. "All right then."

She placed a hand on the door, ready to give it a good push when Adam touched her shoulder. "While it's nothing life-threatening, he's pretty beat up. Prepare yourself."

"Thanks." Mike started to follow her and she glared at him. "I'd like to see him alone first, if you don't mind."

He started to protest. Adam hushed him and opened the door for her. She let it shut in Mike's face.

Finally, she was in the room. At least it wasn't ICU. Her lips tightened. But he might need ICU after she got through with him.

Once again, she forced herself to push the anger aside for the moment. Without taking her eyes from the man in the bed, she shed her heavy down coat and let it fall into the vacant chair next to the window. Her heart constricted, her breath whooshed from her lungs. Adam was right. Kyle looked pretty beat up. The left side of his face sported several shades of purple, blue, and yellow. The IV dripped steadily into his left arm and his ribs were taped. Bruised, not broken. Hurt and sore, but nothing he wouldn't heal from.

Summer stepped closer and clasped his hand to curl her fingers around his.

His eyes fluttered. Opened. "Summer," he croaked. "You're safe?"

"I'm safe. For right now. Not so sure about you."

His blue eyes held hers and she let her anger show. He sighed. "So you know."

"I found out when a man named Corbin Hayes showed up in our

45

bedroom this morning and threatened to cut off my finger unless I gave him a laptop and flash drive you stole."

Bright fear flashed across his face. Strange, she didn't think the fear was for himself. Was it for her? He struggled to sit up, wincing with the effort, right hand pressed to his midsection. She moved back and let him. Refused to help him.

But was proud of herself for not slugging him.

He swung his legs over the side of the bed and pulled out the IV. He held tissue over the area until it stopped bleeding.

"What are you doing?" she asked.

"We've got to get out of here. Gotta keep you safe." He grunted and stood, a little wobbly, but on his feet.

Summer was stunned. How could he possibly be standing when he looked like death had come knocking and he'd barely held the door shut?

"There are three US Marshals outside your door," she said. "I think you're pretty safe."

"Not worried about me. I can take care of myself." He paused and grimaced. "When I don't have a car slamming into me."

"Was it an accident?" she asked. If he was in the Witness Protection program, anything was suspect.

"I don't know. I think the other driver died, so we may never know." He reached for the bag in her left hand. "Did you bring me some clothes?"

Almost without thinking, she'd grabbed them on the way out of the house. She handed them to him. "So what do I call you?"

He paused, his face hard, eyes shuttered. "What did Hayes tell you?"

"A lot. Your friends were more than willing to tell me the truth. Which is more than I can say for you."

He whirled on her, swayed, and sat hard on the bed, the gray pallor to his face really kicking up her worry meter. Which fueled her anger. She didn't want to worry about him.

"I'm so sorry, Summer, but I couldn't tell you the truth," he said. "I wanted to, so many times, but I couldn't." He closed his eyes and swallowed hard. When he opened them, she could see the pain glinting there. "And he's not my friend. He's a killer."

"Organized crime?"

He looked down as he pulled on his pants, then slipped into his shirt. By the time he finished, even the gray was gone and he now had about as much color as the bedsheet beneath him. "Yeah. And you can call me David. They know where I am now."

"David." She tried the name and found it bitter on her tongue. "Did you steal the laptop and the flash drive he wants?"

Panting, sweat beading his brow, one hand pressed against his taped ribs, he looked at her. "Yes."

9

The door opened and Mike hovered half in and half out of the room. "Is it safe to come in?"

"Yes," David said. "But we're not going to be here much longer."

Mike walked to the bedside. "Are you okay to travel?"

"I have to be." As soon as he got the dizziness under control. Sitting still helped.

Summer stood there quietly, her eyes bouncing between the men, taking it all in. The lack of expression on her face worried him. He'd been agonizing for months about telling her the truth and had, ironically, planned to tell her today. All of it. The whole terrible story. And then beg her to forgive him.

Only he'd waited too long.

Summer stared at him a few seconds longer, then spun on her heel and was out the door.

"Summer, stop!" David shouted.

"David, get back here!"

David went after her, ignoring the pain thrumming through him and Mike's shout to stop. And the light-headedness that made him want to keel over.

48

Once outside the room, the marshals flanked him. "Where'd she go?"

"The stairs," Adam said. "But you're in no shape—"

David bolted for the stairs, gasping as his ribs and head protested.

"David! You can't do this!"

Swallowing against the nausea, David ignored them and pushed the stairwell door open. He started down. "Summer!" His voice echoed around him. He heard her retreating footsteps and hurried faster, tripped and caught himself on the handrail. "Summer, wait."

Her footsteps stopped and her voice rose from below. "Leave me alone, David. I don't want to talk to you right now."

"It's not safe. They know who you are. They'll use you to get to me."

"Not if we're not together anymore."

Her words cut like shards of glass shredding his heart. Not because he didn't deserve them, but because *she* didn't deserve what he'd done to her, what he'd pulled her into the middle of. "Summer, please." He kept going, desperate to catch up with her. Finally, he saw her, heard the marshals behind him. It wouldn't matter to them that his marriage had just fallen apart. All they cared about was keeping him safe for the trial. He had to get Summer to listen to him. "I don't want to lose you."

"Too late, Kyle . . . David . . . whoever you are."

Her steps resumed.

So did his.

He followed her into the lobby of the hospital, his teeth clenched against the pain. She whirled. "Stop following me. We're done."

"We're not done. I don't accept that."

Fury ignited. She jabbed a finger into his chest and he fell onto the bench behind him. For a moment, sympathy graced her eyes, then they hardened again. "You don't get to make that choice. You made your choice when you lied to me. Stood there and *lied* to me when I told you that was the one thing I could never forgive. How could you? What kind of man does that?" Tears pooled.

David was vaguely conscious of the show they were putting on for those in the lobby and the marshals trying to corral him, but he didn't care. Right now, stopping Summer from walking out the door was his only objective.

He stood, pulled her to the side, and lowered his voice. "A fool. An idiot. A man who made a huge mistake and is asking for forgiveness. Please, Summer."

She jerked away from him, her chin trembling. "Those are pretty words, David, but you've always been good at throwing them around. Too bad you're saying them *after* you got caught in the lies. Well, I'm not falling for them. I don't believe anything you're saying." She stepped back. "There are no appeals in this situation. We're done and that's final."

His jaw flexed. "They may be pretty words, but I mean every one of them." He gripped her upper arms. "Your life depends on you listening to me."

"I'm done listening." She sighed and shook her head. "I need some time. Time away from you."

He groaned. "You can't. They'll find you and—"

"No. You're not going to use that to keep me around." Tears clouded her vision. "I can't believe you did this to me. I just can't—" She pulled in a deep breath. "If you're so worried about me, tell one of your marshal friends to keep up, because I'm leaving."

Adam intervened. "Ma'am, he's right. Mike told me what happened to you with Corbin Hayes. You need to stay with us."

Her lip curled, disgust shooting from every pore. "Right. You men just have to stick together, don't you?" Without another word, she made a beeline for the revolving door.

Summer had experienced a broken heart before. Her father's bitter duplicity and the subsequent custody battle that led to the most miserable three years of her life. Her fiancé's unfaithfulness and heartfelt lies that he was innocent. Only to have his lover come forward and let Summer know exactly how sneaky he'd really been.

But the pain shattering through her now didn't compare. Out on the sidewalk, she glanced around. The darkness was broken by the city lights, headlights from passing cars. She stopped and stared at the nearest vehicle. And realized she was stranded. She pulled out her cell phone and dialed Marlee's number. Her sister answered on the first ring with, "Where have you been? I've been calling and calling. Are you all right?"

"Hey. No, I'm not all right. I'm stranded and I need a ride." Summer refused to apologize. She'd explain when Marlee pulled up in front of her.

"You were supposed to go with me to take Sugar to the vet this morning. You totally stood me up."

Summer smothered a groan. She'd forgotten she'd made that promise two weeks ago before she and David had decided to take the day off together. More pain cramped her heart at the memory. "Marlee, are you listening? I need a ride."

"Need a ride? Where are you?"

"Three hours away from you. In Charlotte, North Carolina." Summer sighed and sank onto the bench at the bus stop.

"North Carolina?" Marlee's screech nearly deafened her.

Cars passed her, people hurried on their way, and Summer sat. Lonely. Defeated. Weary. And scared. She looked back toward the hospital and saw David limping toward her, the marshals not far behind him. The determined expression on his face sparked her anger once again. She jumped up and started walking again. "Listen, Marlee—"

"What are you doing in North Carolina? You're supposed to be here. How could you stand me up? Do you know how worried I was? How could you be so selfish?"

Summer groaned and closed her eyes. Why had she called her sister?

Brakes squealed.

Time moved in slow motion. Van doors swung open.

"Summer!" David's voice echoed around her.

She spun on her heel, saw David shoved by the nearest marshal into the door of the closest shop.

A hard hand grabbed her upper arm.

Mike Thomas lifted his weapon and Summer knew she was dead if she didn't help Mike protect her. She yanked at her attacker's grip and swung a leg out with a powerful roundhouse kick. The grip lessened and a whoosh escaped the man.

Satisfaction flowed at the solid connection, only to have the fear return at his retaliation. He lifted his weapon. Summer dropped like a rock to the hard concrete. Two shots sounded and she waited for the piercing pain of the bullets.

When it didn't happen, she opened her eyes to see Mike standing over the fallen man, kicking his weapon out of reach. The young man's eyes latched on to hers. Venomous fury, pain from his wounds—and fear—glared at her. His breath rattled and he spat blood. She shuddered and backed away from him. Adam raced after the disappearing van. Burnt rubber assailed her nose and she choked on the fumes.

But she was alive. And not a captive of the men who wanted her husband dead.

The sick feeling in her gut said life as she knew it was definitely over.

10

David's punch landed with a solid thud against the marshal's chin. Just hard enough to gain his freedom, but lacking the force that would break the man's jaw. He bolted from the store with pained curses ringing in his ears.

None of that mattered. Summer needed him.

David pressed a hand to his screaming ribs and raced back out into the street to see Summer sitting in the middle of the sidewalk.

He rushed to her. "Are you all right?"

He grasped her upper arm and helped her to her feet. She snagged her phone from the concrete and stuffed it in her pocket. Her blank stare, automatic actions, and repeated shivers told him she was in shock.

Mike yelled, "What are you doing? Are you crazy? Get back inside."

"I'm not going anywhere without my wife." Beneath his palm, he could feel her trembling increase.

Then she moved. Fast. She jerked away. "They were going to kidnap me. They gave me twelve hours to find that computer. My twelve hours aren't up yet."

She lifted a shaky hand and swiped her hair away from her face.

David's fingers itched to help, but he figured it would be a good way to lose a few digits.

She was still—understandably—fired-up mad at him. Real fear gripped him as he considered the fact that she might never get past her anger. And he would only have himself to blame.

Sirens screamed, law enforcement descended. Mike's fury rivaled Summer's as he glared at David. "We don't need this, David. All this attention isn't a good thing. We need to get out of here before the cops start asking questions."

David nodded. The trial was so close, he couldn't start being stupid now. Or more stupid than he'd already been. He looked at Summer. "He's right, getting out of sight isn't a bad idea."

Summer bit her lip and glanced around. "Fine."

David breathed a small sigh of relief. She had a hot temper sometimes, but she wasn't an idiot.

Together, with the marshals flanking them, they started to move toward the store, then David stopped. He stared at the young man who'd been shot and ignored Chase's prodding to hurry it up. "Pauli . . . ," he whispered.

"Who's Pauli?"

"A good kid." He shook his head. "What's he doing involved in this mess?"

"We'll figure it out later, now go," Chase ordered.

They moved to the store David had forced his way out of. Holding the door open, Chase Tollison glared at him. David glared right back. Summer moved past the marshal and David thought he caught a glimmer of respect in the man's eyes before he shuttered them.

Once inside the store, Mike and the other marshals ushered David and Summer to the dressing room.

Mike looked around. "No windows. One entrance, one exit. We should be good for a short time." He got on the phone to make arrangements for another housing situation.

Summer's wounded stare cut him to the core. He should have done so many things differently. He thought he'd have more time. "I'm sorry."

Tears flooded her emerald eyes. "I am too, David."

He knew she wasn't apologizing. They both knew she had no reason to be sorry. None of this was her fault.

Mike lowered his phone and said, "We've got a new location. A car will be here shortly. We've emptied the shop and it's secure as of this moment. The car will pull up to the delivery entrance in about twenty minutes. Be ready to move."

David registered Mike's words, but his attention stayed on Summer. "I know you're hurt and angry and you have every right to be, but you've got to put that aside for now and come with us."

She jerked and flushed. "I need to go home. Marlee needs me."

"You really think you'd even make it home before someone grabbed you?"

Summer sank into the chair abandoned by the dressing room attendant. "No. I probably wouldn't." A fact that had her glaring lasers at him again. "I can't believe my life has turned into some action adventure movie." She stood and paced to the end of the dressing room, then back. "Tell me everything. I want the whole story. Every last teeny, tiny detail."

FRIDAY
8:30 P.M.

Summer saw David swallow hard. "Every detail, huh?"

He shifted on the dressing room bench and she noticed how pale he looked. Upon closer examination, she could see the strain running after her had taken on him. He looked wiped out and ready to drop. Tough. She pushed aside the sympathy trying to spring up. She needed some answers. "Is everything about you a lie?"

He flinched, dropped his head back against the wall, and closed his eyes. She didn't ask him again. He'd either tell her or not.

But he had about two seconds to decide before she walked out of the store.

And into the hands of the men who'd just tried to snatch her from the sidewalk in front of the hospital. She settled in for a wait.

Her phone buzzed for the hundredth time since she'd been cut off from talking to Marlee. Her sister had probably called out the National Guard by now. She had no choice but to talk to her. Summer grabbed the device from her front pocket and pressed the green talk button. "Hi, Marlee."

"Are you okay?" The screech hit her highest decibel level yet and Summer winced.

"I'm fine. Take it down a notch, will you?"

"Well, what do you expect? What happened? Tell me—"

"Marlee, I'm fine."

Her sister stopped her tirade. "Okay. Good." She sighed, then blurted, "Oh! I almost forgot. Nick needs you to cosign his loan for that little trailer on the lake. Do you think you could meet him at the bank at four o'clock next Friday afternoon?"

Summer ground her teeth. David's words came back to haunt her. "One day you're going to regret all you do for them."

"They're my brother and sister, Kyle," she'd argued. "What am I supposed to do? Turn them away when they need help?"

"They're leeches and they take advantage of your giving nature without a second thought. Take my word for it and run while you can." His bitterness hadn't made sense to her at the time and she'd just ignored the warning.

Now, she wondered if Marlee was even in touch with reality. A sick feeling engulfed her. Had she done this? Molded Marlee into this needy, clingy creature? Or was she giving herself too much power? Marlee had a mind of her own.

"Marlee, I'll deal with that later. I'm in Charlotte, North Carolina, remember? Three hours away?"

"What are you doing there?"

"Kyle's in the hospital."

A pause. "What happened?"

"It's a long story."

"Is he all right?"

"For now."

Marlee lost interest. "What should I tell Nick?"

Summer almost couldn't find her voice. Marlee's blatant selfishness and lack of concern for her and David spoke volumes. Sadness engulfed her. "I'm not even sure when I'll be home or when I'll be able to talk to you next. Tell Nick I'll call him when I can."

A pause. "You said you were okay."

"I'm okay for now—"

"And Kyle is with you."

She frowned. "Yes."

"So you have time for him, but not for me. When is it going to be my turn, Summer?"

Really?

She almost said something like having more time on her hands in the near future—after she left her lying husband—but the truth was, she wasn't even sure she'd tell Marlee a word of what had happened. Although she supposed she'd have some explaining to do when she announced her upcoming divorce. Bitterness sliced through her.

First her father; then Joshua, her lying ex-fiancé; now Kyle.

David.

Whoever.

"Did you hear me? He's in the hospital!" She couldn't help raising her voice. The whole conversation was beyond ridiculous. "I've got to go, Marlee, I'll call you later." She hung up with her sister still sputtering in her ear. Weariness settled on her shoulders as she powered the iPhone down and slipped it into her purse.

She looked at David.

He'd listened to her side of the entire exchange. Shock stood out on his face. "You hung up on her."

"Yes, I did, what of it?" she snapped. Then winced. Just because she was finally admitting to herself her sister's true colors didn't mean she had to turn into a shrew.

Although the knowing look on his face made her want to smack him. But she couldn't. This latest conversation with Marlee had just switched the light on for her. She forced the three words from her lips. "You were right."

"I'm sorry." Real sympathy shone in his gaze. "I didn't want to be."

"You warned me. How did you recognize it and I couldn't?"

"Experience."

"Who?"

"My brother."

"Your real brother or the one you made up?"

His lips tightened, but he said, "The real one."

"You guys ready to move?" Mike asked from the doorway.

David's face shuttered, hardened to a granite look Summer had never seen there before. A tremor ran through her.

Who had she married?

As he took a gun from Mike's outstretched hand and slipped it into a shoulder holster with only a faint grimace indicating he still felt the pain from his accident, she not only wondered who she'd married, but what.

She looked at Mike. "You arm your protectees?"

Mike grunted. "Not typically." He shot a glare at David. "But then he's not a typical protectee. He says he either has a gun or he goes out on his own."

She lifted a brow at David. "So you carry a gun?"

He studied her. "I'm former special forces. I was an Army Ranger, Summer." He returned Mike's glare. "And I didn't have a weapon with me when Corbin Hayes showed up. If I had, things might have been a little different."

"How?"

"Don't guess we'll ever know. Doesn't matter now. I'm not going to be caught without a weapon again."

She gaped. She'd known he was in the military, but had no idea about the rest. "But all of your Air Force medals and—" She remembered the Army tags from the box.

"Part of my cover. It's obvious I'm military, so instead of trying to cover that up, we just decided on a different branch."

"That's why you never talked about it," she murmured. "I thought it was because you had bad memories or something."

His eyes flattened. "I do."

She eyed the gun. "And all of our trips to the shooting range?"

"Just staying sharp. Keeping my skills up and ready." He paused. "And making sure you were comfortable with using a gun in case you ever needed one."

"Unbelievable," she whispered.

"Let's go, people. Everyone get your vests on."

Summer gulped as she watched David velcro the bulletproof vest in place. Then it was Summer's turn. David helped her, then Mike's rough hand on her arm propelled her toward the back entrance of the store and into a black Chevy Tahoe. She shook her head as she clipped the seat belt around her.

David settled in beside her. Too close. She shifted to attach her left hip to the door. He didn't miss her movement but said nothing even though his lips tightened. Mike slipped in on the other side of David and slammed the door shut.

Adam slid behind the wheel and Chase took the passenger seat. "Let's get out of here."

Through the black tinted windows, Summer just noticed another

SUV in front of them. She glanced back and saw another behind. She looked at David. "Are you the president or something?"

Mike snickered.

David sighed. "No, I'm not the president."

"He's a guy who's going to put mob boss Alessandro Raimondi away," Adam said. "Right now, David's more important than the president."

"Raimondi? The one who wants the laptop that I didn't know existed until this morning?" Had it only been this morning? She felt like at least a week had passed since her ominous visitors had rocked her world.

"Yes."

Darkness covered the city. Summer closed her eyes against it all, wanting to shut everything out. And right now, she wasn't even sure she wanted to talk to God.

Guilt flooded her. Mentally, she knew she should be on her knees praying for his guidance and protection, but right now, she was just too tired, too confused, and just plain too stinking angry.

11

In the hospital trauma room, Alessandro Raimondi stared down at his nephew's gray face. Nineteen-year-old Pauli Greco. His sister's youngest boy. Her baby. The child she wanted kept out of the business.

The child who was now dead because Raimondi had allowed him to take part in an assignment he hadn't been ready for. Pauli's eavesdropping and subsequent demand had led to him being a part of the plan. But why he'd been allowed to come along didn't matter.

"I should have said no," Raimondi whispered.

"You didn't have a choice." Pauli's twenty-nine-year-old brother, Agostino, drew in a ragged breath and pushed aside tubing and trash left behind by the doctors and nurses. Symbols of failed efforts to save Pauli.

"About some things, I have no choice. This life I lead, I had no choice about." He touched Pauli's now cold cheek. "Him? I had a choice about." Sickness swirled in his gut. First Georgina and now Pauli. Fury burned a hole in his chest. His nephew's heart no longer pumped blood, but every beat of Raimondi's cried out for revenge. David Hackett. Just thinking the man's name nearly brought on a migraine. "I want him dead."

"Not without suffering."

"Oh, he'll suffer." They fell silent, each lost in their own thoughts and grief. Raimondi rubbed a hand down his cheek. "We'll get him tonight. And if we don't, we'll get those he loves." He pursed his lips. "Hayes said there was a picture of two children on their dresser. Find out who they are. We may need to use them."

"Noted. How are you going to find Hackett?"

"I have my ways. Don't worry. It will be done. By tomorrow morning, Summer and David will be dead."

"What about the laptop?"

"We'll have that too."

Agostino nodded and rubbed his eyes. "Mama is going to be inconsolable. She'll never forgive either of us for allowing Pauli to go with us. Especially after what happened with Georgina . . ."

Raimondi heard the rough grief in Agostino's voice along with the subdued rage. "Yes. That's why she can't know how he died." His sister loved Raimondi's daughter, Georgina, like her own. She'd birthed four boys, but Georgina was the daughter of her heart. And David Hackett had dealt Georgina a crippling blow. Raimondi's heart seethed.

Agostino's eyes jerked up and met his uncle's. "You think you— we—can keep it from her?"

"We have to. This is my fault. I should have stopped this. Kept him safe."

"He insisted on being a part of it. He was a man, able to make his own choices."

But Raimondi shook his head. "It won't make a difference to your mother. All she will know is that her baby is dead."

A pause fell between them. Then Agostino asked, "What will we tell her then?"

Another long pause, then Raimondi looked up at his nephew. "We tell her that he's dead because David Hackett gunned Pauli down in cold blood."

Agostino frowned, and for a moment Raimondi wondered if he would argue, but soon the young man's brow smoothed, his jaw hardened, and he gave a short nod. He leaned over and kissed his dead brother on the forehead, then turned on his heel and strode through the double doors.

12

David clenched his teeth against the shafts of pain shooting through his ribs and slowly turned over on the bed to look at the clock. Adam had handed him a pill bottle and told him to take one for pain. He couldn't do it, couldn't take a chance and dull his senses when he might have to run at any time, might have to protect Summer.

He'd lived with pain before, he could do it again.

When they'd arrived at the safe house last night, Summer had said, "I'm tired. I can't take anymore. We'll talk tomorrow." Then disappeared into her bedroom.

Should have been their bedroom.

David sighed and sat up with a wince. Five in the morning. He might as well give up on trying to sleep. He leaned back against the headboard and dropped his chin to his chest. *Lord, I did what I thought was the right thing at the time. When I married Summer, I wasn't a Christian, but I'm a different man now. I know there are consequences to actions and I've made some pretty rotten choices. Please don't let the fallout be disaster. Again. And spare Summer no matter what else happens.*

As he often did, David thought of Ron, an older man who'd

saved his life last year—in more ways than one—and wondered where he was.

David grabbed the remote from the end table, shifted on the bed trying to find a comfortable position, and finally gave up. He clicked the small flatscreen television on and found a national news channel.

His door creaked and he grabbed his weapon, aiming it.

Adam stepped inside and closed the door behind him.

David let out a breath and lowered the gun. "You trying to get yourself killed?"

"No, I saw the light under your door. Figured you were awake."

"You forget how to knock?"

"Sorry. Didn't want to wake anyone else up."

David gestured toward the chair in the corner and grimaced at the movement. "Have a seat."

Adam sat. "You should have taken one of the pain pills."

"Would you?"

Adam shrugged. "Maybe. If I had a couple of superior marshals guarding me."

David almost smiled. "No you wouldn't."

"True enough."

The reporter on the television caught his interest and David upped the volume. "And in New York, a murderer with a connection to the Mafia is set to go to trial in just under three weeks. Sam Gilroy was caught on video shooting and killing one of his employees, Carl Hyatt. Mr. Gilroy's partner, David Hackett, was thought to be in the building at the time of the murder since his car was seen in the parking lot early that Saturday morning. However, Hackett has been missing since Sam's arrest a little over a year ago."

A picture of David from a little over a year ago flashed on the screen. He'd had dark black hair then, not the reddish blond he now sported. And he'd had a goatee and mustache. David reached up to rub his clean-shaven face.

"Sam's trial is big news," he muttered.

"It's the Mafia connection."

"Have they said who the judge is going to be for the trial?"

Adam gave a slow nod. "Judge Parker Holland."

"Holland. Figures."

"Yeah, he seems to draw a lot of the Mafia cases."

David hesitated, then nodded. "Yes, he does."

Adam must have noticed his reticence. "What is it?"

"Nothing really." David took another hard look at the TV. "He has a good reputation for being fair and honest even though those connected with the Mafia seem to get too many breaks, if you ask me."

"If the cops don't do their jobs right, the judge can't hold them."

"I know, I just don't have to like it."

"From what I've heard and read, he's a stand-up guy. Former military, got the nickname Steamroller as a criminal lawyer." Adam shrugged. "He's one of the best, isn't he?"

"So it would appear."

"Then it's a good thing he's got this case."

"Right."

Adam sighed. "Look, I know you and Summer are having a rough patch right now, but . . ."

He stopped and David looked at him, curious as to what the man had to say. "Go on."

"I mean, I know it's not my business and we don't even know each other that well . . ."

"Will you just spit it out?"

Adam gave a low chuckle. "Yeah." He rubbed his chin. "Summer seems like a fine woman. A good one. She's strong and obviously has a temper. She's also smart and I . . ." He shrugged. "I hate to see you two give up on a good thing."

"I have no intention of giving up," David retorted.

"Good, good. Because family is everything, you know?"

David studied this man who now stood before him. He had a

feeling in a different time, a different place, they would have been good friends. "No, I don't know that. I've never had much of a family, but this last year with Summer has shown me what I've been missing." He ran a hand through his hair and felt the tug on his ribs. "I'm not giving up on her. Ever."

"Good."

David shifted and then stopped trying to get more comfortable. It wasn't going to happen. "Just out of curiosity, how did Mike get Summer to agree to go with him?"

Adam grimaced. "He told her a little lie."

Oh great. Another lie. "What was that?"

"He said she had to go with him because his car was parked in front of your house and Raimondi had already run the plates and found out he was a cop."

"Ah. Summer should know better. If Raimondi had someone run the plates, the marshals would have been all over that. And Mike's information would never have come back he was law enforcement."

"Summer was a little shook up at the time. When she's thinking more clearly, she'll figure it out." Adam shrugged. "Mike was doing what he had to do to keep her safe, saying what he had to say. Maybe she'll appreciate that one day."

"We'll see." He figured another lie would just send Summer deeper into her pit of anger. Not a happy thought.

"What's on that laptop that's so important anyway?" Adam asked.

David studied the man. "Pictures."

"What kind?"

"The kind my buddy Sam used for blackmail. The kind someone didn't want released to the media."

Adam narrowed his eyes. "Who are the pictures of?"

"I don't know. I have a vague description of the man, but other than that, his face has been blurred out."

"What's he look like?"

David shrugged, then winced. "He's an older man, I think. Either that or he's prematurely gray. And really, it's not even gray. He's got a shock of pure white hair that stands out on his forehead right here." David showed him on his own head. "And then there's a tattoo."

"A tattoo? Of what?"

"A snake. On his left bicep."

"So he should be pretty easy to identify if those pictures got out."

"Oh yeah."

Adam rubbed a hand down his face. "What were the pictures of?"

"He was meeting with mob boss Alessandro Raimondi."

"I see."

"So, depending on who he is, he may not want people to know he's in cahoots with Raimondi."

"That's for sure." Adam gave him an easy slap on the shoulder. It still hurt. "I'll leave you alone. You need to rest if you can. To-morrow's going to be a long day."

He left and for the next fifteen minutes, David watched the news and felt his eyes grow heavy in spite of the constant throbbing in his ribs, the shooting pain in the left side of his face, and the gnawing hunger in his belly.

He closed his eyes.

A scuffle outside his window sent his eyes wide. His muscles tensed and yet he didn't move. Didn't hardly breathe as all of his special forces training shot to the surface and sent his senses on high alert. He glanced at the clock. He'd been asleep about an hour.

He moved off the bed, ignored the aches and pains screaming at him, and pulled on the jeans he'd tossed over the chair.

David wrapped his fingers around the grip of the Glock and slipped next to the window. The house had an alarm system, but they wouldn't care about that. Once they were in, the distracting noise might even work in their favor. For most attackers. Fortunately for David, he knew how the game was played. At the edge of the window, he tried to see around the blinds and couldn't.

With one finger, he dipped the blade just enough to see out. His blood went cold.

Three shadowy figures, barely illuminated by the half-moon, moved like eels through the darkness, gliding, writhing up to the front of the house, then dividing, one going to the east side, the other toward the west. The third one slithered up to the front door.

David moved as fast as his injured body would allow. In the hall, he nearly ran into Adam, who had just come from the den.

"They're here," Adam whispered. "Backup's on the way."

"I'll get Summer." David slipped into her room, grateful she hadn't locked the door.

She lay still beneath the covers, earbuds still in her ears, iPod on the pillow beside her. She slept in her usual spread-eagle position that normally had him hugging the side of the bed. He rubbed her silky shoulder and she jerked into a sitting position, her hair whipping into his face. He breathed her familiar scent and wished he had time to linger, kiss the side of her neck like he did almost every time he had to wake her . . .

Sleep fled from her gaze and anger blazed. Before she could lambaste him, he said, "They've found us, we've got to go."

The anger faded as his words registered. Without a word, she threw off the covers and swung her legs over the side of the bed to grab the clothes she'd tossed on the floor. He swallowed hard and looked away, his sense of loss nearly smothering him. How he loved her . . .

"How much time do we have?" she asked as she stuffed the iPod in her purse and slung it over her shoulder.

Tamping down his feelings, he grabbed desperately for the wall he used to have no trouble erecting when he didn't want to feel something. With Summer, it never seemed to work. "None."

"Then let's go." He could hear the fear behind her attempt to sound brave.

"Not so fast. Wait on the marshals. Get your vest on, now."

"We're here." Chase Tollison had his weapon ready. Adam was on the phone right behind him.

"How'd they find us?" Summer asked as she snapped the last button on the vest.

David shook his head. "Don't know. We'll worry about that later after we're safe."

"Where are we going?"

"Good question." David clasped her chilled fingers and pulled her after him. Adam led the way. Chase pulled up the rear. "What's the plan?"

"Get to the car and go from there." His fingers pressed the earpiece tighter into his ear. "One's on the roof."

"There are three of them," David said. "I saw them approach and split up."

Adam grunted. "They don't know who they're tangling with. Head toward the back door."

"The back?" Summer asked.

"There are three vehicles. One parked at each exit," David murmured. "Safest way out right now is the back."

Summer nodded and scooted up behind him, her fingers tightening on his. He hated that it took danger to get her this close. But this was the route he'd chosen. Now he needed to focus on traveling it.

Sirens sounded in the distance.

Then the home alarm started blaring. A gunshot rang and David ducked, pulling Summer down with him to the floor. He rolled and huddled over her, trying to discern where the shot came from. She shoved against him and he grunted with the sharp pain that sliced through his ribs, but he refused to move.

Adam stood next to them, crouched, weapon aimed down the hall behind them.

"The car, David, to the car," Mike yelled over the ear-shattering noise. He turned from the den window.

David rose. Pain traveled through him, but he pulled Summer to her feet.

Chase motioned to the back door as a bullet pierced the window next to Mike. Mike ducked and swore, then dared another glance through the broken window. "Backup's here." Into his radio, he said, "Don't shoot. Repeat. Don't shoot. We're still inside. Hold your fire."

David hoped they listened. After staying alive and outwitting Raimondi this long, he had no desire to die by friendly fire. Summer ran a hand through her hair, her eyes darting from one marshal to the next. Then to the door.

He squeezed her fingers. "Hold tight, babe."

A shadow moved from the living room, lifted his weapon. David lunged to the left with Summer, Adam lifted his gun and fired. The figure grunted and spun back into the dark of the room he'd come from.

"Go!" Adam pointed to the door as he raced toward the man he'd just shot.

Mike herded them toward the exit while Chase brought up the rear.

As Mike reached for the knob, the door burst in.

David shoved Summer down and spun, arm outstretched, the heel of his palm connecting with a chin. The man howled as his jaw snapped. With a swipe of his foot, David clipped the surprised attacker's legs out from under him. Chase came from the left and tackled him the rest of the way to the floor.

13

Summer rolled away from the tangle of bodies. Her heart beat in her throat as she lived this nightmare David had dropped her into. Scrambling back, she watched the fight unfold. David clipped the man on the chin again and the mask slipped. Adam brought the grip of his weapon down to crack against the attacker's head. His pained cries cut off and he dropped like a rock.

David's white face said he was in pain. His granite expression said he didn't care. She hoped his vest had provided some protection to his battered ribs. He held a hand to his side and moved away as Chase came from the living room to give a nod of satisfaction at the unconscious man on the floor. "Two down. One to go."

"Where is he?" Adam asked.

"Dunno." Chase's gaze darted around the room.

Summer found herself doing the same, probing the shadows and scanning the doorways.

"Let's get them out of here before he puts in an appearance," Mike said as he took the lead and exited the house. Summer heard the car door open. "Come on. Come on. Stay low and move fast."

Summer knew the words were for her benefit. Without asking, she knew David had done this before.

She slid into the vehicle followed by David, then Mike. Adam took the wheel. "Where's Chase?"

"He'll stay behind and clean up the mess, then meet up with us later."

Summer clasped her hands between her knees and closed her eyes. She wondered what time it was, then nearly laughed. Did it matter? She also wondered if the crazy feeling inside was hysteria. Probably. She took a deep breath and closed her eyes. Felt David's arm slide around her shoulders. More than anything, she wanted to lean on his strength and shut out the fact someone wanted to hurt her. So they could hurt her husband.

Husband . . .

Summer stiffened as the car pulled away and fell in line behind the other two identical vehicles. "Are we even married?" she whispered.

David froze, his arm tightened. She pulled away to look into the eyes that had captivated her from the moment she'd seen them at the bank. She'd been talking to the teller and elbowed her purse off the counter. Items had scattered. David had helped her clean them up and she'd been unable to take her eyes from him. When he'd asked for her phone number, she'd been giddy with disbelief. And joy.

"Yes, we're married," he said.

"How? You signed a fake name."

"No. It's my real name now. A whole new identity compliments of WITSEC that makes my signature legal."

She swallowed hard. So, at least she was really married to him. She wasn't sure how she felt about that. "You could have faked it. You didn't have to go to all that trouble. I never would have known and after the trial you could have walked away a free man, no strings attached." She couldn't help the bitterness.

His eyes narrowed. "I could have." He paused. "I didn't want to."

Four simple words that carried a huge punch. A small piece of her reveled in the knowledge that he would go to all that trouble to make sure they were legally married. Another part of her was furious that he'd trapped her in a lie, one that would take time and money to dissolve.

If she really wanted to go that route.

But what else could she do? He'd *lied* to her.

The one thing she'd told him she could never forgive. And it wasn't just that he'd lied, but he'd done so with absolute conviction shining in his eyes. She shuddered, wondering what else he'd lied about.

He was going to tell you, she argued with herself.

But he didn't.

But he really married you when he didn't have to.

Might have been better if he hadn't.

Then she could have walked away.

Right. She pulled her iPod from her purse and shoved the earbuds into her ears. Jupiter Wind's lead singer crooned in her ear, reassuring her that God was with her, telling her what hope looked like. When the next song came on, she couldn't help the humorless smile that curved her lips. How appropriate. She sang along silently.

> I'm walking on a tightrope
> And my feet are slipping.
> I'm about to lose control
> I'm hanging on a thin wire.
> And my hands are sliding
> And I'm crashing to the ground.

When the chorus came on, she made it her prayer.

> I know you're gonna save me
> 'Cause I know you'll never let me go.

Summer heaved a sigh. He'd said, "I didn't want to."

And those four little words did more for her heart than she wanted to admit.

14

"What's on the laptop?"

David spun to find Summer standing in the doorway to the bedroom of the second safe house. He winced at the fast movement, his bruised ribs protesting.

She wasn't smiling, but at least her ferocious glare had faded to a hard-eyed stare.

"Everything's really on the flash drive, but you can't access the flash drive with just any computer. The flash drive is a special one used by organizations like the Department of Defense."

"Nice that the bad guys have access to the same equipment."

David shrugged. "You can buy them online. On the flash drive is everything you can imagine. Information, pictures, dates, money transactions, all linking Raimondi to numerous illegal activities. Stuff Raimondi doesn't want falling into law enforcement hands."

"And you stole it."

He sighed, glanced around the room, and wondered if it was bugged. Finally he nodded toward the bed. "Sit."

She did so. Grudgingly.

Arms crossed, she kept her gaze glued on him. The distrust there pierced like a flaming arrow.

"I'm sorry I lied to you."

"I am too, Ky—David." She rubbed a hand over her eyes. "That's going to take some getting used to."

Did that mean she was going to be around to get used to it? Hope flared, then dimmed when the distrust stayed firmly planted on her face. He sighed. "Summer, I—"

"Who are you?"

He looked away, then back. "I'm a man who made a mess of his life and only by the grace of God was able to attempt to do something to restore it."

She blinked. "By stealing a laptop from the Mafia?" She sighed and closed her eyes. "Oh David."

"I had to. Summer, I was working as a CI for the FBI."

She stared at him. "A confidential informant?"

David ran a hand over his bruised ribs. "To make a long story short, I was in the Army. Special Forces. But I was also part owner in a business. It was what I did when I wasn't on assignment and it provided a good income. When I got home after a long eight-month assignment in Afghanistan, my partner had apparently decided to get into some illegal activities with organized crime using our business as a front while I was gone."

She winced. "How did you find out about it?"

"The FBI approached me. At first I didn't believe it, but the seed of doubt was there. I asked them to give me a week to snoop around and see what I could find out."

"What did you find?"

"Enough to convince me they were telling the truth. Sam was involved with the Mafia and he was using our business just the way the FBI said he was."

"So you started working with them."

"Yeah, but they weren't real interested in Sam. They wanted the big guy. Raimondi. In the first six months, I managed to gain access to his private residence. I planted listening devices, copied whatever I could from whatever computer I came across. But Raimondi is paranoid careful. He never says much over his office phone, he doesn't keep anything on his personal computer, and his staff is extremely loyal because Raimondi treats them like equals."

"Sounds like a stand-up guy," she muttered.

"Then it came to my attention that Sam was going to frame me for murder."

Summer paled. "Murder?"

He nodded. "That business partner I told you about? Sam Gilroy. He killed a man and it was recorded on his laptop."

"Then how would he frame you for the murder?"

"Simple. He didn't know he recorded it, but I did. He was working on a video presentation when Carl Hyatt came in and threatened to go to the building inspector about some substandard materials Sam was using. Sam couldn't let that happen, because if the business was flagged and shut down for an investigation, Raimondi's business would come to a halt. As would all the nice money Sam was pocketing.

"And so he killed him?"

"Yes."

"What about the video?"

"Carl walked in during Sam's recording. After Sam killed him, he had to get him cleaned up. I guess by the time he finished all that, he'd forgotten what he was in the middle of. He simply closed his computer and went home."

"But you got the video?"

"Yes. Later. I couldn't just walk in his office and take it. He carried that laptop with him pretty much everywhere. He left it locked up in his office occasionally, but I was pushed for time. I had to get the laptop before he found the video file with the murder on it. I had one plan. Get the laptop with the flash drive and disappear.

And do it fast." He rubbed his eyes. "I knew I was a dead man. Seconds after I walked in and found Carl dead, Sam was already plotting how to get rid of me. I knew I was going to have to take what I had to the Feds, but I wasn't leaving until I had that evidence. When I came back to work Monday morning, Sam had everything cleaned up and three guys in the office with him."

"Who were they?"

He smirked. "Men who were in Raimondi's pocket. They were also very well-known citizens with a lot of pull in the city. Sam told me that if I said anything about the murder, he had enough evidence to get me tried and convicted. I knew I had to get into his laptop and get that video before he realized what he'd done and erased the evidence. Finally Sam just flat-out asked me what I planned to do. I told him I'd thought about it and wasn't going to do anything, that his business was his business and as long as he kept the illegal part of what he was doing out of the legal side, I'd turn a blind eye."

"But you really wouldn't, would you?"

David shook his head. "No, of course not. I was just buying time to get that laptop. I was hoping to throw him off. I think it worked, because he didn't say anything more and for the rest of the morning acted like everything was normal."

"I can't believe this," she whispered. "Were you going to tell the cops about Carl?"

"Yes. As soon as I could turn over the video."

"This is just crazy. It's like I'm in some messed-up, twisted action movie." He heard the tears in her voice. "This is not what I signed up for when I married you." The last word squeaked out and he moved to hold her.

Only to have her push him away.

The physical pain of her rejection didn't sting nearly as bad as the emotional.

She twisted away, then back. Sucking in a deep breath, he watched her gather her composure. She put her lawyer face on and clasped her hands in front of her. "Okay. So. You told Sam you weren't going to do anything."

He nodded. "But Sam didn't trust me. Like I said, I could tell it was only a matter of time before he had me killed."

"So you played along with Sam, acting like you weren't happy with him but weren't going to do anything like turn him over to the cops."

He shifted. "Yes. In the meantime, I was planning how I was going to get that laptop."

Summer sat still, watching him. At least she was listening.

"I got lucky—Sam hadn't planned for one of our clients to show up that day, but he did, right before lunch. There was just no way for Sam to get out of inviting this client to lunch. I pretended to be on a call when they stopped by and asked me to join them, and I told them I'd catch up with them at the restaurant. Instead I got into Sam's office and started looking for the video on his computer. I had a hard time finding it. Apparently he realized what he'd done and deleted it. Or thought he did."

"But you found it."

"Just because you delete something from your hard drive doesn't mean it's gone."

"Right."

"At first I just wanted the video, but in my search, I found all kinds of information that would be helpful to the FBI. I tried copying it, but it wouldn't. I realized that the flash drive was one of those special ones that can be programmed to work only with a certain computer. I'd used them myself in the Army." He leaned forward, desperate to make her understand why he'd done what he'd done. "You can't copy anything to another device. So I just grabbed the laptop with the flash drive still in the port and walked out of the building. I haven't been back since."

"So why haven't you turned the laptop over to the FBI? If they have the evidence, Raimondi would have no reason to kill you."

"Oh, he has a reason. I betrayed them. Stole information and am cooperating with the authorities."

"But you still haven't given them the laptop."

"No way. I've told the Feds a lot of what was on it and that I'll give it to them a few days before the trial so the prosecuting attorney can properly prepare. They'll have a forensics accountant ready to go, subpoenas issued for the bank account holders and all that. The trial is three weeks away and I'm ready to hand it over. In fact, I was planning to go get it on Monday. But now this—" He shook his head.

"Then let's go get it. Or better yet, tell them where to find it and let them go get it."

David pinched the bridge of his nose. "I would if I knew who I could trust," he said softly. "That laptop—or really, the flash drive—is for my—our—protection. In case Raimondi and his cohorts manage to get their hands on me. See, they don't want to kill me yet. They want me alive so I can tell them where the laptop is. If I fall into their hands, the laptop is simply a way I can buy time to escape. It's my only bargaining tool. I gave the FBI a sampling of what was on that laptop and they're ready to get their hands on the rest. And that's why Raimondi is desperate. He's pretty sure I haven't given the laptop to the FBI yet. But Raimondi knows his time as a free man is short lived."

"So you can't copy anything off the laptop. The flash drive and the laptop go together."

"Right. I was able to get the video off the hard drive where he recorded it. But all of his organized crime dealings were saved on that special flash drive. He used an Imation Enterprise s250 flash drive. It's the kind of flash drive that top secret government officials use. The drives have strong hardware encryption, password protection, retry limits, and all that. You can even remotely disable and destroy the thing, but I managed to get that turned off before I had to hide it. The other thing is, you can control where the drives may be used based on IP addresses or range. I tried to get into the drive after I took it and couldn't access it." He shot her a look. "And I'm good. I'm very good with that kind of thing. But I just didn't have enough time to work with it. I had to hide it before I could crack it."

"So it's hidden now."

"Yes. And I'm the only one who knows where."

"But you said you saw all that stuff on his computer. Names, dates, bank accounts . . ."

"The day I went to copy the video, Sam had some files open from the flash drive. He was careless and didn't shut it down when he left for lunch."

"So if something happens to you . . ."

He shifted. "I've made provisions that if something happens to me, the location of the laptop will be disclosed to the proper authorities. Only Raimondi doesn't know that and neither do the authorities."

"So Raimondi thinks the only way to recover this evidence is to kidnap you."

"Yes. He thinks he can get the information out of me one way or another."

She swallowed. "You mean torture you?"

He nodded and his eyes went dark. "Or you."

15

Summer nibbled on the scrambled eggs Adam had cooked. They were good, but she wasn't in the mood for food. She felt nauseous and tired and scared and—

"You okay?"

She looked up to see Chase enter the kitchen. "I've been better."

"I'm sure."

The sympathy in his gaze made her sigh. "I'm his weakness, aren't I?" she blurted.

Adam glanced up from the paper he was reading. He and Chase exchanged a look, then Chase said, "Yes."

The fact that Chase didn't have to ask for clarification on her question said a lot. "They'll use me to get to him." She wasn't sure why she needed to say the words out loud or even have the fact acknowledged by someone else. David had told her as much last night. It was silly to need it confirmed.

Chase took the seat to her right. A purple bruise shadowed his jawline. He clasped his hands in front of him and leaned forward. "That looks like what their plan is right now. They probably thought you knew where the laptop was when they paid you that surprise visit. They were watching your house, watching you. Having Mike show up wasn't part of their plan."

David walked in and sat at the table across from her. He looked at Chase and gave a small wince when he spotted Chase's face. "Sorry about slugging you."

Chase shrugged. "If it had been my wife, I would have done the same thing."

The admission seemed to surprise David. Summer thought she saw his shoulders loosen up a bit.

She asked the men, "Mike probably saved my life, didn't he? Forcing me to leave my house?"

"Yes." Adam looked at David, then back to her. "Once they realized you really didn't know where the laptop was, you were expendable." He paused. "Although, they probably wouldn't have killed you right away."

She nodded, grimacing at the thought. They would have kept her to use against David. Just like they would do if they got their hands on her now. She shot a glance at her husband. Lips tight, jaw tense, he stared at the wall across from him.

"I know you may not want to hear this," Adam said, "but if something like this has to happen, it's good you and David can be together while it's going on. A lot of times families are separated and never know what's happened to their loved one. It can really tear a family apart."

Summer almost gave him a sarcastic answer, but bit her tongue. He was trying to help.

Chase pointed his half-eaten donut at her. "Raimondi's cohorts obviously followed you and Mike to the hospital and tried to grab you at the first opportunity."

She looked at David. "So the only way we'll truly be safe is if we simply disappear."

David's eyes darkened.

"I honestly don't know that you'll ever be safe again," Chase said.

Summer stared at him. "What about after the trial? When they're all in jail?"

David slapped a hand on the table. "We'll worry about that later."

"No," Summer said, the one word sharp and cutting, "we'll worry about that now. I've spent the last year in the dark. Fill me in with the truth."

Adam shifted and shot David a look. "Raimondi's connections reach far and wide. In all likelihood, even if he's in prison, he'll have revenge on his mind."

"So I'm never going to be safe again?" she whispered.

"You will," David declared. "I'm going to see to it. One way or another you'll be safe."

"What about my family?" she asked. "Are they safe?"

David and Chase exchanged a look.

"We have surveillance on them for now," Chase finally said.

"For now? How long is 'for now'?"

Another tense look. "We're taking it one day at a time."

"I want to talk to my sister."

"No." Adam stood. "You can't do that. You can't have any communication with your family until after the trial."

Summer stood, panic flaring. "I have to! You don't understand my family. They depend on me." David leaned forward and she cut him off before he could speak. "Yes, I know they take advantage of me. But they've got to know I'm all right. I can't just leave them hanging like this." She jabbed a finger at David. "You know how she'll react. I need to talk to her, tell her I'm fine and that she won't hear from me for a while. And what about my mother? I'm supposed to go over tomorrow and fix lunch for her." She paced from one end of the kitchen to the other. "I can't believe this." She froze as she thought about Olivia Todd. "And what about my clients? I have to be at work on Monday. How long is this going to drag out?"

Adam rubbed his head and sighed. "We can give your sister a call. We'll have to get a burn phone."

"We don't have one with us. Mike can get one."

"You don't understand. I don't have time to wait. This is my client's life we're talking about. Her girls and their future. If her husband gets wind of this . . ." She swallowed hard. "And my family. Just two calls, guys. Please . . ."

"Then we'll just have to go somewhere to do it," Adam said. "A pay phone."

Summer noted he ignored her question about how long this ordeal would last. She didn't demand an answer. She knew as well as Chase did, this could last for the next three weeks. Her mind started clicking as she mentally delegated her work schedule. Her paralegal, Celeste, would handle most everything for her.

But Olivia was a different matter.

"Don't you have a secure phone?" David asked.

"Yes, but it would be best to make the call from another location. Raimondi has seriously good computer guys on his team." He looked at Summer. "They've probably got a tracker on all your family's numbers. Even encrypted cell phones can be traced by the right people with the right equipment."

Summer felt sick, the nausea she'd felt earlier returning full force. She glared at David, who sighed and dropped his head. She bolted from the room to the bathroom and lost her breakfast.

David helped Summer into the car. She looked pale and wan, worn out from the constant emotional roller coaster he'd strapped her into. With each beat of his heart, his guilt intensified. He had to find a way to get Summer someplace safe until the trial was over. Chase spoke. David knew his words were aimed at the person on the other end of the device Chase had shoved in his ear, so David kept his attention on Summer.

"Marlee doesn't deserve you." As soon as the words were out, he wanted to recall them.

She turned cold eyes on him. "And I didn't deserve you. Sometimes we get what we don't deserve."

He winced as the barb hit home. The pain of his betrayal stood clear in her eyes. He curled his fingers into a fist against his thigh, the desire to smash something overwhelming. But he couldn't. She was right. She didn't deserve what he'd done.

"Why did you marry me?" she asked.

He kept his gaze on the passing scenery as he pondered how to answer her.

"Stop thinking up a lie and tell me the truth."

"I wasn't trying to think of a lie—"

"The truth."

"There's a lot about me you don't know, Summer."

She gave a soft snort. "Tell me something I *don't* know."

He clenched his jaw, then slowly forced himself to relax it. "I wasn't a Christian when we met, for one thing."

She lifted a brow. "And you are now?"

"Summer."

She turned away, but not before he saw the sheen of tears in her eyes. "I told you what my father did to us."

"I know." Summer's father had betrayed her too. He'd divorced her mother and taken her and her siblings away from the woman. Summer had never forgiven him.

"He lied to me. Joshua lied to me. And now you." A tear slipped down her cheek. The sight nearly ripped his heart in two.

"Summer—"

She swiped the wetness away and looked at him. "So why did you marry me?"

"I love you."

Longing swept over her face, her eyes softened. Hope surged. She shook her head. "You said, love. Not loved."

He sighed and closed his eyes. "I needed a good cover. The people after me weren't looking for a married man with a mortgage. There. You feel better you know the truth now?" His bitter words hung between them.

A low moan came from deep within her, a sound so agonizing he froze for a moment. Then grabbed her and wrapped his arms around her.

Her head fell to his shoulder and he could feel her shaking. "I'm sorry, Summer, I'm so sorry," he whispered against her hair. Mike and Chase sat silent in the front and David ground his teeth at the lack of privacy.

The two men said nothing, but he knew they could probably hear quite a bit of the whispered discussion. It galled him to have this aired in front of them, but he had no choice. Not right now. He had to convince her while she was willing to listen. "I'll make it right, I promise."

A shuddering sigh boiled out of her and she pushed him away. "You used me."

David said nothing. He had no argument. She was right. And yet . . . "Yes. In the beginning. But not really."

"What?" Confusion pulled her brows together.

He swallowed hard and whispered, "From the moment we met, I knew you were different. You looked at me with such . . . innocence, such sweetness. I was drawn to you in a way I've never experienced before."

"Of all the banks you could have chosen, you had to walk into mine."

David swallowed hard. Summer had been at the front of the line to cash a check when her purse had fallen over, littering the bank floor with spare change, a brush, her makeup, all of the things a woman carried. He'd helped her clean up the mess, then asked her for her phone number, then out on a date for that night.

She'd said yes.

And his plan had been born. Make Summer fall in love with him and marry him in a whirlwind courtship.

She let out a breathy laugh. "It only took you two months to get me to marry you. I was a gullible fool, wasn't I?"

16

Raimondi gripped his cell phone and held his volatile temper in check. Barely. "Where are they?" He reached out to run a finger down the back of the red-tailed boa. He'd gotten the one-year-old snake two weeks ago. Six feet long, it curled around the base of the lamp on his desk. Just touching the reptile brought his blood pressure down.

"On the move," Hayes said. "I've got our people on them right now. We should have them in our hands shortly."

"So you say. Did you get the information we needed?"

"Yes. Our source feels quite sure Mrs. Abernathy will not let the fact that her life is in danger stop her from appearing in court to defend her client on Tuesday."

Raimondi thought about that. "So if we lose them between now and then, we know where to find them on Tuesday."

"Most likely. According to my source, Mrs. Abernathy is very passionate about helping this particular client."

His office door opened and Phillip, one of his more trusted hired hands, shoved a trembling young man probably in his early thirties into the room.

Raimondi told Hayes, "Hold on one minute. I need to take care of something. It won't take long." He pressed the hold button and looked at Phillip. "You found him."

"Wasn't easy," the man grunted. "But his girlfriend decided she'd rather keep all of her fingers than hide him any longer."

Raimondi grinned. "You're a fast learner, my boy." He stood and stared at Chico. "You failed me."

Chico swallowed. "I didn't mean to. I didn't know he was undercover, I swear."

"And because you failed me, you must pay a very high price."

Sweat broke out on Chico's forehead.

Raimondi picked up the boa and held it for Chico's inspection. The young man blinked and backed away. Phillip pushed him back, closer to the snake than before.

"You don't like snakes?" Raimondi said.

"S-sure. I like them just fine."

"Oh really?" Raimondi arched his brow. "Well, that's good to hear, not many people do." He put the snake back under the light. It curled around the base once more. "Now, down to business. I lost about two hundred thousand dollars' worth of cocaine thanks to you. How are you going to pay me back? Can you go to your bank and make a nice little withdrawal?"

Chico paled. "No sir. I don't have that kind of money."

"No, I didn't think you did."

"B-but I can get it."

"From where?"

"I-I don't know. Just give me a chance. I'll make it up to you, I promise."

Raimondi pretended to consider it and Chico relaxed a fraction. "No. No, I don't think so."

Chico lost even more color. "Please. I promise. I'll rob a bank. I'll do whatever."

Raimondi nodded to Phillip. Phillip placed his weapon at the base of Chico's skull. Chico whimpered and resumed begging.

Raimondi laughed. "I'm just kidding. You can leave."

Phillip dropped the gun and Chico grasped at his chest as though to hold his heart inside before it pumped right through his skin. Raimondi gestured to the door to his right. "Go."

Chico didn't wait to be told twice. He pulled the door open and slammed it behind him. Phillip walked over and slid the bolt home.

Raimondi flipped the switch on his computer monitor. He watched Chico rush down the stairs and skid to a halt. Another careless flick of his finger released his friends that slithered toward the now-panicked man who realized he'd just walked into a den of vipers. Literally.

"Idiot. He really thought I would let him go? Oy, they fall for it every time." Raimondi spoke the words aloud, aware that Phillip had already left the room. On the monitor, Raimondi watched Chico race back the way he'd come and grab the doorknob, which, of course, wouldn't turn. The door rattled and Raimondi heard a faint pounding, a soft scream. He'd soundproofed the area to the point he could hear some, but not a lot. Raimondi watched the monitor.

Chico turned and pressed his back against the door and, in a panic, kicked out at the first snake, then the next. Fool. If he would just be still, the snakes wouldn't attack. Raimondi clucked. His victims never failed to disappoint him. They panicked every time.

After the first bite, Raimondi lost interest. For some reason Chico's screams annoyed him. He would be quiet soon enough and Phillip would be back to clean up the mess.

Raimondi flipped off the monitor, picked the phone up, and reconnected with Hayes, who'd been telling him about Summer's court date with her client. "Who's the client?"

"A woman by the name of Olivia Todd. She's fighting her husband for custody of her two young girls. If Summer doesn't show up, it's very likely that Mrs. Todd will lose custody. Her husband's a well-to-do stockbroker. Lots of money." He grunted. "And an abuser. I'm tempted to take the man out and save them the trouble of going to court on Tuesday."

"No. If you want to kill him, I'm fine with that, but wait until after Tuesday." Raimondi calculated. "Okay, that's three days from now. I want Hackett before then, but if he manages to elude us, we'll have to grab him and his wife on Tuesday at the courthouse. Security is tight there. It'll be hard to do."

"I've got ways to get past that."

"Then get it set up just in case we need to go that route. I don't want to, but there's too much at stake and I need the laptop and David dead before the trial."

"Like I said, I've got an inside track to the courthouse. We'll get them there if we have to."

Raimondi watched the snake slither across the desk and down onto the floor. "I have a feeling David will do pretty much anything to keep us from hurting Summer."

Hayes snorted. "He's a former Ranger. He'll know we're just going to kill her anyway."

"Very true, but it'll be up to him how much she suffers before she dies."

17

Summer sank into the warmth of her coat and watched the scenery fly by while she played with the cross necklace around her neck. She thought about what it meant. He'd given it to her for their first-month anniversary.

A symbol of their kindred faith. Of their love centered on the One who had brought them together. Only now she wasn't sure who she married, much less what he truly believed—or if God had even had a hand in anything. Chase stomped on the brake. Summer jerked forward against the seat belt.

"What is it?"

"Sorry," Chase said. "Traffic." He looked in the rearview mirror at Mike and demanded, "Why didn't we know about this?"

Mike was already on the phone. "Get off and take an alternate route. We can't be jammed in like this."

Adam had his laptop open, typing furiously. "If you can go up the shoulder to the next exit, we can get around this."

"Anyone behind us?" David asked.

"Not so far." Chase spun the wheel and moved onto the shoulder to go around the mess. Summer caught her breath as an 18-wheeler pulled to the right to block them. Chase laid on the horn. The trucker stayed put. "Unbelievable. Run his plates."

Mike shifted on the seat beside her.

Three slow minutes passed. They inched forward. Summer's tension escalated with each second. Dizziness hit her and she realized she was holding her breath. Breathe, she told herself. Just breathe.

The trucker stayed half in the lane, half on the shoulder. Adam snapped, "Get the company dispatcher to tell him to move."

"No time for that. I want off this road." Mike pushed open the door and stomped up to the passenger side of the truck. Summer saw the door open, Mike flashed his badge and waved his hand. A gunshot sounded and Mike dropped. The truck door shut and the driver gunned the engine.

Another shot from behind them and the car jerked. "Go! Go!" Adam's shout rang through the vehicle.

Heart thudding, Summer spun her head to see three men bearing down on them, weaving through the traffic, weapons drawn. "Behind us!"

Adam already had them spotted. He knocked his computer out of the way and shoved his door open. "Stay down!" To Chase, "Get them out of here."

Could Adam hold them off? And what about Mike?

David grabbed her hand and opened his door. "Come on! We stay here, we're dead!"

Chase spared him a glance. "Stay put." The car limped forward. "They got two of our tires."

"What about Mike?" Summer asked.

David's grim face and tight jaw said he thought Mike was beyond help.

Another shot and Summer ducked as the bullet slammed into the window. Glass shattered. David pulled her from the vehicle. She managed to snag her purse and then sucked in a terrified breath as she scrambled after him.

Adam and Chase hollered, but David ignored them. His right hand gripped her left. "Hunch over and run," he told her. "Make yourself as small a target as possible. Stay right with me."

His unflappable cool gave her confidence and steadied her shaky legs. David moved between terrified motorists. If he was bothered by the pain of his ribs, she couldn't tell. He moved like he did this on a daily basis.

Shots chased them down the highway as they weaved in and out of the cars. "We're putting these people in danger," she huffed.

"Keep going. To the left and down that hill."

A bullet zinged past her right ear. More gunfire, screams, horns honking. Summer tried to block the sensory overload of sound. David's grip tightened. Her feet flew across the ground. They scrambled down the hill. Thankfully, it wasn't very steep.

Yet steep enough that they were now out of range of bullets. David pulled her along and she fought to keep up. She was in good shape, but no match for the husband who ran five miles every morning. He found the sidewalk. "There's a hotel."

"Won't they expect us to do that?" she panted.

"I'm hoping they expect us to keep running as fast and as far as possible."

She followed him, dodging other people on the sidewalk. David slowed, a hand pressed to his ribs his only indication they pained him.

She wanted to push him to go faster, but knew he didn't want to draw attention to them. So they strolled, hand in hand, like they hadn't a care in the world. "How did they know we were on the highway?"

"I don't know." He stopped outside the hotel and looked around. "We need to figure that out, though. Either there's a mole with the marshals or they were tracking the car somehow."

Summer frowned.

David led her into the nearest store. "Stay here out of sight of the street. I'm going to get a room and we're going to lay low while we figure out a plan."

"Stay here?"

"I've got cash and I don't want to check in as a couple. That's what they'll be looking for. Not a single guy."

She nodded. "Just hurry."

David smoothed her hair away from her face and pressed a kiss to her lips. "I'm going to make up for everything, Summer, I promise."

Pain lanced through her and she gave him a small shove. "Go get the room." He muddled her thinking when he was so close. Everything in her wanted to shout that she forgave him, that it didn't matter about the past. But she couldn't do that. The memory of him looking her straight in the eye and promising to never lie to her just wouldn't leave her alone.

He was a good liar. How did she know he wasn't lying now?

She didn't.

"Keep an eye on the street," he said. "If you see anyone suspicious, get into the men's room."

"The men's room?"

Frustration crossed his face. "They'll look for you in the ladies' room first."

"Anything to throw them off. Okay."

"We're taking a lot of calculated risks. It's all a gamble. Hopefully, this is one that will pay off."

"I'll be waiting. Go."

He jogged across the street. Summer let her gaze pierce the surrounding area. So far she saw no one that stood out, no one who looked like the three goons who'd tried to kill them on the highway. She swallowed hard. Were Chase and Adam okay? And Mike? Had he been shot or had he just dropped when he heard the gun go off? And what about her family? She pulled out her cell phone and stared at it. Then stuck it back in her pocket.

She didn't dare.

But what about her family? Worry cramped her stomach. She reached up and grasped the necklace, rubbing her thumb over the ridges of the cross as she prayed for wisdom—and a plan.

A sedan drove by the store. Slowed. And stopped on the curb.

She moved deeper into the clothes rack behind her.

"May I help you?"

Summer jerked and whipped her head to the left. The necklace popped off in her hand and she gasped. "Oh no."

A saleswoman in her early forties stood watching her, brow raised. "Do you need any help?"

"Uh . . . I'm just . . ." She forgot about the necklace even as she tightened her fingers around it. Two men got out of the car. One in a dark suit, the other in khakis and a leather jacket.

"Ma'am?"

Summer turned back to the saleswoman. "I'm running from my husband," she blurted. "That's him. I don't know how he found me, but he did. If he catches me, he'll kill me."

Shock blanched the woman's face white. Then red. She stuck her chin out. "Follow me."

"What?"

"I have a place you can hide. Then I'll get rid of him."

"But I don't want to put you in dan—"

"Hurry. I'm Casey and I've been where you are." She glanced at the window. "Come on now, he's coming."

Summer shut up and hurried after the woman, her spine tingling as the bell above the door announced the arrival of the men who wanted to kill her.

18

David slid the room key into his pocket and stepped to the glass entrance door to the hotel. He glanced across the street where Summer was supposed to be waiting for him. When his gaze landed on the dark sedan parked in front of the store, his stomach flipped. Fear for Summer invaded him.

He pushed through the door and crossed the street, his hand reaching for the weapon in the shoulder holster Chase had provided him.

Once inside the warmth of the store, he stepped immediately behind a clothing rack near the right front corner. Through the slitted opening created by two of the denim shirts, he scanned the area in front of him. Three customers who hadn't even looked up at the dinging of the bell and one employee talking to the two suits at the cash register.

No Summer. That he could see.

He moved closer. David recognized the taller of the two as Raimondi's nephew, Agostino Greco. A chill swept through him. Raimondi had called out the big guns. Agostino didn't usually step up to the front lines to get his hands dirty. But when he did, he was deadly and efficient.

The woman shook her head. "I'm sorry, sir, I haven't seen this woman."

"We've tracked her to this store. Do you have security video?"

"Of course."

"Then we'd like to see it."

"Absolutely not."

"Look, lady—" The taller of the two men jabbed a finger at her.

Agostino laid a hand on his shoulder. The other man let out a curse and spun on his heel to pace and shove aside clothing on the nearest rack.

"Hey! You've no right to manhandle my inventory. Back off or I'll call 911." She grabbed the handset from the base and shook it at him.

David saw alarm on the other customers' faces. One woman swallowed hard and pulled out her phone as she backed toward the door.

The others followed, their instinct telling them this might be a good time to get out.

The bell chimed once, twice. David let out a slow breath. Through the window behind him, he saw the three women pause on the sidewalk. One had a phone pressed to her ear.

The cops would be here soon. Agostino shot a glance at the door. He knew it too.

"Ma'am." Agostino kept his cool as he turned his attention back to the woman. David had never seen the man lose it. "She's a fugitive. And dangerous. We just don't want to see anyone get hurt." The false concern in Agostino's voice grated all over David's nerves, and if Summer hadn't most likely been hiding somewhere nearby, he would have been tempted to do a little bodily damage. Instead, he exercised self-control. And prayed.

"Neither do I," the employee said. "I haven't seen that woman.

Now if you want to come back with a warrant, we'll talk about viewing the security footage."

David processed the information. The men had identified themselves as law enforcement. And still she wasn't talking. *Thank you, Lord.* Where was Summer?

Frustration stamped itself on the tall man's face. He leaned in. "If you're lying to me, I'll be back."

"I'll be here." She stared him down and he turned with a ripple of curses.

David gave a silent cheer for the woman's unwillingness to be bullied by the two men. He didn't think either of them would hurt her. Yet.

He hung back in his hiding place, keeping his cool, slowing his pulse by sheer will. Relief and worry filled him at the same time. Relief that Summer wasn't in the wrong hands and worry about her location. Had she seen Agostino and his partner enter and somehow manage to escape the store?

David saw Agostino heave a sigh, as though by drawing in the air, he could pull in more patience. He gripped his partner's arm and nodded to the door. "Thank you for talking to us."

The two men came close enough for David to reach out and touch. He held his breath as they paused.

Agostino said in a low voice, "We'll find her, Gianni, but not if you lose your temper. She's here somewhere. Let's get out and bide our time. You take the back door, I'll cover the front."

Gianni's nostrils flared over his tight lips, but he gave a nod and stepped outside. David waited for the door to shut. He sidled around the rack toward the store's interior and stood there. Waiting.

The owner of the store moved to the front door and locked it. Then she whirled and returned to the back of the store. She swept behind a black curtain and David could hear voices. Murmuring.

He stepped from his hiding place. "Summer?"

A gasp.

The woman pushed the curtain aside, her eyes wide and scared. "How did you get in here?"

"I've been here. I don't want to hurt Summer. I'm here to get her someplace safe."

She studied him a moment. "You're not with those clowns that just left?"

"No ma'am. Not even close."

"It's all right, Casey," Summer said as she came from the back. Her eyes met his. "He'll keep me safe."

David winced at the thin thread of sarcasm.

Casey looked uncertain.

Summer walked toward him and he took her hand. "They're covering the front and the back." He looked at Casey. "Is there another way out?"

She lifted a brow. "The roof?"

Summer watched David shove the roof-access door open and climb out. He turned and offered his hand. She slung her purse over her shoulder and grabbed his wrist. He hauled her up and out beside him with one effortless pull—and a gasp. She looked at his white face. "The ribs?"

"The ribs." But he shook it off and let his hand slide from her wrist to her finger.

In spite of his obvious pain, strength emanated from him.

Strength he'd always used to protect her. Always gentle, always aware that he could hurt her physically. And always careful not to.

When he let go, she stumbled and reached out to steady herself on David's arm.

Her cross necklace slid through her grasping fingers and fell through the opening to the floor below. "My necklace!"

He stopped her from turning. "Let it go, I'll get you another one."

"I don't want another one. I want that one." The admission

surprised her, revealed things to her. She was still in love with her husband no matter how much he'd betrayed her. She was mad and hurt and not thinking straight, but she still loved him.

The first moment she'd laid eyes on him, he'd taken her breath away. Today was no different other than the fact that she forced herself to ignore her desire to wrap her arms around him and bury her head against his shoulder. She couldn't do that. One, she was still hurt from his lies. And two, time was not on their side.

"This way. Be careful." He kept a firm grip on her hand and led her across the roof to the next building. Then the next and the next. Finally, he stopped. "Here's where we go down." The ladder disappeared in a curve over the side of the building.

Summer looked over the edge and gulped. "That's a long way down, David."

"I'll be right below you."

"Won't people think it's weird to see us coming off the building?"

"Yeah, which is why we're going to wait until the coast is clear or until dark."

"Dark? That's hours from now."

"I know." He got to his knees and looked over the side of the building. "We're three stories up. That's not too bad."

"Might as well be fifty." He didn't argue with her. She asked, "Can you see anyone?"

"Yeah. They keep circling this block." He watched, his shoulders tense.

"Don't we need to let someone know you're okay?"

"Not yet. I'm not so sure I need to let any of them know where we are."

"Why not? They're the US Marshals."

He stared off into the distance. "Because Raimondi keeps finding us."

"But how?" She paused. "You don't think one of the marshals is telling them where we are, do you?"

"I don't know. But it's something to think about." He shook his head and turned to watch the area they'd come from. She tried to figure out what he was looking for. "We're pretty well blocked from view if anyone comes up, but that means we can't see them either."

She ignored his last comment. "Really? You think someone's feeding Raimondi information?"

"I can't see Adam or Chase being a snitch. Or Mike either." He pursed his lips. "I mean, why wait until now? Three weeks before the trial?"

Summer thought, then offered, "Unless Mike thought he'd be able to get you to give up the laptop before now."

David rubbed a hand across his chin and stared at her. "Good point."

"Was Mike shot?"

"I don't think so. The shot came from behind us. I saw him get up pretty quick after that. It was reflex. Hear a shot, hit the ground."

They fell silent. Summer finally asked, "What are we going to do?"

"That's what I'm trying to decide."

"Well, we can't avoid these guys by ourselves." She looked at him. "Can we?"

He studied her, his eyes shuttered. "No, probably not."

"I see your brain working. What are you thinking?"

"They're here! They gotta be!" The shout from below drew their attention and Summer offered up a silent prayer. *Keep us hidden, Lord.*

Summer looked over the edge and saw one of the men from the store pacing and yelling at his cell phone. "They went in, but they didn't come out and they're not in the store. We searched it." A pause. "Check the roof."

Summer and David dropped to the asphalt. His jaw tightened and he caught her gaze. "Okay, now we have to move again. They're going to be up here any minute."

She looked around. "Where do you suggest we move to? We're kind of at the end of the line here."

He peered over once again. "The ladder has to be lowered from the next level. They can't get up on this side. As soon as he disappears, we go down."

"No waiting for dark, huh?" She gave a nervous rub of her hands. She didn't like heights.

"Afraid not."

Adrenaline surged again.

He continued to watch over the edge, then swung his leg over. "Follow me."

19

"Should have put a tracker on him," Mike muttered as he paced from one end of the hotel room to the other. The bullet had grazed his forehead. He'd slapped a Band-Aid on it and taken four ibuprofen to combat the monster headache now pounding in his skull. But at least he was alive and able to track down his wayward witness.

"He'll call," Chase said.

"He's not going to call," Mike countered.

"Why wouldn't he call?" Adam asked.

"Because he's gonna go off on his own." Mike wore another layer off the carpet.

Chase looked at Mike. "That's crazy. He doesn't stand a chance. Just him and Summer? He'll get them both killed."

Mike shook his head. "He's a former Ranger. He's got contacts he can call and places he can hide."

Adam frowned. "Then why did he consent to WITSEC?"

Mike rubbed a hand down his face. "Because I talked him into it."

Chase walked to the sink and filled a glass with water. "Why did he need talking into it?"

"Because he's a former Ranger with contacts he can call and places he can hide," Adam muttered.

Mike shot Adam a dark look. "I assured him any time he felt

like the marshals weren't doing their job, he was free to take off and take care of himself."

Chase slammed the glass onto the counter. Mike winced and was surprised the thing was still in one piece.

"You told him what?" Chase said.

Mike shrugged. "I would have told him anything to keep him nearby." At Chase and Adam's censoring looks, Mike ran a hand over his head, hating the need to defend his actions to his peers. "Look, he was ready to ditch me after he gave me the video of Sam Gilroy committing murder, even though he knew Raimondi would be coming for him. I wanted him where I could keep an eye on him. I wanted him alive for the trial. I didn't want him found in a back alley somewhere."

"So you told him what he wanted to hear."

"Yeah." He shrugged. "Well, it wasn't a lie. No one forces anyone into the WITSEC program. He knew that and I knew that, but I wanted to convince him of the benefits of staying. I did and he stayed. Reluctantly." He paused. "Meeting Summer was the clincher. The day he met her he quit fighting me on it, quit pacing like a caged lion and settled down into becoming Kyle Abernathy and enjoying domestic bliss."

Mike let Chase and Adam digest this. Chase finally asked, "So who would he call for help?"

"The guys in his former unit probably," Mike said.

The three fell silent.

Chase paced to the door and back. He always reminded Mike of a sleek panther ready to strike at any given moment. When he unleashed that strength, it was an amazing—and scary—thing to see. Mike had seen it once. He'd rather not see it again.

Chase spun on his heel. "All right. So who are the guys in his unit?"

Mike shot him a perturbed glance. "That's confidential."

"And you knew who they were ten minutes after you had him

in custody." Adam snorted. "We've seen you use your own connections."

With a lifted brow, Mike kept quiet. What Adam said was true. He was well connected and used those connections to ferret out any info that would benefit him as a handler.

"Why'd he leave the unit?" Adam asked.

Mike pursed his lips. "Not sure. He refused to tell me." And he truly didn't know.

More silence as they thought.

Mike sat and leaned forward, his head in his hands. Responsibility sat heavy on his shoulders. If he didn't get David back and the man missed the trial, his career was over. Done. He might as well put his gun in his mouth and pull the trigger. Anger surged. Why hadn't David called? He looked up. "Summer's still got her phone with her. Let's see if we can get a location on her."

Adam pulled the laptop around to face him. "She had it turned off."

"Maybe she'll turn it on." Mike kept his temper under control. Going ballistic wouldn't help anything.

Except maybe make him feel better.

"What about David? Does he have a phone?"

"He didn't when he got out of the car."

"I've got Marlee Chastain's phone up," Chase said. "So far she's received two calls since Summer and David took off. The first one traced back to Summer and Marlee's mother. It lasted just over an hour. The second one was from a woman by the name of Kristen Lee."

"That's a co-worker of Marlee's," Mike said.

"That call lasted fifteen minutes."

"So no calls from strange numbers."

"Nope."

"Then keep tracking. It'll happen."

"How'd Raimondi know we were there, Mike?" Chase asked.

"They were right behind us on the interstate. Mere minutes. Like they were following us."

Mike frowned. "I don't know how they found us."

Adam leaned forward and clasped his hands between his knees. "Three times they've found us without any trouble. They're tracking us somehow."

Chase stared at Mike. "Or someone's telling them where we are."

Mike stiffened. "What are you saying?"

Chase didn't look away. Neither did Adam.

Mike's heart sank. "Really?" Wounded, he stood and paced to the window, then whirled to face them. "How long have we worked together? You honestly believe I would work for Raimondi?"

Indecision flashed across Adam's face. Chase simply watched him. Then said, "I sure don't want to, but I know it's not me or Adam."

"So it's me by default."

"Okay, Mike, it's not you," Adam said. "Then who is it?"

"Who says it has to be anyone?" he asked slowly. "What if it's David?"

Chase lifted a brow. "David?" He let out a humorless laugh. "Why would he sic Raimondi on his own tail?"

"And besides," Adam said, "he'd never put Summer in danger. He loves her."

Mike shrugged. "I don't know. I don't have an answer for it. All I know is they're tracking us somehow or someone higher up is letting Raimondi in on our locations."

"Then maybe we need to go off grid," Chase said.

Mike rubbed his chin. "You mean once we get Summer and David back, don't tell anyone where we take them?"

"Yeah. Not even the boss. Just us."

Mike nodded. "That might be an option to think about."

20

David reached up and helped Summer down off the ladder while watching the street, his nerves taut and expecting action.

"Where are we going?" Summer gasped.

He gripped her hand and pulled her after him. "To the hotel."

"That's crazy, David. We have to get as far away from those guys as we can."

"That's what I'm praying they're thinking too."

"What if they're thinking what you're thinking?"

Together, they crossed the street, David looking both ways. And not just for cars. They ducked into the hotel and he stood to the side of the glass doors, Summer tucked behind him. "If they're thinking what I'm thinking, then . . ."

"Then what?"

"We'll need to think of a new plan."

"What's the old plan?"

David heard the exasperation mixed with fear in her voice. "There." He pointed. "They're coming out of the shops."

Summer gasped and pulled back. "You don't think they hurt Casey, do you?"

"Casey?"

"The woman who helped me hide from Raimondi's men. The one who helped us escape to the roof."

"I wouldn't think so, but we'll put a call in to the cops to go check on her. Will that make you feel better?"

She nodded.

He stayed put, watching. The men consulted an iPad and David wondered what they were looking at. Then Agostino stomped to the black sedan and motioned for his partner to get in. The partner argued, but finally acquiesced. They drove off and David let out a slow breath. "Okay, let's get up to our room and start planning."

She jerked to a stop. "Our room? As in one singular room? Don't you mean rooms?" She emphasized the s.

David sighed. "Summer, you can't be alone. I know you hate my guts right now, but I won't leave you to the mercies of the Raimondis."

She bit her lip and stared at him.

David ran a hand through his hair. "Look, it's a suite. You can have the bed and I'll stay on the couch if it'll make you happy."

"Happy?" She scoffed and her eyes went sad. "Yeah," she said, her voice so soft he had to strain to hear it. "That'll make me happy."

"Okay then."

They rode the elevator to the second floor and David motioned for her to stay put. "Let me check the room."

She frowned but didn't argue. It took him less than ten seconds to clear it.

Summer strode to the bathroom and stopped. Without turning around, she said, "I don't hate your guts."

"What?"

"You heard me."

"Where are they?" Raimondi growled into the phone. He eyed the cages of his pets. Snakes. They were very therapeutic for him.

The red boa had quickly become his favorite and he kept the snake nearby so he could run a hand over it during these stressful times.

"I don't know." Impatience tinged Hayes's voice. "Their trail stops at the shop. Either they're hiding really well or they found the tracker."

"Tear that shop up and find them."

"That's what I told Agostino and Gianni to do. They're not there, but the tracker says they are."

"So they found it and ditched it."

"It looks like it."

Curses ripped from Raimondi's throat. "Why is it so hard to grab two people? Agostino and Gianni are *your* responsibility. They report to *you*. This is what you *do*! This is your *job*. You're an assassin, for the love of—" He felt the vein in his temple begin to throb and took a deep breath. In a low, quiet, lethal voice, he said, "I want them in my custody. Now. What's the next step? What do we have to do to get them?"

"First of all we have to find them."

"Then do it. Or you'll pay for your incompetence."

"I have an idea on how to do that. To lure them out of hiding in order to get at them."

"I don't even need to know what the plan is. Just do it."

He hung up and reached for the boa, lifting the snake with a gentle touch. Raimondi placed a cheek against the scaly skin. Instantly, the pounding of his heart eased. "Ah yes, my friend, you know how to turn a bad day into a better one."

When he calmed down, he set the snake aside and watched it slither to curl under the sunlamp Raimondi kept for the reptile. He eyed the glass aquarium cages and smiled at his collection. A diamondback rattlesnake. A rare red coral kukri, found in India— he'd paid well over a million dollars for that one.

A knock on the door pulled his attention from his obsession. "Come in."

The door opened and his sister entered. Her swollen eyes attested to her grief. His heart ached for her and yet he didn't have time to deal with her hysterics. Not now. But he rose and walked to her. He took her hands in his and kissed her cheek. As he led her to the brown leather sofa, he said, "What brings you by here today?"

"Revenge," she whispered. "I want revenge for Pauli's death, Alessandro. I can't sleep, I can't eat, I can't function."

"You will have your revenge. David Hackett will pay for what he's done to this family."

"First Georgina, now Pauli . . ." She shook her head. "I don't understand. What did we do to make him hate us?"

He squeezed her hands. "Some people don't need an excuse to hate. They just do."

She sighed. "Is Georgina here?"

"I haven't seen her today."

The red boa slithered close and she jumped to her feet with a shriek. "Why do you insist on having those awful creatures? In a cage is one thing, but roaming free?" With a shudder, she backed toward the door. "What about Rosalinda? Is she here?"

"Yes, in the kitchen, I believe." The last time he'd seen his wife, she was baking cookies to tempt Georgina from her room.

"Fine." With one more glance toward the snakes lining his wall, and one last shudder, she left.

Raimondi chuckled as he leaned over to pick up the boa and place a kiss on its head. "You, my scaly friend, have great timing."

21

Summer headed straight for the shower. She needed to be alone. Totally and completely alone. David didn't say anything, just let her be. He knew her well enough to stay away right now. She lathered her hair and thought.

She really didn't hate his guts. In fact it bothered her that she was having a hard time holding on to her anger.

And that made her mad.

She should be furious. She should be giving him the cold shoulder and doing everything in her power to make him squirm by reminding him of his guilt, his incredible gall to lie and think he would get away with it without suffering any consequences.

So why wasn't she?

Because she was hurt. Hurt once again. Someone who'd professed to love her the rest of her life had uttered those words as though they held all the meaning of ordering lunch at the drive-thru. It hurt.

Maybe the anger would come back, but right now, she just ached with a sense of loss so deep she wasn't sure how to even begin processing it.

When she finished the shower, she wrapped the towel around her and sat on the toilet to stare at the wall. *What am I going to do, God? How could you let this happen? I thought he was the one you wanted for me and now this? I don't understand what you're doing, why you're allowing this to happen. And I really don't like it.*

Summer wasn't terribly religious. She'd grown up going to church because her mother needed some free day care a few times a week. But the lessons had sunk in and she'd become a Christian at the age of sixteen at a church youth retreat. She thought maybe it had been because she'd desperately wanted a father to love her and, lacking one in her home, the thought of having one with her all the time, in the spiritual sense, really appealed to her.

Well, of course that was part of it, but there was more to it than that. She'd really thought God had a plan for her life and had tried to live accordingly.

And now this. She hadn't foreseen anything like this.

"I must have messed up somewhere, God, because I don't see how marrying a man who wasn't who he said he was and now running from someone who wants us dead was a part of your plan." Nausea and exhaustion swept over her. She had to get some rest or she was going to simply pass out.

A knock sounded on the door. "Summer? You all right?"

"I'll be out in a minute."

"I've got some clean clothes for you. May I come in?"

"Yes."

He opened the door and passed her a backpack. She took it without looking at him and rummaged through it. It had all of the essentials. "Where'd you get this?"

"A friend. Dress before you come out, okay?"

"He's here?"

"Yeah."

Lovely. David was having friends over while all she wanted to do was sleep and shut out the world if only for a brief time. She sighed. "I won't be long."

Within minutes she was dressed in her favorite brand jeans and a purple short-sleeved shirt. She pushed the sweatshirt aside for later. Even the undergarments were her size and the brand she favored. She had to admit it felt wonderful to slip on clean clothes. She left the towel wrapped around her wet head and stepped into the living area of the suite. David and another man who looked to be in his early fifties sat on the couch. An arsenal of weapons graced the dark wood coffee table.

The sinking sensation in Summer's stomach took over again. She swallowed hard. So. This was her life now.

David motioned her over and the man with him stood. "Summer," David said, "I want you to meet a friend of mine. This is Ron."

Summer shook Ron's hand. Salt-and-pepper hair, dark eyes, and a five o'clock shadow made him seem menacing somehow, dark. Then Ron crinkled a smile at her and she saw a light in his eyes that overshadowed the darkness. "Good to finally meet you, Summer."

"Thanks for the clothes."

"My pleasure."

Her nose twitched. She smelled food and her stomach rumbled in anticipation. She nodded to the weapons. "What's going on?"

David pulled a black backpack from under the table. "Making sure we have what we need to survive."

She flicked a glance at Ron, then back to David. "Shouldn't we be leaving? They're probably tracking your phone."

Her husband shot her a gentle smile. "I didn't use my phone. I used the hotel phone to call a number they don't have in their system. They can't track us. Yet."

"But they'll be checking hotels, right?"

"Yes. They may or may not check this one since it's so close to where we disappeared. They'll figure we ran for a while."

"You hope."

"Yeah."

Summer sighed and walked to the mini fridge and pulled out a bottle of water.

Ron asked, "Are you hungry?"

"Starving."

Ron pushed a brown sack toward her. "Tomato soup and a roast beef sandwich on toasted whole wheat bread. Plus an apple."

She stared at the bag as though it would bite her. David had married her without loving her and yet he'd managed to find the kind of clothes she liked and had Ron bring her favorite meal. Something he hadn't had to do. They were running from killers and he thought about small details that would matter to her.

Summer took the bag and moved to the small round table. "Thank you." She sat in the chair and began eating while the guys muttered back and forth. When the conversation lulled, she asked, "How do you two know each other?"

David paused, exchanged a glance with Ron. "Ron saved my life."

"Tell me."

Two simple words that demanded a great deal. He rubbed a hand down his cheek. "Ron was hitchhiking and I picked him up."

Summer lifted a brow at him. "When was this?"

"About a year ago."

"November sixteenth," Ron said.

Summer's gaze shot to his. "What? That was the week after we got back from our honeymoon. The week you were on that business trip to New York. The one that came up at the last minute and couldn't be put off." She laid her spoon on the table. "You didn't have any business in New York, did you?"

"Oh I had business all right. It just wasn't what I told you."

"Of course it wasn't," she muttered. She sighed. "So why did you go to New York?"

"I had to get that laptop."

"But why? You already gave the video to the cops and Sam was in jail."

"I went to get the laptop. About thirty minutes after I walked out of Sam's office with the laptop, someone tried to kill me. I knew I had to act fast, so I hid the laptop and flash drive. I was worried Sam would figure out where I'd hidden them and tell Raimondi. I got paranoid. I had more than myself to think of now." He shot her a meaningful glance. "I got to New York, got the laptop and the flash drive, but I was attacked and," he shrugged, "the rest of the week I was in the hospital recuperating from a car wreck—"

"You were in a wreck and you didn't call me?" Summer glared at him.

"I couldn't. If they found out where I was and you'd come to the hospital, that would have put you in danger."

The anger faded from Summer's eyes.

"I had a lot of time to think about my life. That's when I asked God to make me into the kind of man who deserved to have a wife like you."

She blinked. "A wife like me?"

"Good, kind, innocent . . ." He swallowed hard. "Everything I wasn't, but at that point, wanted to be." He shook his head and glanced at Ron. "I couldn't let Raimondi find that laptop. That computer was the key to getting the guys at the top of the food chain." He clenched his fingers into a fist. "And I wanted those guys. Carl Hyatt was a good man. He didn't deserve to die. At the time of his death, there was nothing I could do about it. But now that I had the laptop and the flash drive, I couldn't lose it. That information meant justice for a lot of people. Sam was just a low man on the totem pole." He narrowed his eyes. "I wanted the guy at the top and so did the FBI."

"Oh, David," she whispered. He could see the horror in her eyes. "But how could you let Carl Hyatt's death go, how could you not report it?"

He ducked his head and prayed for guidance, for patience for Summer to let him finish telling the story. "I know how it sounds, but you have to understand, that's the way it works sometimes." He sighed and shook his head. "So anyway, with Sam in jail, things should have calmed down."

"But they didn't," she said.

"No. They escalated. Sam was connected to the Raimondi family. The mob or organized crime."

"And they were mad at you because you had Sam arrested."

"Yes. That was one thing."

"What was the other?"

"They didn't care so much about Sam, mostly they were upset because I had Sam's laptop." He stood and paced to the table where she sat, then to the bedroom, then back to the couch. "But Sam was one of theirs. He worked for them and made a lot of money for them. They were using our business to launder money, hide weapons at some of the construction sites. You name it, they're into it. With Sam's arrest, a full investigation of the company would ensue."

"I remember seeing something about that on the news."

"It made the national networks," David said. "They knew I was the reason Sam was arrested, Sam's laptop was missing. They put two and two together and came up with the right answer. If they found me, they'd find the laptop."

"Why would the marshals agree to protect you if you didn't have anything to give them?"

"Because I agreed to testify at Sam's trial and I also agreed to get the laptop and flash drive and turn it over to them. Eventually. In turn, Mike convinced me to stay in the WITSEC program for a limited time. But I knew they wouldn't stop coming for me as long as that laptop was still out there."

"So you left after our honeymoon to get it. That still doesn't tell me how you and Ron met."

Ron stood. "I'll let David finish his story. I've got to be going." He looked at David. "Let me know if you need anything else."

"Will do."

The men shook hands. Ron gathered the leftover weapons and was gone almost as fast as he'd appeared.

David picked up the Smith & Wesson Model 60 and hefted it. Small, lightweight at twenty-four and a half ounces, it would slide nicely into the ankle holster Ron had also provided. The little gun wouldn't do much in a long drawn-out gunfight, but the extra five rounds were an extra five chances of escape should they need them.

"Pick your weapon."

She stared at him, her lips tight. "This was why you taught me to shoot, wasn't it?"

David sighed. "Part of it."

"And the self-defense training?"

"Yes." He gave her a slow smile. "But the self-defense training was mostly because I liked the way the sessions ended." With her in his arms.

She didn't even blush. Or return his smile. "You can finish your story later. I'm exhausted."

"Summer—"

"And I still need to call Marlee. Did Ron leave you a phone that can't be traced, by any chance?"

He fished in his pocket and held it out to her.

22

Summer dialed Marlee's number and waited, nerves tense, mentally preparing herself for the tirade she knew was coming.

By the end of the third ring, she almost allowed herself to relax. She could just leave a message.

"Hello?"

The tension came back full force. "Hi, Marlee."

"Summer! Where are you? What are you doing?"

"One question at a time. I can't tell you where I am. Some bad guys are after me and I have to hide out for a while."

"Well, thank you very much. I'm guessing it's the same bad guys that came after me and broke my arm yesterday?" Panic and fear mixed with the anger in her voice.

Summer stood still. "What?"

"Yeah, what do you think about that, sister dear? You get mixed up in something and I suffer for it."

Her sister's hard words sliced at Summer's heart. "Marlee, I'm so sorry."

"And I think they're watching the house." Sobs finally broke through. "Oh, Summer, I'm so scared. I don't know what to do or where to go. You weren't answering your phone and Mom and Nick left yesterday to fly out to Houston to meet with that specialist and I'm—"

"They did? I didn't know they were doing that this week. I thought that was next week."

"They changed it. And is that all you can focus on when I'm telling you my life is in danger?" Marlee's high-pitched squeal made Summer grimace.

"Calm down, Marlee."

"Calm down? Calm down? I—" Her sister's voice cut off with a scream and Summer blinked.

"Marlee? Marlee?"

"Well, hello, Mrs. Abernathy."

She froze. And spun to stare at David. He was looking at the weapons, the contentious conversation between her and Marlee nothing new for him. "Who is this?"

His head snapped up. That part was new.

"You don't recognize my voice?"

"Corbin Hayes," she said, proud of the lack of fear in her voice.

David stood. Then leaned over to write something on a piece of paper. He held it up. SPEAKER.

Summer pulled the phone from her ear and pressed the button. "Very good, Mrs. Abernathy. Now, listen closely. You messed up our plans when you ran off."

"Gee, so sorry." She couldn't help the sarcasm. An agonized scream echoed through the line. "Marlee!"

"Now play nice or pretty little Marlee here will have to suffer a little longer."

Summer swallowed. David was writing again. He held up his note. PLAY ALONG.

"I'll play nice," she whispered. "Don't hurt her."

"That's more like it."

"What do you want?"

"The same thing I wanted the last time we met. Your husband and the laptop he stole."

"I told you I didn't know what you were talking about."

"But you do now." He paused. "I hear an echo. I must be on speakerphone. Who's there with you?"

"The marshals who've been keeping me safe."

David nodded his approval.

"Ah, well, that means I must be going. I'm sure they're sending help for poor Marlee. Too bad they'll be too late."

Marlee's frantic scream was silenced with a final click.

Summer turned on David. "You said there was someone watching out for my family."

"They were. I don't know how Hayes managed to get to her. Did you call her cell phone or her landline?"

"Her home line." She ripped the towel from her head. "I've got to go to her."

David grabbed her upper arm. "Summer, you can't do that."

"You have a better suggestion?" she snapped.

He sighed and rubbed his eyes. "Yeah. I'll call Mike. Cops will be at her house in minutes."

"Then do it."

The phone rang and Mike didn't recognize the number. He pressed the device to his ear and barked, "Thomas."

"Summer's sister is in danger. Get some cops out there now and get her some protection." David paused. "If she's still alive."

"Where are you?"

"Don't worry about that now. Get someone out to Marlee's house. Now. I'll call you back in ten minutes for an update."

Click.

Mike growled but got busy. All it took was one call. The cops and an ambulance were en route to Marlee's house. He dialed the number David had called from.

"They on the way?"

"Yes."

"Thought you had people watching them."

"We did."

"Then they weren't very good at their job."

Mike muttered a curse. "I'm expecting a call any mo—" His phone beeped. "That's Bennie. Let me call you back."

Click.

He switched to the other line. "What do you have?"

"She's on her way to the hospital."

"She's still alive?"

"Yeah. But it looks like they decided to use her to send a message."

"Message received. Thanks." Mike hung up and dialed David's number again. David answered on the first ring. "She's in the hospital," Mike said. "Alive."

A sigh of relief reached his ear. Then David said, "Good."

"Now, where are you? You need to let us come get you."

"Not yet."

Click.

Mike threw his phone across the room.

David hung up with Mike and Summer pounced. "Well?"

"She's hurt, but she's alive."

Summer flinched. "How did they get to her?" Anger boiled inside her. Could no one make a promise and be depended on to keep it?

"I'm not sure, he didn't get into that."

"I've got to go to her."

"She's three hours away, Summer. Mike's got US Marshals on her door."

"And that's supposed to be a comfort? He had them on her house and we see how well that worked out."

David snapped his mouth shut. He gave a slow nod, conceding she was right.

Summer paced and ran a hand through her hair. "Look. My brother and mom are out of the state. I'm not terribly worried about them right now, but Marlee . . ." She bit her lip. "She needs to come with us."

"What?"

"We need to keep her with us. To keep her safe. If she's well enough to travel, I mean. She can't stay there."

"But the marshals—"

"You practically told me you don't trust them anymore." She marched to the window, stood to the side like she'd seen him do, and peered out. "We've been here for several hours and no one but your friend Ron seems to know where we are. We haven't been attacked or shot at or—" She closed her eyes and took a deep breath. Worry for Marlee ate at her. "I want her here where we can keep her safe." She softened her tone and her stance. "Don't you understand, David? I've been keeping her safe for twenty years. I can't just abandon her now."

"You're not abandoning her, but—" he held up a hand to forestall more arguments—"but I get what you're saying." He sighed. "All right." He got up and paced from one end of the suite to the other. "We'll have to trust them."

"I know. But we don't have a choice. Not if we want to get Marlee. If they're watching her." She rolled her eyes. "Although, if they're doing as good a job at the hospital as they did her house, we could just walk in and walk out without them knowing we were ever there." Sarcasm dripped.

"It wasn't Chase, Adam, or Mike on your sister's house," he reminded her.

"I know. But they were trained by the same people." She scowled.

"So you want to trust them or not?"

"What if trusting them means getting killed?"

"I could ask for different marshals."

She tilted her head and squinted at him. "Would they do that?"

"I don't know."

Summer rubbed a hand over her lips. "No." Her gaze flicked to the weapons. "No, let them bring Marlee here. If we're attacked again, we'll know."

"No. No way, Summer. That's putting you in danger as well as Marlee."

She frowned. "I'm already in danger. Marlee's already in danger, David. If we don't do what Hayes says, he's going to kill Marlee anyway. You and I both know it." She planted her hands on her hips. "We have to know who we can trust and we have to know fast. The only way to do that is to set a trap and see what we catch."

David kept his gaze on her. She watched his eyes change. Respect and admiration glinted there. "You're an amazing woman, you know that?"

Silence fell between them. Her mouth worked, but nothing came out. She swallowed hard and tried to grab on to her initial anger she'd felt when she first learned of her husband's deception. She finally said, "Just call Mike."

Summer relaxed a fraction as David dialed the number.

Within seconds, Mike was on the phone. David said, "Bring Summer's sister here." Summer could hear the expletive from across the room. David winced. "I'll tell you where we are when I get your word that you'll bring Marlee into the protection program. We want her safe. Obviously having your guys just watching her house occasionally isn't working out too well for Marlee." David listened a few more seconds, then hung up. "Mike's working on it."

"Is she well enough to travel?"

"She's got a black eye, a broken arm from a previous attack, and an assortment of other cuts and bruises, but she's going to be all right."

Summer pressed her fingers to her eyes. "I can't believe this. So where was this previous attack?"

"Apparently, someone caught her coming out of the grocery store last night and worked her over in the parking lot. She was just released from the hospital this morning. A friend took her home. And now this."

Summer felt sick. Her stomach rumbled and she took a deep breath to stem the rising bile. She dropped her fingers from her eyes. "Can he trace that phone you're using?"

David shook his head. "He can probably get a pretty good idea of the location if he checks the towers it's pinging off of, but he can't trace it straight to us."

His phone rang and he put it on speaker. "That was fast."

Mike grunted. "She freaked about the idea of leaving with the marshals. She said she doesn't trust anyone but her sister and you."

Summer sighed, then hardened her resolve. "Fine," she said. "We'll come get her."

"No way," Mike protested. "Absolutely not."

"We're on the way," David said.

"She had a pretty hard knock on the head so she's not being released from the hospital until in the morning. They want to keep her overnight for observation."

"Then we'll see you in the morning."

Mike growled and threw his phone against the wall. Again.

Chase lifted a brow. "You keep that up, you'll need another phone case. Again."

"How many of those indestructible cases have you destroyed since becoming David's handler?" Adam asked.

"Six," Mike snapped.

"Huh," Chase grunted. "I would have thought it would have been more than that."

Mike glared. "Marlee doesn't trust us and won't leave the hospital with anyone but Summer and David. So, he and Summer are going to the hospital to get her sister. And David won't tell me where they are."

"Then we meet them at the hospital."

Adam stood. "We don't have any clue where they are or even if they're still in the vicinity. Why don't we go back to Charleston and get a hotel near the hospital? That way we can be there to intercept them."

"And once they're back in our hands, we're not letting them go."

Chase barked a laugh. "If David wants to go, you won't have any choice but to let him."

23

"I need to make another call with your handy little untraceable phone," Summer said and held out a hand.

"To who?"

"My client, Olivia Todd. We're supposed to be in court on Tuesday and she and I have things we need to discuss."

He hesitated. "That's fine, but first things first."

"What?" She dropped her arm to her side and curled her fingers into a fist. She really needed to talk to Olivia.

"We need a car if we're going to the hospital to pick up your sister."

"Okay. So what are we going to do?"

He thought for a moment. "Didn't you say your friend who owns the store lives above it?"

"Yes. Her name's Casey."

"Okay then. You're going to walk across the street and ask Casey if we can use her car."

Summer ran a hand down her cheek, then pinched the bridge of her nose. "What if they're still out there?"

"I don't think they are. We've shaken them for the moment, but I'll be right behind you and watching." He reached out to cup her chin. "I won't let anything happen to you, Summer."

She jerked away from his touch. "Don't make promises you can't keep." His sigh reached her. Guilt swamped her. She lifted her chin. No, she wouldn't feel guilty. He'd done this. "So, after we get the car, we come back here?"

"No. We hit the road. Once we're seen leaving here, I don't want to come back."

She stared at him. Then gave a slow nod. "All right."

"You ready?"

"Sure." She glanced around. "Are we taking everything Ron brought?"

"It's just a couple of backpacks. We can manage that."

Summer packed hers and stuffed the Smith & Wesson Centennial 642 Airweight into the shoulder holster Ron had brought. She liked the weapon. It was light and easy to carry. She had shot one before on the numerous occasions David had insisted she go with him to the shooting range. She'd always enjoyed their outings and had never suspected he had an ulterior motive for taking her. He was military. He liked guns. She liked what he liked.

Now she knew better.

Her stomach turned as betrayal washed over her once again. Instead of saying anything, she pulled on the heavy sweater to conceal the weapon. She picked up the backpack she hadn't had a chance to unpack and slung it over her shoulder. "What's on that laptop, David? Specifically?"

"Just all kinds of names and dates." He paused. "And there's one file labeled 'blackmail.'"

She swallowed hard. "Who was Sam blackmailing?"

"I don't think he was. I think he just had evidence that he could use as blackmail."

"Who was the evidence against?"

"I don't know."

"I don't understand then."

"Sam had pictures on the laptop of a tall man meeting with

Raimondi, shaking hands and looking all friendly like. His face had been blurred out, but he had a shock of white hair up here." He pointed at the hairline of his forehead. "If I had a name to go with the pictures, he might be recognizable. The other distinguishing mark is a tattoo on his left bicep. It's not visible in all of the pictures, of course. In fact, in almost all of the pictures he has long sleeves on. But in one, he was leaning over reaching for a drink on the table. He had short sleeves on and I got a good look at it." He tapped his chin. "Someone went to a lot of trouble to get that picture with the tattoo."

"What does it look like?"

"The head of a snake."

"Ew." She wrinkled her nose.

He gave a gentle smile. "I know how fond you are of snakes."

She shuddered. "Not."

"You okay with the plan then?"

"I'm good with it."

"You're sure?"

She snorted. "No, but I don't guess we have any better options. We need a car." She drew in a deep breath. "So, I'm going to get us a car."

David watched Summer walk across the street and knock on the door of the store. With each step, his heart beat with love for her. And a desire to keep her safe. She knocked again and David scanned the street, keeping Summer in his peripheral vision. Now six o'clock in the evening, the sun had disappeared. The cold air surrounded him, made him long for a fireplace, a cup of coffee, and Summer's sweet kisses.

Summer pressed the buzzer and rapped her knuckles on the glass this time.

He waited. Watching. Two men started toward her.

129

David straightened, unlatched the strap across his weapon and moved to intercept them. Just as he was going to call out to Summer, they passed her without a glance. He let out a slow breath and took his hand from his gun.

Another sweep of the street didn't raise any flags. He crossed the street to where Summer still stood and placed his back against the wall.

She glanced at him, her leg jiggling nervously, her fingers twisting together. She waited.

Finally, the door cracked and she leaned in. "Hi, Casey. Do you remember me?"

"Of course. Come in."

Summer stepped inside and David followed. Casey gasped as he shut the door behind him. Fear lit her dark eyes. "What do you want?"

"Don't worry, we're not here to hurt you." Summer took her new friend's hand. "We need another favor."

"Is your husband still after you?"

Summer winced. "It wasn't my husband after me." She nodded to David. "He's my husband. But the men after me want to see us dead."

"Why?" Casey's round eyes grew wider.

"Because we have something they want."

"Okay." Casey held up her well-manicured hand. "I don't need to know anything else. I've had enough trouble today." She swept her hand out and for the first time David noticed the chaos surrounding them.

"What happened?" he asked.

"I left to get a bite to eat. When I came back, this is what I found." Fear stood out on her features. "Along with this."

David took the note she held out to him. "Talk to the cops and we'll come back."

"You need to call the cops."

Casey's jaw hardened. "I've lived through worse." She shook her head. "They were looking for something."

"Did they find it?"

"I have no idea. I don't know what they were looking for." She rubbed her eyes. "What do you need from me?"

"I'm so sorry this happened," Summer said. "I'm sorry we've involved you in this."

"Like I said, I've been involved in worse. Now, what do you need?"

"Your car."

She gaped. "My car?" Her lips pursed. "Okay, wasn't expecting that one. You really need my car?"

Summer nodded. "We need to get going. I know it's crazy to have a complete stranger ask you this, but will you let us use your car?"

"But, what am I supposed to do for transportation?"

David spoke up. "We just need it overnight. I'll have someone drive it back to you tomorrow." He slid to the window and looked out. Still clear.

Casey looked from him to Summer. "I don't want to know what this is all about, do I?"

"Probably not," Summer said.

Casey hesitated only a few more seconds, then walked to the counter and pulled a set of keys from a drawer. She removed one from the ring. "I'll call my sister or mother to come pick me up if I need to go anywhere. This is the spare." She handed it to Summer.

David pulled a stack of bills from his wallet and handed them to her. "For your trouble."

Casey took them, mouth still open. "I feel like I'm in a Lifetime movie or something."

"Tell me about it," David muttered. He took Summer's arm. "Let's get out of here."

Summer pulled away from him and hugged Casey. "Thank you."

"I guess when I told the Lord to put people who needed help

131

in my path, he was listening. The least I can do is the same." She gave them a slight smile. "Just stay safe."

They headed for the door. "Oh, wait," Casey called.

David turned.

Casey opened another drawer and pulled out a necklace. "You dropped this when you were running yesterday. I kept it in case I saw you again."

Summer stared at the piece of jewelry, then looked at David and back to the cross. Her jaw hardened. "That's all right. I don't need it." She turned and headed for the door while David's heart hit rock bottom.

Casey lifted a brow and looked at David. He held out his hand and she dropped the necklace into it. Shoving it in his pocket, David followed Casey and Summer out the back of the store. Casey's dark blue Ford Explorer sat just outside the door.

Summer climbed in the passenger side while David adjusted the driver's seat. Summer said to Casey, "Thank you again."

Casey waved them on their way.

Summer turned to David. "I really need to call Olivia. Could I please have your phone?"

He glanced behind him as he backed up. "I'll stop at a gas station. I don't want to use this phone any more than necessary."

Summer sighed and leaned her head back against the headrest.

"I had to do what I did, Summer. All of it. Including deceiving you."

"No, you didn't."

He clamped his lips shut as he wove through town, his eyes swiveling between the rearview mirror and the road. She didn't understand.

And he was afraid she never would.

Summer woke with a jerk. She hadn't meant to go to sleep, but had conked out soon after clipping her seat belt around her. Darkness covered them, broken only by the headlights of the passing cars. "Where are we?"

"About an hour away."

"Want me to drive?"

"No. I'm good."

"Want to talk about what you're thinking about?"

"Not right now."

The stilted conversation grated across her nerves, so she shut her mouth and stared out the window into the darkness. When David got his mind wrapped around something, it didn't do any good to push him. He'd either talk or he wouldn't. The zing of hurt surprised her. She'd consistently pushed him away for the last two days, and now that he wasn't pushing back—it hurt. Her emotions made no sense. Frustration filled her. She wanted to punish David for his deception and lies. And she wanted to hug him and pretend none of it ever happened.

Tears made her blink. "Could you stop at that pay phone so I can make that call? Once Marlee's with us and we're back with the marshals, who knows when I'll have a chance."

"Yeah. I'll stop right before we get to the hospital."

"Thanks."

They rode in silence the rest of the way. Summer straightened when he pulled into a gas station. He drove straight up to the pay phone and Summer rolled down her window. She dropped the coins in and dialed Olivia's number, praying the woman would pick up when she saw an unfamiliar number on her screen.

The phone rang. And rang. And finally went to voice mail. "Olivia, this is Summer. I'm sorry I've been out of touch. I need you to call me at—" She looked at David and he shook his head. "Well, actually, you can't call me." An idea hit her. "If you need me, keep leaving messages on my voice mail. I'll do my best to call when I can. But I will be there Tuesday on time, I promise." *Unless I'm dead.* But she kept that thought to herself. "Just keep everything status quo until Tuesday. Hang in there, my friend. Stay strong and keep praying."

She hung up and closed her eyes. All of this had to happen now during this case. If she wasn't absolutely sure Raimondi was the one after them, she'd swear Olivia's abusive husband had something to do with all the terror raining down on them.

But she knew the men after them didn't have anything to do with Silas Todd. No, her husband could take all the blame for that one. She shoved her earbuds into her ears, leaned back, and did her best to tune out the world and focus on the words of the song. She needed some hope right now.

24

At the buffet, Olivia helped Sandy spoon macaroni and cheese onto her plate, then a chicken leg and some green beans. It was Sandy's birthday and she wanted to eat out. That was all. She didn't want a video game or new clothes or whatever it was kids were into these days. When asked, "What do you want for your birthday?" she'd answered, "I want to go to the Veggie Bar restaurant with you and Laura."

"But what about a gift?"

Sandy smiled. "That would be my gift and I'd get to share it with you and Laura."

Olivia noticed the child said nothing about wanting her father there. Noticed, but wasn't surprised.

"All right, then, darling, that's what we'll do."

Sandy grinned, stretching the small scar that ran from her bottom lip to her chin. Permanently scarred by a man who was supposed to protect her. Fury boiled in Olivia's gut. She should have left sooner. She should have walked out the first time he hit her. But she'd let her fear rule her. Only when he went after Sandy could she find the guts to leave.

Olivia followed her daughter back to their booth and thought about their room at the shelter. It wasn't a bad place. It just wasn't home. But it was safe. From her window, if she stood just right, she could look out and see the gates. The locked gates. With the security guard stationed in the small house. Evan Pritchard. Probably in his early sixties, but he was lean and still had a full head of hair without a speck of gray in it. Secretly she wondered if he colored it.

"Why are you smiling?" Laura asked, finally looking up from her plate.

"I was just thinking how blessed we are."

Laura raised a brow. "Seriously?"

"Seriously. Think about it. We have a bed to sleep in, food to eat, and friends to hang out with." She took a deep breath. "And we're safe." Her children so needed to feel safe.

Laura snorted. "We'll never be safe as long as that monster is walking the earth." Sandy whimpered and Laura immediately lost her attitude. "Except maybe at the shelter." She pretended to think about it. "Yeah, I think there, we're safe. Don't you, Sandy?"

"I-I don't know. Are we?"

Laura reached over to hug her baby sister. Olivia's throat tightened, but she didn't say anything.

"Yes. We are." Laura said it with such firm conviction that Olivia almost believed her too.

Sandy visibly relaxed. "Good. I like it there. And I like Mr. Pritchard. He's nice."

The fact that her child could trust another man after what her own father had done to her spoke volumes. And gave Olivia hope.

They would be all right.

She picked up the big piece of cake she'd cut from the dessert tray and set it in front of Sandy. She'd placed a candle in the shape of a 9 at the center. Then she reached into her small purse and pulled out the lighter she'd splurged on for just this occasion. She lit the candle and started singing, "Happy Birthday to you—"

"—Happy birthday to you," joined a voice to her left. The waitress.

"Happy birthday, dear Sandy," Laura sang loud.

"Happy birthday, to you," the patrons at nearby tables joined in.

Sandy beamed, then in a move that was completely out of character with her more reserved personality, climbed out of the booth, and gave everyone a curtsy. After the clapping died down, Sandy returned to her seat and dug into her cake.

Olivia closed her eyes for a brief moment of thankfulness. For a brief snippet of time, all was right in her child's world, and while Olivia didn't have the money to spend on a present, she didn't mind digging a little deeper into her pocket for this dinner. They had to eat anyway and this was Sandy's favorite place.

She glanced toward the door and felt her heart freeze. "Silas," she whispered.

Sandy's fork clattered to the floor. Laura simply lifted her head and glared. But Olivia caught the fine tremor that went through the girl's body. She slid out of the booth and walked toward the man she'd once loved. "What are you doing here?"

"It's my daughter's birthday," he said. "I took a chance you'd bring her here." He pulled a box from his jacket pocket. "I brought her a present."

Not wanting to make a scene, she kept a smile on her face, but whispered through gritted teeth, "Go away."

His eyes narrowed and he stepped toward her. "Make me," he taunted.

Olivia felt sick. Once again Silas had managed to ruin a lovely moment. He brushed past her and stepped over to the booth. Laura had switched places with Sandy and put the girl between the wall and herself. The protective gesture was nearly Olivia's undoing. "Silas, please—"

"Please what, Olivia? Please let me come home? Please forgive me for breaking up the family? Please forgive me for running off and not even telling you where I'm staying? Please, what?"

Olivia's gaze darted from one table to the next. Even though

Silas kept his voice low, they were drawing attention. She sat in the booth and forced a smile for the girls. "Sandy, Daddy's brought you a gift."

Sandy ducked her head and began to cry, then hiccup and wheeze.

Olivia couldn't stand it, couldn't play this game. She fished Sandy's inhaler from her purse and handed it to Laura, who turned her back on her father and helped her sister. Then Olivia stood and faced down her husband. Fear twisted every nerve she had into double knots. "Just leave us alone."

In the booth next to them, a man stood. Olivia sucked in her breath at the sight of his badge clipped to his belt. And the gun on his right hip. "Is there a problem?"

Silas cleared his throat. "Not at all. Just delivering a little birthday gift to my daughter."

"Mighty good thing to do."

"I thought so." He shot Olivia a smirk.

"Now you've done it," the officer said. "The door's behind you. Why don't you go find it?"

Silas's smirk disappeared. "What's it to you?"

"Mister, I've worked more domestic violence cases in my career than you'll ever be able to read about and I have a special dislike for people like you. I'm guessing you're an abuser of women and little kids." He stepped forward and pointed a finger about a centimeter from Silas's nose, and Olivia gasped as her husband's face darkened. But that didn't stop the officer. "Now, you get away from them before I arrest you."

"For what?" Silas argued.

"Disturbing my meal." He looked him up and down. "And for having a bad attitude. Want me to go on?"

Silas glared, his nostrils flared, and Olivia couldn't drag her eyes away from the two men.

Silas gritted, "Do you have any idea who you're talking to?"

The officer smirked. "I don't care if you're the president of the

United States. No one gets away with bullying a woman and her kids on my watch. Now scram."

Silas curled his fingers into a fist and Olivia stepped back, the back of her knees hitting the booth.

"Do it," the officer said, eyes narrow, muscles bunched.

Silas dropped his arm, then lifted it to point a finger at Olivia. "I'll deal with you later."

He placed the box on the table without another word, turned, and left the restaurant. Olivia swallowed hard and tried to control the shakes that set in with the ebb of her adrenaline.

"Thank you," she whispered.

The officer stepped closer. "I'm Detective Johns. From the conversation before I interrupted, I gather that you've left him."

"Yes."

"Good move. If I thought you were going home to him, I wouldn't have interfered."

She shook her head. "No. Other than a court date, I'm done with him. Only now, I'm afraid he's going to follow me—" She sighed and shook her head. "Never mind. Thank you, though."

"He won't follow you. Finish your meal, enjoy yourselves. My partner and I will escort you wherever you're staying. We'll make sure you're not followed."

The lump in her throat made it almost impossible to speak, but she managed a grateful nod.

The girls hadn't said a word and didn't eat another bite. Olivia choked down another spoonful of her melting ice cream, then gave up. She couldn't force another bite down, not even for her girls.

Ten minutes later, when they walked away from the table, Olivia didn't bother to point out to Sandy the gift her father gave her. She had a feeling Sandy knew exactly what she was doing when she left it sitting on the table.

25

"I got 'em."

Raimondi drew in a deep breath at Corbin's announcement. "Where are they?"

"They're on the move again. I'm not sure what happened to those lost hours, but we just picked up a call to Olivia Todd from a pay phone near the hospital in Charleston, South Carolina."

Raimondi chuckled. "I figured that's where they would go after you finished with the sister. So you didn't kill her?"

"No. I decided she might be worth more to us alive than dead."

Raimondi thought about that as he filled the water bowls in his pets' cages. "That was only when we didn't know where Summer and David were. Now we know. Go ahead and kill her." A pause on the other end of the line made him frown. "Hayes? You have a problem with that?"

"I'll kill her, that's no problem. I'm working on a plan to get all three of them at the same time."

"Do not kill David before we have the laptop in our possession."

"I won't."

"His sister-in-law is another matter. You can get rid of her."

"All in good time. Will you let me handle this? I have the sister-in-law in my sights. I have plans for her, plans that will end with her dead, but first, I want to see if she has any more uses."

"Like what?"

"Bait."

Raimondi heard the sly pleasure in Hayes's voice and wondered what the man had in mind for the woman. Then he decided he didn't care as long as she wound up dead.

"What about Summer?" Hayes asked.

Raimondi dropped the frozen rat into the boa's cage. "Ah yes, the beautiful and spunky Summer. Let's keep her alive for the moment. Bring them to me the moment you have them."

"Yes sir."

"Because I think I might enjoy having them as guests for a while." He turned and looked at the black door to his right. "Yes, I'd like to show them my hospitality. I've been a bit bored lately with all of the things going wrong. I think they might provide a bit of entertainment if you brought them to me."

Hayes gave a low chuckle. "You're a sick man, Raimondi."

"Sick? No. David just needs to get what's coming to him." He sighed. A low mournful sound. "What's sick is the fact that it's just so hard to find good help these days. Just when you think you can trust someone, they turn on you. As quick as a snake."

David blinked as the Sunday morning sun rose. He nudged Summer. "Wake up, hon. Time to get this started." He'd parked at the emergency entrance to the hospital where security was nearby. If anything happened during the night, at least help was close. He'd decided against a hotel room and Summer had agreed. She'd slept for six hours uninterrupted while he'd dozed in patches. But that had been his life for so long, he was used to it. Sleeping with one eye open had taken on a whole new meaning when he'd joined the Army.

He shifted and his back protested along with his healing ribs.

She groaned and rubbed a hand down her face as she pulled her earbuds down and tucked her iPod in her purse.

He smiled. "I'm glad some things haven't changed."

"What do you mean?"

"You falling asleep to your favorite music."

"Oh. Yeah." She gave him a faint smile. "I always used to do that as a teen. Especially when I was living with my dad. I suppose it's my way of escaping."

"Praise and worship is a good escape."

She shrugged. "It's not so much an escape now as much as it's just another way to hear from God. A way of listening to what he has to say through the words of the song." She pulled in a deep breath. "Is it time?"

"Yeah. You ready for this?"

She took a deep breath. "I just pray we're wrong. I don't want any of them to be in on betraying us. The thought of one of them being a part of Raimondi's mob just . . ." She shivered.

"I know. I've gotten to know Chase and Adam pretty well. I think they're stand-up guys."

She stared at him. "Anyone can appear as a stand-up guy with enough motivation."

He winced and was grateful when she didn't dwell on that topic. "What about Mike?"

"Mike does his job. He's good at it and he doesn't let anything distract him. I would call him a friend in the loosest sense of the word."

"You think he'd take a bribe?"

David shook his head. "I have no way of knowing that." His lips tightened and he looked at the entrance to the hospital. "Ready?"

She nodded. "Ready."

26

Summer and David made their way into the hospital. As the revolving door swooshed around, Adam and Chase stepped into the lobby area to greet them.

"Watching for us, huh?" David asked.

Chase frowned at him. "Yeah. You're not making this job any easier."

David lifted a brow. "Sorry about that. When the bad guys keep showing up, it makes a man wonder."

Adam rocked back on his heels. "You think we had something to do with that?"

David sighed. "It's hard to know these days. I guess if we wind up dead, we'll know."

Chase glared. "I take exception to that."

David almost smiled. The two men were truly wounded that he suspected them. Either that or they were excellent actors. It made him feel slightly better. "Where's Mike?"

"Staying with Marlee," Chase said.

"He got the short straw," Adam muttered.

Summer lifted a brow. "How is she?"

"She's doing better," Chase said. He shot a snide look at David. "She doesn't trust us either."

"Don't take it personally," Summer said. "She doesn't trust any man."

"She's borderline hysterical, demanding to see Summer and refusing to cooperate with anyone." He sent Summer an apologetic look. "She's not anything like you, is she?"

Summer shook her head. "No. She's not." She pulled in a deep breath. "Why don't you take me to see her?"

"That works for me."

Chase led the way. Summer followed with David at her side. Adam pulled up the rear.

One elevator ride later found them walking down the hallway toward her sister's room. Mike stood outside talking with a uniformed officer. When he saw them coming, his eyes narrowed and his lips tightened. The way his nostrils flared, Summer figured he'd like to lambaste both her and David.

But he didn't. He simply said, "Glad you're still breathing."

David nodded. "Figured I'd better get us away from Raimondi's guys before they finally succeeded in getting to us."

The mild-mannered prod had Mike's nostrils flaring again. Adam made a choking sound behind her and Chase snorted. Mike turned to Summer. "You want to see if you can get her to cooperate? Otherwise we're leaving her here."

Summer didn't bother arguing with the man. She brushed past him and into Marlee's room. Summer gasped and Marlee opened her eyes. Upon seeing Summer, she burst into tears. Summer moved to her sister's side and very carefully took her in her arms, not wanting to jostle her sister's arm. "I'm so sorry, Marlee." A cast encased her left arm, bruises on her forehead and cheek stood out.

Marlee sniffled. "They broke in my house when I was talking with you on the phone and they said they had to make sure you knew they were serious and they wanted some stupid laptop and—"

Summer placed a finger over Marlee's lips. "Shh. It's okay now.

144

You're going to come with us and everything's going to be fine."
She prayed her words weren't a lie.

"Where have you been? I tried to call but you wouldn't answer
your cell phone or your office phone. You've never not taken my
calls and then you called and said you were in Charlotte and I just
needed you to help me." Summer listened as Marlee prattled on.
Summer had turned twenty-nine on her last birthday. Nick was two
years younger and Marlee was a mere baby at twenty-two. She'd
graduated college last year with a degree in interior design and
hadn't settled on any kind of employment other than waitressing.
Occasionally.

Summer sat back in the chair, aware David had entered the room
and stood waiting. Mike, Chase, and Adam still remained outside.
"You've been giving the marshals a hard time, I hear."

"Yes. US Marshals? I don't understand. What are you involved
with? What is going on?" Marlee's string of questions ended on a
screech that made Summer wince.

She grabbed her shoulders. "Stop it."

The order shocked her sister. She snapped her lips closed and
stared.

Summer's ears rang at the sudden silence and she blinked. Should
have done that a long time ago. "There is a man who is after some
evidence David has. That laptop."

"David? Who's David?"

Summer swallowed hard, her initial anger and shock over discovering her husband wasn't who she thought he was bubbling back
to the surface. She shoved it down. "Kyle is David."

"I'm sorry. What? I don't understand."

Summer explained. At the end of her explanation, Marlee gaped,
her gaze swiveling back and forth between Summer and David.
"That's insane."

"Tell me about it," Summer muttered. Then she lifted her chin.
"So this means you're in danger. Mom and Nick should be fine

for now. Hopefully by the time they get on a plane to come home, this will all be over."

"And we'll all be alive to talk about it," David said.

Marlee looked at David. "So you've lied about everything? All this time?"

Summer squeezed her sister's hand. "Don't."

Marlee gaped at Summer. "And you're okay with this?"

"No, of course not," Summer snapped. She'd had enough. Her nerves were tight enough without having to explain her crazy emotions to her sister when she wasn't sure she understood them herself. "I'm still in the shocked, processing stage. But now that I know the whole truth, I'm dealing with it. For the moment, let's just get out of here and get someplace safe."

Marlee glanced at the door. "And you trust those guys out there?"

"About as far as I can throw them."

David climbed in the car after the women and slammed the door. His heart thundered in his ears as Summer's words echoed. "Now that I know the whole truth . . . Now that I know the whole truth." *Oh sweet Lord, please let me know the time and place to finish the story.* The truth. He'd told her most of it. There was just one part he'd left out. If he told her that particular part right now, she'd leave him for sure.

David clenched his fingers into a fist against his thigh. No, that part would have to wait. If she left him now, she would die. He couldn't risk it.

Instead, he'd risk his marriage once again. Only when the trial was over would he tell her about Georgina.

In the SUV, David sat against the passenger door behind the driver's seat, Mike's cell phone pressed to his ear, making arrangements to have Casey's car delivered to her. Summer sat next to him and Marlee on the other side. He hung up, saw Marlee wince and cradle her injured arm. She shot him a glare as Mike shut the door after her. He ignored her and reached for Summer's hand. She let him hold it but laid her head against the back of the seat and shut her eyes. Mike climbed in front with Adam at the wheel. Chase would follow in the decoy vehicle with two other marshals.

"Where are we going?" Marlee's tired voice echoed through the vehicle.

"To a safe house," he answered. "I need your phone."

"I don't have a phone. I was sort of busy getting beat up, remember?" she snarled. "And wait a minute, I need to go home. What about my clothes, my stuff? I'm not packed or anything."

David bit his tongue. Fortunately, Summer didn't. "This isn't a vacation, Marlee. Your needs will be taken care of. In case your broken arm isn't warning enough, your life is in danger."

"Because of him," she snapped and shot a glare at David.

He refused to look at her and curled his fingers around the itch in the center of his palm.

Summer let go of his right hand and David had to fist that one too. "Maybe so, but right now, the main thing is getting safe and staying that way."

"I can't believe this. This is totally going to wreck my life."

David saw Summer's fingers mimic his. He placed a hand over her fist and squeezed. She took a deep breath and exhaled slowly as her hand relaxed.

Adam said, "We're going up the road a few hours. We have a hotel suite reserved. It's got two rooms. Y'all can figure out the sleeping arrangements."

"I'll share a room with Marlee right now," Summer said.

David winced and said nothing.

Summer stared straight ahead.

Marlee smiled and finally quit her griping.

27

The rest of Sunday afternoon had been spent driving and holding on to her patience by a mere thread. They'd driven for several hours with one restroom break. Just when Summer had been ready to succumb to a Marlee-induced migraine, they'd stopped at the hotel.

Room service had taken care of her growling stomach and three ibuprofen had sent her headache running. Unfortunately, Marlee had everyone on edge with her constant complaints and insistence on returning home. David had disappeared into the first bedroom on the left with the statement, "When you can't take it anymore, you can join me."

Summer had endured. Now it was Monday morning and Summer left Marlee sitting on the bed whining about the fact she was going to miss her date that night. Tantalizing smells came from the covered dishes on the breakfast bar and her stomach rumbled. Summer made her way to the well-stocked full-sized refrigerator. She opened a bottle of orange juice and swigged it.

Adam sat on the couch in the small suite, his long legs stretched out to prop his feet on the glass-topped coffee table. "Need something a little stronger?"

She cut her eyes to the man. "If I were going to start, now would be the time I would do it."

A small smile curved his lips. "She just needs to grow up a little."

Summer lifted a brow.

Adam shrugged. "Okay. A lot."

"Where's Mike?" She started a fresh pot of coffee. It looked like Adam had finished off an entire pot by himself.

"He went to check out the hotel, scouting for anyone or anything suspicious."

"Like what?"

Adam shrugged. "You know, like anyone hanging out in the lobby who doesn't look like they should be there, that kind of thing."

"Right. What about Chase?" Summer pulled two mugs from the cabinet, paused, and put one back. David could get his own coffee. Her pettiness shamed her, and with a sigh, she pulled it down again.

"His dad's in the hospital. Chase has power of attorney and they called him to come in."

"Oh no. I'm so sorry." Sympathy for Chase flooded through her.

"He called. It's not as serious as they thought, so he'll be back in a couple of hours."

"Oh. Good." Silence fell between them as Summer ate and tried to relax her frazzled nerves. The food didn't help. Maybe conversation would. "Do you have any brothers or sisters?"

"Two brothers and three sisters."

"Wow. A big family."

"Yeah." He gave a fond smile.

"You're all close?"

"Definitely. When we're not playing practical jokes on one another and fighting."

The way he said it made her believe he didn't truly mean fighting. "Practical jokes?"

"Oh yeah. We've come up with some doozies."

"Your poor mother."

The dimple in his left cheek deepened. "She does get annoyed with us, but she's a good sport."

"Are your brothers and sisters older or younger?" She sipped the orange juice and moved to the small table to sit and wait for the coffee to brew.

"The two brothers are older, the three sisters are younger."

"Which one is the worst practical joker?"

He grinned. "Me."

"I figured."

Adam glanced toward the other room and Summer followed his gaze. David appeared, his hair still damp from the shower. Her heart cramped at her loss. She loved him so . . .

"Morning," Adam said.

"Morning." David's eyes slid to Summer. "Was that Marlee I heard still whining?"

"Well, it sure wasn't me," Summer said and sighed.

He nodded, and Adam said, "I could arrest her and put her in a holding cell. She'd be pretty safe in there all alone."

David looked interested. "On what charges?"

"Disturbing the peace, aggravated assault on my ears . . ." He shrugged. "I could come up with a few more."

Summer rolled her eyes. "Really, guys?"

"You want to arrest me?"

At Marlee's soft question, Summer jumped up. Her sister had heard the entire exchange. She looked small and vulnerable, hurt and angry, all at the same time.

Adam flushed and dropped his head.

David swallowed hard. "Of course not, Marlee."

"Then—"

"Your whining is getting old," Summer blurted. "It's setting everyone's nerves on edge." Summer was surprised at her ability to be so blunt with Marlee.

Marlee's shocked expression said she was surprised as well. David looked like she'd announced she was joining the Peace Corps and leaving the country. Summer wasn't sure where her backbone was coming from when it came to dealing with her sister, but she wasn't going to question it.

Marlee flushed. "I'm being that obnoxious?"

"Yes," the three answered simultaneously.

Marlee's eyes widened, then she pursed her lips and gave a short nod. "I'm sorry. I'll try to tone it down."

Summer lifted a brow. "Thanks. That would be nice."

Her sister rubbed her right hand over her cast as though she were chilled. "So. Is there anything to eat? I'm starving."

Summer passed her sister the covered dish. Marlee sat down and dug in while Summer waited for the criticism of the food.

When it didn't come, she allowed herself to relax a fraction.

When they'd all eaten their fill, Summer stood and walked over to sit on the couch.

Which may have saved her life when the building rocked. Summer screamed as plaster cracked and the chandelier crashed into the chair where she'd just been sitting.

28

"Summer!" David squinted through the haze, trying to locate her. Insulation, plaster, and chunks of the ceiling rained down on him. Disoriented, he held a hand to his head and willed the dizziness to stop.

When Summer didn't answer, panic seized him. Another blast tilted the floor and David fell to his knees, head spinning, ears ringing. He heard Adam's voice over Marlee's screams. David finally got his breath and crawled toward the couch, the last place he'd seen Summer.

Suspecting a bomb and expecting to feel the building come down around him at any moment, David knew they didn't have long to get out. He found Summer on the floor, coughing. Water spurted from the sprinklers in what was left of the ceiling.

"Marlee," Summer gasped. She swiped the water from her eyes.

"She's all right. I think I can still hear her." He found her hand. "Are you all right?"

"Yeah, just got hit in the back with something and had the breath knocked out of me. And my ears are ringing."

Relief nearly made him giddy. She pulled away from him. Adam was still on the phone with a 911 operator, he figured.

"Where's Marlee?" Summer gasped.

"I'm right here." Fear made the girl's voice thick. "Can we get out of here? I don't want to be buried alive." A sob caught on her last word, and Summer wrapped an arm around Marlee's shoulder. Her sister held her left arm against her chest.

"It'll be all right."

"I'm going to open the door and see if we can get out," Adam said. "We're on the top floor so there's no jumping. Stay back."

David pulled his weapon and noticed Summer had hers as well. Satisfaction darted through him. He'd taught her well. His motto hadn't changed from the moment he started carrying. Keep your gun closer than your enemies. Marlee looked shell-shocked. At least her mouth was closed.

The one time he wouldn't blame her for screaming.

Adam opened the door. Chaos littered the hallway, wires hung from the cracked ceiling. But at least the door opened and they weren't trapped in the room. Other hotel patrons scrambled to find their way out.

The yells and cries were almost as deafening as the explosion. Adam led the way, his shoulders tense, jaw set. David pulled up the rear, his heart pounding, adrenaline flowing.

Summer followed behind Adam, stepping over the debris. Many wept in terror even as they plunged toward the stairs. One woman muttered the Lord's Prayer. She tripped and fell to her knees. David reached down and helped her to her feet before falling in behind Summer and Marlee.

The lights flickered and went out.

Darkness surrounded them. Panicked screams echoed. David reached for Summer and gripped her fingers to make sure she didn't stumble.

Adam placed his fingers in his mouth and let out a piercing whistle. The screams fell silent. "Everyone stop," Adam said. "See if the generators kick in."

Seconds passed.

Then an eerie glow came from the generator-powered lights hanging from what was left of the walls.

"All right, keep going." Adam began again.

David let go of Summer's hand and kept a wary eye on the people around them. His heart thudded in his chest.

"It's a trap," he muttered.

"It was a bomb, wasn't it?" Summer asked. Her voice shook as she herded Marlee after Adam.

"No doubt."

Her lips clamped shut but even in the dim light, he could read the look she shot him. They'd been found yet again.

Dust and plaster swirled. Breathing hurt. His lungs felt like someone was prying them from his chest with a crowbar. His ribs protested the continued abuse and his eyes watered. He swiped them with the corner of his shirt. Which simply transferred the dust from his shirt into his eyes. He blinked and pressed the back of his hand to one then the other. It helped. He had to be able to see if he was going to spot a threat.

Summer copied his movements as did Adam.

They made it to the stairwell with the others. A baby cried, a mother whispered reassurances.

David wanted to get the men responsible for this and wrap his hands around their throats. One by one.

But first. Safety. He slipped his weapon in his shoulder holster and motioned for Summer to do the same.

With a frown, she did.

Summer had hoped the interior of the stairwell would have been spared and allow them to descend the four flights without issues. She should have known better. The people pressed and panic reigned. They followed the crowd down.

"Everyone needs to calm down," she whispered.

"Yeah," David agreed. "They do."

Someone shoved against her back and she slammed into David. He caught her, steadied her. Then placed his fingers in his mouth and let out an ear-splitting whistle that echoed in the enclosed space. Shocked silence greeted him. Adam turned with a raised brow.

David yelled, "Everyone listen up. Panicking is not going to get us out of here. We have a US Marshal here who's going to take the lead and tell you what to do. If you want to live, be quiet and listen."

Adam shot him an exasperated look, but took his cue. "These stairs are dangerous. Stand away from the railing—or what's left of it." People shuffled to obey. Muted cries still sounded, but at least they seemed grateful to have some leadership.

"Hey," a voice called from below. "There's a big hole in part of the stairwell between the second and first floors. But if we can get past it, the rest of the ones look stable enough."

David pulled Summer and Marlee behind him. Adam dropped to his stomach and moved to the edge where the railing had been ripped apart. "What do you see?" David asked.

"He's right."

Sirens sounded in the distance, barely discernible, but Summer heard them. They were on the east end of the building. Through the wall next to her was the outside. Hope stirred. Help was coming. She sent up a silent prayer of thanks. Marlee's fingers tightened. She'd heard them too.

Adam scooted back away from the edge. "We'll have to help lower the elderly, women, and children over the gap. I think most of us young guys can jump it."

Summer said, "Get those over who can't make it themselves. Marlee and I can jump it too."

Marlee whimpered.

Or not. She would be hampered with the cast.

David nodded.

Adam got everyone's attention again and laid out the plan. "Anyone have any objections?"

"No. Let's just get out of here." A young man in his early twenties spoke up. Sweat coated his face. Blood flowed from a cut on his forehead. Summer dug in her jeans pocket and pulled out a clean napkin she'd slipped in before eating breakfast. She handed it to him and he took it with a grateful look.

"What makes you think this is the best way?" An older man challenged. "If those stairs keep crumbling, whoever's trying to get over will go down with them."

"True," David said, "but I think it's a chance we're going to have to take. Unless you have a better idea?"

"What about going back up and down the other side?"

"The other side might be just as bad."

"Or it might be just fine." Eyes narrowed, he thrust his chin out.

David shrugged. "Go however you want to go. I'm going that way." He pointed down.

The man shifted, and as David turned his attention to helping Marlee over a piece of concrete, Summer saw the weapon underneath the sports coat.

She caught her breath and her gaze slammed into his. He gave her a half smile. "I'm a cop."

"Then why don't you get up there and help some people?"

He gave her a measured look and scooted past her. She tugged on David's hand. "That guy that challenged you says he's a cop. He's got a weapon under his jacket."

David's eyes sharpened. He maneuvered his way around the people waiting their turn to be helped over the hole with Summer and Marlee at his heels.

"Hey, no cutting in line!"

She turned to see who complained and to apologize, but she didn't have the chance.

A hard shove sent her stumbling to the edge of the stairs where the railing had broken away. Heart in her throat, her foot slipped, caught on the debris, and she felt herself go over the edge.

29

David heard a scream and whirled to see Summer slip off the edge of the stairs. He lunged and wrapped a hand around her wrist. Her pulse hammered wildly beneath his palm. At least he thought it was hers, it might have been his own crazy pounding heart he felt.

He pulled and others grabbed her clothing, and finally she was back on the hard cement, panting. Sweat dripped from her forehead and he wiped it away. He looked into her scared eyes, trying to hide his own terror. It wasn't a long fall and it might not have killed her, but she would have been badly hurt. "Are you all right?"

She gasped, then swallowed hard. "I think my shoulder's been wrenched out of the socket, but yes, the damage is minimal." She glanced at the concerned gazes of those who were like her and just wanted out. "Thank you."

A young woman holding a toddler said, "That guy with the gun under his jacket was in a big hurry. He pushed past and got you with his shoulder. He just jumped down to the first floor and went out the door."

Adam appeared. "Everything all right?"

"For now." David tightened his grip on Summer's arm and pulled her with him. Adam took charge of Marlee but said to David, "I want to be the last out."

"Right. Gotcha."

"So let's help these others and then we'll do what we've got to do to save our own skin."

David understood what Adam didn't want to voice in front of Marlee and Summer. If the bomb had been planted with the hopes of killing David and Summer, it was a long shot. Not that there wouldn't be deaths, but that the bomb would cause the deaths of the two people who were the targets.

Therefore the killers would be watching those coming out of the hotel.

And when Summer and David stepped out, whoever planted the bombs would be waiting to grab them in the chaos. There was probably a sniper on the roof of a building across from the hotel.

"You got a plan?" he asked Adam as he helped hand over a small child to his waiting mother. The woman looked pale and sick. He hoped she wouldn't pass out. She didn't. Child cradled in her arms, she disappeared down the stairs to the exit.

"Yes."

"All right, I've got a backup one if yours doesn't work."

Adam shot him a perturbed look. "It'll work." He helped an elderly couple over the hole, then looked back at David. One by one, David and Adam helped everyone in the stairwell make it to the bottom floor. Thankfully, the exit wasn't blocked and they were met by rescue personnel.

David watched the last person exit, then turned to Adam. "All right, what's your plan?"

"We get out of here."

David lifted a brow. "That's your plan?"

Adam shrugged. "I didn't say it was a good one."

"Where are they now?" Raimondi pressed the phone to his ear as he watched the news coverage. The bomb had done its job. The middle of the hotel was practically gone. Each end still stood. Deaths were reported, but no official number had been released. They were calling it an act of terror. He snorted. They could call it whatever they wanted as long as he was able to get to David Hackett.

"Still in the hotel." Corbin Hayes sounded satisfied. A premature satisfaction, Raimondi felt sure.

"Are the men ready to move in?" he asked.

"As soon as I spot them, I'll give the word."

"The sister and the marshals are expendable," he said. He picked up the remote and upped the volume.

"That's good because that might be the only way we're going to get to Summer and David."

"Do we have everything set up in case we need to get to them in court tomorrow?"

"I'm still working that angle. Let's just hope we don't have to wait that long. I know you want this taken care of way before then."

"Indeed, that would be best." Raimondi hung up. He muted the television and turned to sink into the recliner.

A knock on the door pulled his attention from the television screen. "Come in."

Agostino stepped in. "Hello, Uncle."

"What news do you have?"

"Nothing. I just thought I would come wait with you."

Raimondi gestured to the recliner next to his. "Sit."

Agostino sat.

Raimondi rose and poured his nephew a glass of bourbon. He handed it to Agostino. "How is your mother?"

"Grieving. She's in bed and won't get up."

"When is the funeral?"

"Tomorrow."

Raimondi nodded. "She will go."

"How is Georgina?"

He pulled in a deep breath. "She will be fine."

"It's been over a year and she hasn't let go of him."

"It's not up for discussion. She will be fine." He took a sip of the bourbon. "As soon as I present her with David's head on a platter."

Agostino frowned. "I thought she didn't want him hurt."

Impatience threaded through Raimondi. "She doesn't know what she wants. If falling in love with David Hackett is any indication of her judgment, then clearly she has none."

"But—"

"Enough. Bring them to me."

30

Summer cast glances at an uncharacteristically quiet Marlee. Her sister stood silent and pale, her lips quivering every so often. David and Adam seemed to have worked out some sort of plan and were now determined to put it into action. Rescue workers filtered in through the exit door. Several made their way up the stairs, carefully maneuvering around the hole.

Two stayed behind. One looked at the four of them. "Everyone all right?" At their affirmative, he said, "Come on, come on, let's get out of here."

Adam flipped out his badge. "We're going to need your help."

If Adam had reached out and slapped the man, he couldn't have been more surprised. For a moment he didn't move, then said, "We don't have a lot of time to discuss this. What's the issue?"

In less than ten seconds, using short concise sentences, Adam explained the situation.

The fireman nodded. "Hold on a sec."

He spoke into his radio and within another five seconds had five other firemen coming through the door. He outlined the plan to get them out of the building alive.

Summer broke in. "It's too dangerous."

Adam's phone rang even as the firefighters started stripping out of their gear. He snapped it to his ear and listened. He looked at David. "We got our sniper. He's under arrest and awaiting questioning."

The firefighters paused and exchanged glances. The building shuddered and a chunk of concrete landed in front of Summer. The firefighter who'd taken charge shot dark looks at the stairwell even as he handed his gear to David.

A young man in his early twenties hesitated. "Captain, you sure about this?"

"We're rescuing people. You know the creed. 'Give me strength to save a life . . .' That's what we're doing."

"Yes sir."

Once the four of them were dressed in firefighting gear, David pronounced them ready. "Let's do it."

Adam nodded. "Can't thank you guys enough for this."

"I'm Chip Hancock, fire captain for company 12. I come from a family of firefighters and law enforcement." A slight smile curved his lips. "Can't wait to tell Dad about this one." He shoved his ax into David's hand. "Act like you're helping me to the ambulance." He glanced at the others. "The rest of you do the same. Then get on the truck. I'll manage to get away from the ambulance and drive you wherever you need to go."

"You got it."

Summer hitched her breath. A sniper? But why? Didn't Raimondi want them alive? It didn't make sense and she had no more time to think about it before she was hustling out the door. Finally. Her tension came not only from the anxiety of being a target, but from the fear of being trapped in a collapsing building.

Once outside, Summer clung to the captain, doing her best to make it look like she was holding him up when, in reality, if it hadn't been for his arm around her waist, she might have collapsed onto the hotel's asphalt. She pushed him toward the ambulance, then turned for the fire truck as he'd directed her to do.

The gear was heavy, weighting her down. She was surprised she could keep moving. She heard Marlee whimpering behind her and prayed no one from the Raimondi family could hear her. David and Adam crowded next to her. They climbed into the truck and waited.

Within no more than a minute, but what seemed like an hour, the captain climbed into the driver's seat and the truck took off.

She clung to the seat. David wrapped an arm around her. She looked at him. "If they're watching, won't they find it strange that a fire truck is leaving the area when the fire is still going?"

"Maybe, but it's our only hope right now."

"I want to go home," Marlee wailed. "Please, please, let me go home." Her sister had had enough. She broke down, sobs racking her slender frame. Summer's heart clenched with the need to comfort, but she was so tired, she could barely move. Adam sat up front, giving the driver directions. David placed a hand on Marlee's shoulder. Summer couldn't tell if he meant the gesture to be a comfort or a warning.

Ten minutes later, they pulled into the parking lot of a warehouse. Lights burned and the doors flew open. Marlee managed to dry her tears and get herself under control.

The fire truck stopped beside a waiting SUV. Two other SUVs waited, just like the previous times they'd had escorts. Within seconds, Summer, David, Adam, and Marlee had stripped the firefighting gear off and handed it over to the captain and the other firefighters who stood staring.

She hugged the captain. "Thank you."

He flushed. "Yes ma'am." His gaze flickered over the others. "Stay safe."

One of the marshals spoke up. "Please don't say anything about where you delivered them."

"Not a word."

"We're leaving and won't be here long enough for it to really matter, but . . ." He shrugged.

"I was never here."

He left and Summer slid into the vehicle followed by the others.

Ten minutes later, they were in the driveway of a small building on the edge of a middle-class neighborhood. The marshals gestured for them to go inside.

Summer hung back. "How do we know we can trust them?"

"Because they didn't take our guns," David murmured in her ear.

She wasn't sure if he really thought that or if he was just trying to comfort her. She stepped inside and noted that the place had been decorated to be functional, not fancy. "What is this place?"

"A debriefing hidey-hole."

David gripped her upper arm and led her to a chair. She sank into it. Adam did the same for Marlee, who'd stopped her weeping and sat mute, staring straight ahead.

David turned to the man closest to Summer. "They found us again."

Short and to the point. Summer decided she liked that about her husband. Her husband who'd lied to her. The husband she was very, very angry with but still loved with everything in her. She'd pushed aside her past hurts and fears and allowed him to lay siege to her heart. And he'd stomped all over it. A renewed sense of betrayal and a tidal wave surge of anger swept through her. She clamped her lips together and waited to see how this meeting was going to play out.

"I'm Bennie Holcombe. I'm with the marshals." Bennie was tall, a couple of inches over six feet. Muscles bunched under his jacket. Dark eyes glittered at her.

"Where are Mike and Chase?" David asked. He didn't seem intimidated by the man's vast size.

"We just got word that Chase was injured in the hotel bombing. He was returning to your suite when the bomb went off. He's being treated at the local hospital."

David grimaced. "And Mike?"

"Mike's been removed from duty as your handler."

Summer gasped. "Why?"

"Because someone keeps tracking you down. There's a leak somewhere and we can't seem to plug it."

Summer shivered. She'd been sprayed by the sprinklers and without the warmth of the heavy firefighter's uniform, the wet cold seeped into her bones. She wrapped her arms around her waist. "Or we're being tracked somehow."

A young woman in a plain blue sweatshirt pulled several blankets from a shelf behind her. She handed one to Summer and one to Marlee who quickly wrapped herself in it. Summer did the same and felt slightly warmer.

"How?" Bennie asked.

She shrugged. "I don't have any idea, but if none of the marshals working with us are traitors, then it only makes sense that they're tracking us somehow."

Bennie motioned to the woman beside him. "This is Holly Spencer. Why don't you women go with her and we'll see if there's anything on you."

Marlee sank into her blanket.

"Marlee should be fine," David said. "They were tracking us before she came into the picture."

"Check her anyway."

Marlee dropped the blanket onto the chair and rose, her casted left arm clutched to her stomach. She followed Summer and Holly into a back room.

David went with one of the other marshals. In a side room, David asked, "What's your name?"

"Vic Hastings." The two men shook hands.

"You got a shower in this place?"

"Yeah. And dry clothes. Just go through them and find something in your size."

"Thanks."

165

David stepped into the bathroom while Vic went over his clothes. Ten minutes later, he was showered and changed into a pair of jeans, a white T-shirt, and a Dallas Cowboy dark blue sweatshirt. He even found a pair of socks and combat boots that fit. When he stepped back into the room, Summer and Marlee were nowhere to be seen. Still showering and changing. He approached Vic, who turned and looked at him. "We found it."

David blinked. He hadn't really expected them to find anything. "What?"

"This." Vic dropped Summer's necklace into David's outstretched palm.

31

Summer decided she'd never take showers for granted ever again. Or soap. Or clean clothes.

She brushed her hair and stared into the foggy mirror. She wasn't interested in cleaning it. It didn't matter what she looked like at this point. All that mattered was survival. Marlee came into the bathroom via what amounted to a changing room and stepped up beside her. She swiped the mirror with a towel. She leaned forward and examined her face.

"I look like I've aged ten years," she scowled.

"No you don't. And at least you're alive."

"Barely."

Summer sighed.

Marlee took the brush from her and led her to the toilet seat. "Sit."

Summer didn't have the energy to argue. She sat.

Marlee positioned her so she could have full access to Summer's hair. With long gentle strokes, she brushed.

Summer felt some of the tension seep from her. "Thank you."

"You used to let me brush your hair for hours when we were younger."

"I know. I love it."

"I figured out that was one way to get you to spend time with me."

Summer blinked. "What?"

"You were always so busy working or with your friends. I was so much younger. Mom was either at the doctor or one of the bars downtown trying to find her next boyfriend that I felt lost, alone, invisible."

Summer swung around with a gasp. "I never knew that."

Marlee shrugged and flushed. "I suppose that's why I acted the way I did."

"And still do." The words were out before Summer could swallow them.

Marlee jerked, then let out a short laugh. "Yes, I suppose so."

Summer sat in silence while Marlee maneuvered the fingers of her broken arm and worked her hair into a tight french braid.

"Doesn't that hurt your arm?"

"A little. I'm just using my fingers to hold the hair and doing most of the work with my right hand."

"That's amazing you can do that." She paused. "Why didn't you go into cosmetology? You've always been great with hairdressing and stuff."

Marlee sighed. "I didn't figure it was a 'good enough' profession for you."

"What's that supposed to mean?"

"Well, you're a lawyer. I figured I needed to do something better than becoming a hairdresser." The bite to her words crawled up Summer's spine.

"But I never said—"

"You didn't have to. Didn't you listen to your own lectures on making something of my life?"

Summer snapped her lips shut. Was she really that demanding and judgmental?

When she was done with the braid, Marlee stepped back and said, "I know I can be a brat. I'm sorry."

The admission and apology surprised Summer. She sighed. "I probably made it easy for you to be one. You were so mad at me for marrying David. Why do you dislike him so much?" She'd never voiced the question until now.

It hovered between them and Summer wondered if Marlee was going to respond. With a sigh, her sister laid the brush on the counter. "Because he moved too fast, swept you off your feet." Her sister looked down. "Took you away from me."

"Oh, Marlee, he didn't take me away—"

Marlee looked up, eyes fierce. "Of course he did. Now when you have a day off work, who do you spend it with? Now, on the rare occasions that you actually cook a meal, who do you share it with?"

Summer stared. Speechless. "But he's my husband. That's what married couples do."

"Not to the exclusion of all others," Marlee argued. "I have to fight tooth and nail to get any time with you." Her shoulders slumped. "It's just so different than it used to be. I don't like it. You were my one constant, the person I knew I could count on. Then you got married and it all changed."

"No, no. That's not true." Was it? Had she excluded Marlee since getting married? She didn't think so, but if that's the way Marlee felt—

She gripped her sister's right hand. "If that's how you feel, then we need to figure out when we can spend time together. Just you and me. We'll put it on the calendar."

Marlee gave her a small smile and nodded. "Sure. Let's do that." Then she frowned and looked around. "Assuming we live to see another day."

A knock on the door made Summer jump. "You two about finished in there?"

Summer opened the door to David's handsome face. His eyes swept over her and the longing there nearly had her falling into his arms. She wanted to forget his deception and the fact that everything she knew about him was a lie. But she couldn't. She had to be strong. To help Marlee through this craziness and make sure they all stayed alive.

"We're ready."

Summer and Marlee followed David into the main area. Marlee went to the blanket she'd left on the chair and wrapped it back around her. Summer didn't think it was that chilly in the building, but Marlee had always been one to freeze no matter the temperature outside.

She watched her sister squirm a bit and get comfortable. Marlee closed her eyes and leaned her head back against the cushioned headrest. Summer sighed. Already, she'd tuned everything out around her.

Summer turned to ask what they'd found, but stopped when she saw her necklace laid out on the table in front of Vic. "What's going on?"

David said, "The tracker was on your necklace."

She gaped. "What? But how—" The memory of Corbin Hayes reaching out and taking her necklace in his hand flashed across her mind. "When he broke into my house, he admired my necklace."

Vic nodded. "The tracker is very small. Unless you looked at the back of the cross, you probably wouldn't even notice it."

"I usually don't even take it off."

David's lips thinned, parted. Summer wondered if he'd say anything about why she didn't have it around her neck.

He didn't.

"So, what do we do now?" he asked.

"Get you guys out of here so we can set a trap for Raimondi's boys."

"Does that mean Mike's back to being my handler?"

Vic and Bennie exchanged a look. "No."

"Why not?"

"He's working on something else right now."

David stared and Summer could tell he was wondering what the true story was, but these guys weren't going to share it. David must have decided not to waste his breath trying to get it out of them. He shrugged. "Fine. Now what?"

Bennie looked at his phone. "Chase is on his way from the hospital. He wasn't hurt that bad. He and Adam are going to escort the three of you to your new location."

Summer rubbed her eyes. "Look, I know this isn't important to you, but I have a very important trial coming up tomorrow morning. I need to be in court. I *will* be in court."

"We can't guarantee your protection if you don't follow our instructions," Bennie said.

David looked at her. "Summer, you're going to have to let one of the other lawyers in the firm take this one. What about Grady?"

Summer straightened her shoulders and narrowed her eyes. "No. Absolutely not. Olivia is counting on me. Her *girls* are counting on me. No one else knows this case like I do." She paused as she glanced back and forth between the marshals and David. "No one *cares* about this case like I do. I *have* to do this."

"Not if it means you wind up dead."

She gave him a hard stare and said in a killer-soft voice, "Then you better make sure your friends don't let that happen."

David looked at Bennie. "Well?"

Bennie shrugged. "All I can promise is we'll do our best. We escort judges to and from the courthouse on a regular basis. We can do the same for Summer."

"Then will you come up with a plan and let us in on it before nine o'clock in the morning?"

"I'll come up with a plan, but my best advice to you—" he looked at Summer—"to both of you . . ."

"Is?" David asked.

"Trust no one."

———

"Have you found him yet?"

Georgina's quiet question pulled Raimondi from his computer. She stood in the doorway, tall and regal. And with black circles beneath her dark brown eyes that attested to her sleepless nights. It had been over a year and still she thought of the man who'd betrayed her. Still she grieved her lost love. And now she grieved for Pauli, the cousin she'd adored. A six-year difference between them, he and Georgina had been playmates, with Pauli scrambling after his older cousin and making a nuisance of himself from the time he could walk. Georgina had loved every minute.

He opened his arms to her. She lifted her chin.

Raimondi sighed and dropped his arms. "No. Not yet. But we will."

"You're not going to hurt him, are you?"

"I should."

"Don't. Please. I asked you to find him for me, but not so you could exact some sort of revenge."

"Then why do you want me to find him?"

"Because I want to talk to him."

Raimondi shifted, his impatience hard to keep hidden. "Why would you have anything to say to him?"

Her eyes took on some of the fire that had been missing ever since David Hackett had walked out of her life. "I need him to look me in the eye and tell me he never loved me. I need him to tell me why he just left, walked out and never looked back. I need to hear that from him."

Raimondi growled his dissatisfaction. Georgina was such an innocent. But there was no way she could not know what her father did for a living. She'd never mentioned it. From the time she was old enough to read the papers, she'd never brought up his job or the family business. She preferred to keep her head buried and think he was a very successful financial consultant. And Raimondi was happy to let her believe that.

Until now.

"He betrayed you. He betrayed this family."

"Then he must have had a good reason." She narrowed her eyes. "I just wonder, what could that reason be, Papi?"

"Do you really want to get into this?"

She stared at him, her frailness touching his heart even as his mind devised ways to cause David Hackett immense amounts of pain.

Tears flooded her eyes and she bit her lip. "It's been over a year, Papi. And nothing. His partner's in jail, his company has been sold, and no one knows where he is. It's like he dropped off the face of the earth."

"He left you a note."

Her lips twisted. "That's not good enough. I want to hear him say it. Tell me why he would walk away from me." Her eyes issued a challenge. She thought he was the reason David had left. And she wasn't completely wrong.

But there was no way she was talking to David before Raimondi killed him.

No way at all.

"Trust no one," Bennie had said.

Good advice and yet he needed Chase and Adam for now. He had no choice but to trust the two men. David's mind spun. Where was Mike? He'd tried calling and his phone had been cut off. Not a good sign. As the black SUV ate up the miles, he relished the forced proximity to Summer.

He closed his eyes and thought about the one part of the story he'd yet to tell her. *God, I wish I'd known you before I made a mess of everything.*

What was he going to do?

He was going to tell her. Just not yet.

Or did he even need to go there?

No. He needed to come clean. Be honest. No more lies.

Summer's head tilted against his arm. He looked down to find her eyes shut, nostrils flaring slightly as she breathed.

Was she asleep that fast?

Marlee stared out the other window. Adam drove and Chase rode in silence.

Now that the tracking device had been discovered, there should be no more trouble with Raimondi's guys. At least until the trial.

His tension could ease for the moment, but David knew Raimondi wasn't finished. He also knew Summer was determined to show up in court tomorrow morning.

He knew why she was so vehement that she was the only one who could represent her client. Lawyers switched off all the time, covering for one another. But this case was different for Summer. She'd been obsessed with it from the beginning. Olivia and her two girls had come to mean so much to Summer. It was almost as if they represented a test of some kind. A test she was determined to pass.

David leaned his head against the window and shut off his brain. An old trick he'd mastered in the Army. He knew he needed to rest. To sleep while he could. He needed to be ready to fight back when Raimondi struck again.

"You guys all right back there?" Chase asked.

David opened his eyes. "Yeah. You?" Chase had a nasty cut above his right brow that some medical personnel had butterflied shut.

"I'll live. I was getting ready to get on the elevator when the bomb went off. A piece of the ceiling slammed into me. Just gotta learn to duck a little faster."

Adam said, "I think it's time to hand over the laptop, don't you?"

David let out a snort. "My only piece of insurance? Not a chance."

"You still don't trust us?"

David didn't answer for a moment as he thought about the question. He said, "I think I trust you. I don't necessarily trust the program."

"We haven't lost a witness since the inception of WITSEC in the seventies. At least no one who followed the rules."

"I'm not very good at following rules." He paused. "And there's a first time for everything. Unfortunately."

Adam and Chase fell silent. David had trusted Mike and Mike trusted Adam and Chase. They were good men. At least they seemed to be.

When Adam pulled into the parking lot of the next hotel, David gritted his teeth. They took their security measures and within minutes the five of them were in the presidential suite shedding the bulletproof vests.

"I'm hungry," Marlee announced.

"We'll get room service." David glanced at his watch. A little after 1:30.

"I'll call." Marlee picked up the phone. "I know what Summer likes, what about the rest of you guys?"

Her friendliness made him blink. And wonder what she was up to. But he gave her his order. Adam and Chase did the same.

David palmed the phone in his pocket as a plan formed.

32

Alessandro Raimondi was proud of his family. He was proud of the long line of crime that he came from. And he was proud of the fact that if his hired help couldn't tie up loose ends, he wasn't afraid to step in and do the dirty work himself. Something his grandfather had passed on to his father and his father to him. Raimondi had taught his three boys well, but had bowed to his wife's wishes to keep his daughter out of the business. And to have David—

"Yes sir? May I help you?"

"I'm here to see one of your prisoners." He gave the woman the name. She motioned him through. Raimondi stepped through the metal detector, suffered a wand search, and left all of his belongings behind. Including the fake ID. He pressed the mustache harder onto his upper lip and blinked at the grittiness caused by the colored contacts he'd acquired for this occasion. He didn't want his face on camera. He sure didn't want anyone knowing he was meeting with this particular prisoner.

Knowing the meeting would be videotaped, Raimondi thought carefully how he would word his questions. He just hoped the man he was meeting with would play it cool.

Raimondi followed the guard into the private meeting area

he'd requested and sat at the table to wait. Seconds later, the door clanged open.

He turned and smiled. "Hello, Sam."

Sam squinted. "Do I know you?"

"Have a seat."

Sam sat slowly. The guard stood by the door.

"You've aged," Raimondi said.

"Prison does that to a person."

"Watching your back, huh?"

Sam's eyes widened as recognition finally hit him. Raimondi lifted a finger to his lips. The guard shifted and took a step toward the table. Raimondi leaned back and crossed his arms. The guard relaxed. Sam's gaze flicked to the door and back to Raimondi. He took a deep breath, then mimicked Raimondi's position. "What brings you here?"

Raimondi offered a careless shrug. "Just thought I'd visit an old friend."

Sam licked his lips and Raimondi gave a slight smile. He relished Sam's uneasiness, knew the man was wondering if this was going to be his last day alive.

Raimondi took great pleasure in knowing he could answer that question with a confident "yes."

Summer gripped her notes on Olivia's case. Not that she needed them. She had the flash drive with several videos. One of which would probably be the most condemning piece of evidence against Silas Todd. She almost felt sorry for him. Almost. Hiring a private investigator had paid off big-time. Silas had an ego the size of his wallet. He thought he was invincible. Fortunately his extreme arrogance would be his downfall.

The courthouse came into view and David tensed beside her. Adam and Chase were silent. Summer caught sight of a number of police officers. Her heartbeat slowed a fraction as she realized the marshals had arranged for extra security. Of course they would. And of course David had insisted on coming with her. Something everyone had argued against to no avail.

Uncertainty gripped her. Was she doing the right thing? Refusing to back off the case and let someone else handle it?

No. None of this was Olivia's fault. If Summer handed her off to someone else, Olivia and her girls would suffer. Besides, it was too late now. At least Marlee had agreed to stay put with two marshals guarding her.

The car pulled up to the door at the back of the building. Summer climbed out after David and let them usher her straight into the building. The door slammed shut behind her and she jumped.

Chase patted her on the back. "It's all right."

She nodded and let out a breath she hadn't realized she'd been holding. The Kevlar vest felt heavy and bulky and she wanted it off. David took her hand, and together, they walked toward the conference room. The first room they entered resembled a waiting area. Olivia's girls sat on a love seat. They held hands and stared at the adults with eyes too old. Too weary. Summer went to them and hugged one, then the other. The girls squeezed her neck and Summer breathed in their sweet clean scent.

"It's going to be okay," she whispered. "I don't know how, but it will. God does answer prayers. Remember that no matter what happens today. Promise me."

Sandy merely nodded against her. Laura said, "I'll believe it when I see it."

Summer's heart ached. She remembered feeling exactly the same way. "I'm praying you see it. Soon."

Judge Reed Morton came out of the conference room and greeted them. "No trouble?"

"Not a bit," David said.

"You'll have to wait out here." He looked at the marshals and the two police officers already there for the hearing. "Looks like we have the security we need."

Chase nodded. "We've got more around the building and snipers on the roof of the bank across the street."

The judge had been updated as to the risk, but when he realized the level of security surrounding David and Summer, he agreed to continue the hearing. "Then let's get this done."

Summer shot a glance at David. He was making funny faces at the girls. Sandy smiled behind her hand. Laura rolled her eyes. A pang shot through her. He was a good man.

Wasn't he?

She stepped into the room and immediately focused on the occupants, thoughts of her own personal problems tossed to the back burner.

Olivia Todd sat at one end of the long table. Her husband, Silas, sat at the other. He glared. Olivia stared at her lap.

"Hey," Summer said and touched Olivia's shoulder.

She looked up and relief flared like a blow torch. Summer gave her a reassuring smile and took her place beside the woman. The judge sat at the end of the table next to Silas's attorney.

Introductions were made and Judge Morton started by saying, "We're here to determine custody arrangements for the minors, Laura Denise and Sandra Rene Todd."

David's heart went out to the little girls who sat across from him. A woman the little one had called Aunt Lily squeezed in between them when she'd come out of the restroom. "They've already started?" she asked.

"Yes, I believe so."

She nodded and held out her hand. "I'm Lily St. James."

David shook it. "David Hackett."

Lily slipped an arm around Sandy's shoulders. The little girl leaned into her and winced.

"What's wrong?" Lily asked.

"Nothing. My ribs still hurt sometimes when I move wrong."

David's hands curled into fists. He met Laura's eyes. She looked down at his hands, then back up and gave him a grim smile. "Yeah," she whispered. "Me too."

Her perception shocked him.

Chase peered out the window that had been covered in anticipation of David and Summer's arrival. He spoke and his words were carried into the small earpiece he had in his ear to whoever was listening. To Adam he said, "We're all clear so far."

So far.

He glanced back at the girls. Laura had gotten up to pace in front of the closed door. Every so often she would shoot an anxious look at it. He wished he had a way to make the child feel better, but figured he might make things worse.

She pulled out an iPhone and fiddled with it for several minutes.

"Are you playing a game?"

She looked up at him. "Something like that."

"You want my seat? I don't mind standing."

She eyed the couch. "There's a seat over there. I don't need yours." She must have felt guilty for her abrupt words because she added, "But thanks, though."

"Sure." Maybe he should just shut up. Men were probably not her favorite people.

She studied him a moment longer, then went back to the phone. More pacing.

A yell came from behind the closed door and David leapt to his feet. Laura jumped back and then froze, her back against the wall. Sandy buried her face in her aunt's shoulder, then started coughing.

Chase placed a hand on his weapon and moved toward the room.

David beat him to it. Stepping to the side, he twisted the knob and pushed the door open. Chase stood on the opposite side.

"Everything all right in there?" David called.

Summer came to the door, her tense face and haunted eyes reaching right into David's heart. This case was especially hard for her. "We're fine. Silas is a little uptight, but I think the two officers in the room with us can handle it."

Chase and David nodded. She shut the door.

Sandy looked up from her aunt's shoulder. Her hitching breaths worried David. "She okay?"

The woman nodded and pulled an inhaler from her bag. Sandy took it and used it like a pro. Lily stared at the door with a look of pure hate on her face. David hoped the woman didn't own any weapons or Silas Todd would be in danger of serious harm.

She blinked, shuddered, and sighed. Running a hand over Sandy's hair, she looked at David. "Anxiety-induced asthma."

He nodded. "Maybe she won't need that anymore after today."

Lily's shoulders relaxed a fraction. "That's the prayer."

Laura had been following the conversation. David watched the girl take a deep breath and give a quick nod as though in answer to a question she'd just asked herself. She moved from the wall and walked to the door to rap her knuckles against the wood.

33

A knock on the door startled them. Silas swung his glare from his wife to the door. The knob turned and Laura Todd stepped into the room.

Olivia jumped up. "Honey, what are you doing? You're supposed to be waiting outside."

Her small hand trembled, but she notched her chin. "I want to talk to the judge."

"But you've already—"

"No, I mean again."

Summer glanced at the judge, who leaned forward with a frown. "Young lady, this is a very serious meeting we're having here and you're interrupting."

She met him frown for frown. "And it's my future that you're meeting about so I think I should have a say in it."

"I gave you that chance. You didn't have a whole lot to say."

"Well, I was scared of you before."

"And now you're not?"

"Oh I'm still scared of you, but I'm more scared of my daddy, so may I please talk to you?"

Olivia gasped. Then silence echoed around the room. Silas's

face grew red. He stood. "Laura, you need to stop this nonsense and wait outside. Now."

Laura looked at him. "No. Not until I talk to the judge. I hate you and I want him to know why."

"Laura—" Silas's voice took on a menacing edge that had his lawyer placing a hand on the man's forearm. Silas took a deep breath and settled back into his seat.

Laura asked the judge, "Are you going to make us have to see him?"

The judge sighed. "Honey, I have two daughters." He pointed to Silas. "A father who would fight so hard to keep custody of his girls deserves to see them."

Tears filled Laura's eyes. "Even when he screams at them that he hates them and tells them that he wishes they were never born? Even when he gets drunk and hits them?" she whispered.

"I object." Silas's lawyer leaned forward. "Judge, this is irrelevant. You've already talked to the children."

"Shut up," Judge Morton said.

The lawyer snapped his lips shut, then started to say something else.

Judge Morton nailed him. "You want me to hold you in contempt?"

The man stayed quiet, speaking volumes of displeasure with his body language. The judge turned and shot a ferocious frown at Silas.

Silas slammed a fist on the table. "Laura, why are you doing this? I've never laid a finger on you."

Summer thought Silas's blood pressure might just cause him to stroke out and save them all a lot of grief.

The little girl trembled and stepped closer to her mother. Olivia reached out to hold her daughter's hand.

Judge Morton asked, "Why didn't you mention any of this when you had the chance to tell me earlier today?"

"I couldn't get my tongue to work. I was scared." She swallowed hard. "But I have to do this for Sandy."

"Your little sister."

Laura nodded. "My dad doesn't hit me, but he hits her. He even put her in the hospital with a punctured lung."

"Laura, that's a lie," Silas growled. "Now shut your mouth."

"It's not a lie and I have proof." She dug into her pocket and pulled out an iPhone.

Olivia lifted a brow. "Where did you get that?"

"It's Claudia's. She let me take it home one day after school." She swallowed hard. "The day Daddy hurt Sandy so bad." She tapped the screen. "We were playing with it. Sandy was recording me singing and stuff. Then Daddy came home. He was mad because Mom hadn't started making dinner yet. But she was sick and didn't feel good. She was throwing up and everything, and Daddy wasn't supposed to be home until the next day anyway. He got home early."

Olivia didn't make a sound. Tears slipped silently down her cheeks.

Judge Morton leaned back in his chair. "Go on."

With a glare at her father, Laura tapped a few more times, then handed the phone to the judge. "Sandy left the phone recording. Press Play."

"I object," Silas's lawyer said. "We haven't had the chance to review this."

"Neither have we," Summer snapped.

"Be quiet, both of you."

He stared at Laura, who stood trembling, everything about her shouting her desire to flee and her determination to be brave and make the adults in the room listen to her.

"Press Play. Please, sir."

The judge did.

A child's singing, girls giggling echoed through the room.

Then a door slammed. Curses rent the air.

Silas jumped up once again. "Shut it off!"

"Sit down," the judge roared.

The officers moved toward Silas as he started around the table. His lawyer stopped him. "Sit."

"The video was rigged."

From the phone, Silas's voice echoed, "Where's your mother? Where's that lazy, lying, no good—"

"I'm here, Silas," Olivia's weak voice answered.

"So this is what happens when I'm gone? You haven't even started dinner?" He called her a few more names.

A whimper. "I'll start now, Silas. I'm sorry. I'll start now."

"Leave her alone!" The young girl's voice echoed through the room. Sandy, the younger child.

"Sandy, no!" An older girl's voice. Laura.

Heavy footsteps. Then a sharp crack. A gasping cry of pain. "Talk back to me, will you? Guess it's time to teach you some manners."

What followed was too horrible to listen to. Summer wanted to cover her ears. She didn't. She listened and swallowed the ever-present nausea churning in her stomach, flinching at Sandy's high-pitched screams and Laura's cries for him to stop.

Summer wanted to rail at the man who'd done this to his family, a man who could beat a child. She glanced at the judge. Even he looked horrified.

Olivia wept silently. Silas sat still and glared at them all. And even though she trembled, Laura glared right back.

Judge Morton broke the silence. "Full custody granted to Olivia Todd." He looked at Silas. "No visitation until you get the help you obviously need." He looked at the two officers near the door. "Take him into custody. Charge him with child abuse. I'm not sure on how many counts, but it'll be enough to put him away for a while."

Laura burst into tears and raced around the table to fling herself into the judge's arms. "Thank you."

Judge Morton looked stunned and gave her back an awkward pat. He held her away and looked into her eyes. "No one is going to hurt you anymore." He guided her to her mother. Olivia held her and stroked her hair as Laura closed her eyes and wept.

Silas bolted to his feet with a roar. "No! You can't do this!" He rushed toward his wife. "You're dead!"

The nearest officer slammed into Silas, tackling him to the floor. He whipped his hands behind his back. "And you're under arrest."

Summer sat, stunned by the abrupt end to the ordeal. As the officers led a protesting Silas down the hall, Olivia lifted her gaze. The judge cleared his throat and Laura grinned at her mother through her tears. "I didn't believe her, but Summer was right, Mom. God sometimes answers prayers in a big way."

David and Summer, flanked by Adam and Chase, walked toward the exit. David squeezed her hand. "You did it."

Summer took a deep breath. "Yeah, well, I think I'll give God and Laura the credit for this one."

"Silas was not a happy man."

"Nope."

"Are you okay?"

"I'm better. I'm so glad I was here." She looked at him. "You understand why I had to put my life on the line to be here?"

"Oh yeah. I understand."

She nodded and they continued their trek through the courthouse flanked by the two marshals.

"I don't think I'm mad at God anymore," she said. He lifted a brow and she shrugged. "Remember in the car I was so furious with you? You had said something like I didn't deserve what you'd done?"

Wary, he eyed her. "Yeah."

"I'm glad God doesn't always give us what we deserve. We deserve to be miserable creatures for as long as we're on this earth, and yet he delivers us from evil time and time again."

"And uses children to do it sometimes."

"Exactly. Laura will always know that she was a hero today."

"So were you."

She gave a half laugh.

A pop sounded and Chase dropped.

"Gun!" Adam yelled as he shoved David toward the nearest door. The stairs. Chaos erupted inside the courthouse.

"Chase!" David resisted.

Adam gave him another hard push. "I'll take care of him. You're the priority. Now go!"

David grabbed Summer and pulled her with him into the stairwell. A bullet slammed into the door just above his head. He shoved the door closed and guided Summer halfway down the steps. "Stop here."

Shivering, shaking, she obeyed without a sound. David had his weapon in his hand, ready to use it. The stairwell door opened once again and he lifted the gun.

Adam stumbled through it. "Go, go, go. The car's coming around."

He spoke into his mic. David kept a tight grip on Summer's hand as he descended to the basement floor.

"Who was able to get a gun in here?" David demanded. Security had been so tight.

His question went unanswered as they burst through the basement door. Three black SUVs sat waiting, engines running. Adam opened the door to the middle vehicle and Summer climbed in. David followed her. Bennie sat at the wheel.

Adam said, "Get them out of here."

"What about you?" Summer finally spoke.

"I'm making sure no one's following you. Bennie will take care of you. You've got marshals in front of you and marshals behind you. See you soon." He shut the door.

The first vehicle took off with a squeal of tires. Bennie was right after him. The third vehicle stayed close behind.

They exited the parking garage into the sunlight. David squinted. The SUV in front of them peeled off around a corner. Bennie went straight. He turned to see the vehicle behind them go in yet a third direction. At least they knew what they were doing. If anyone was trying to follow, they'd have to guess which vehicle David and Summer were in. Hopefully they would guess wrong.

David watched the mirrors. No sign they were being followed. He leaned his head back and closed his eyes for a brief moment. Summer sat silent beside him.

The car jerked to the right and David slammed into the door. "Hey!"

Bennie put the vehicle in Park and turned. "Sorry about that."

"What are you doing?"

Bennie lifted his left hand and David found himself staring into the barrel of a Glock 40.

34

Summer pulled in a deep breath. No, no, no. This was not happening.

She noticed David kept his hands where Bennie could see them so she did too. "You?"

Bennie gave a one-shouldered shrug. "Money talks. Give me your gun."

David handed over his weapon. "So what now? You kill us?" he asked.

"Nope, I need you alive. At least for now." He turned the weapon to Summer's face. She flinched and pulled back. The gun followed her. She wished she had her own weapon with her. Because of David's status as still active military and his work with the FBI, he'd been allowed to keep his gun in the courthouse. Summer had had to turn hers over. She hadn't had time to get it before the shooting broke out.

"Now hand over your phones."

David narrowed his eyes and for a moment Summer thought he might refuse, but when Bennie kept the gun on her face, David reached in his pocket and tossed the phone into the front seat. Summer did the same.

With his right hand, Bennie handed back a set of handcuffs. "Put these on him."

Summer took them. Looked at them. And said, "No."

He lifted a brow. "Then I'll kill your sister, and I'll kill you while David watches."

David shifted. "Put them on me, Summer," David said.

She saw his eyes darken, trying to tell her something.

"Behind your back," Bennie ordered.

David shifted and put his hands behind his back. "Do it, Summer."

"David, I—"

"Just do it," he snapped.

The ring of the first cuff encircled his right wrist. Then the second. She left them loose.

"Tighten them. I need to hear a few more clicks."

Summer tightened them and glared at the marshal. "You leave my sister out of this."

Bennie smirked and, without taking his eyes from Summer, said, "She's already in it." He reached over one more time and handed her a phone. "Take a look at this and see if it's a little incentive for your cooperation."

Summer snatched the phone and, with a shaking finger, pressed Play.

David watched over her shoulder.

Marlee's scared face came onto the screen. She glanced up at the person holding the phone, then back to the camera. Tear stains tracked her cheeks. "Summer? I'm sorry. They came in and killed the marshals." A sob escaped and a hand slapped her across the face. She screamed.

Summer gasped and flinched.

A voice said, "Focus. Say it."

Marlee sniffed, her cheek already puffing up. "They're going to kill me unless you give them what they want. That laptop. You've got to give it to them." The video stopped.

Summer threw the phone at Bennie. It smacked him in the forehead. He glared and his nostrils flared. "Temper, temper."

Bennie heaved their phones into the bushes lining the parking lot. Then he opened the driver's door, got out, and opened the door next to Summer. She wanted to cringe, lean in to David.

Instead, she stared at Bennie, refusing to cower. He snagged her arms behind her back and cuffed her. He shoved her back into the seat, and she fell against David with a cry she couldn't hold back. He tensed and she could tell he wanted nothing more than to lunge at the man, but she was in the way. Which was probably a good thing.

She righted herself and glared at Bennie.

He ignored her and climbed back into the driver's seat. "Now, David. I need you to give me directions on how to find this elusive laptop that Raimondi wants so bad."

"So, it's come to this, has it?"

"I'm afraid so. Now which way?" He held up the phone. "One call is all it takes to start killing off everyone your wife loves. Starting with her sister."

Summer couldn't stop the groan that escaped her.

David glanced at her and said, "Get on I-26 and go west, then get on I-40 toward Asheville."

"That's better."

"How are you going to explain our disappearance to your boss?" David asked. "You were the only one in the car we got in."

"I appreciate the concern, but you don't need to worry about that. I've got it taken care of."

"Where's Mike?" David asked.

"Again, not your concern."

"Oh come on, Bennie, did you kill the man? What's the big secret at this point?"

Silence from the front seat. Summer felt her heart drop. "You did, didn't you?" she whispered. "You killed him."

"Mike was too nosy for his own good. Figured out some things he should have left alone."

David blew out a breath. "He didn't know about the tracking

191

device on Summer's necklace so he figured someone from the inside was leaking our whereabouts. He went to you, didn't he?"

"Like I said, it doesn't matter."

But David wasn't done. Summer could almost hear his brain whirling. "When he told you his suspicions, you didn't know about the tracking device either, did you? So when Mike told you he thought someone on the inside was ratting us out, you got nervous because you'd been feeding Raimondi information."

More silence.

David let out a harsh laugh. "You weren't sure if he suspected you and was feeling you out, getting your reaction, or just had the misfortune to pick you to report his suspicions to. So you killed him to make sure it didn't matter. How close am I?"

"Pretty close," Bennie said. The coldness in his voice made Summer shiver.

David clamped his jaw shut and Summer could see his desperate struggle to control himself. For a few moments, he stayed quiet. His arms moved, restless against the back of the seat.

Finally, he stilled and took a deep breath. Her heart pounded in her throat and terror clogged her lungs. His wallet fell to the seat between them. He turned his head and caught her eye. "Get ready," he mouthed.

She frowned. "For what?" she silently asked, moving her lips to form the words, making sure Bennie wasn't watching in the rearview mirror.

"Escape," he whispered.

"How?"

He shook his head. They rode in silence for the next hour. Summer leaned her head against the window, her nerves shot, her stomach threatening upheaval at any moment. She swallowed hard and closed her eyes to offer up prayers to the God she struggled with.

Please, God, if you're there, do something. I don't know why you've let this happen, but I don't want to die.

A tear leaked down her cheek and she swiped it against her shoulder.

Please, God. Save us.

"What now?" Bennie's question made her jerk. Her wrists ached and her shoulders protested the awkward position, but she just bit her lip and watched David's face.

"Keep going and turn at the next exit. Follow that road until you see a bunch of trees."

"Great directions, Hackett. Street names?"

"I don't remember. Just drive. I'll tell you where to go."

With an annoyed sigh, Bennie did as directed, following David's instructions. He got on the phone and talked low with whoever was on the other end. After they hit I-40 and headed into North Carolina, every once in a while David would give Bennie another set of directions.

Summer shivered, her heart pounding, adrenaline still rushing. Trees thickened, highway noise died down. Why was David taking them out to such a remote area? Killing them and hiding their bodies would be incredibly easy. She wanted to scream at God to make this stop, to make it all go away. Instead, she sat silent and prayed while she watched David for whatever she was supposed to be ready for.

And then David caught her eye.

She lifted a brow.

He motioned with his head for her to slide closer.

With a glance at the rearview mirror, she did.

Bennie didn't seem to notice.

And then she felt David's hand behind her, working the cuffs.

His hands were free? How?

Who cared?

She felt the cuff release from her left hand. Slowly, she pulled her hands apart, never taking her eyes from the mirror.

Bennie slowed to go around a sharp curve and David struck.

35

David gripped the cuffs, the fingers of each hand wrapped around the loops. In one sudden, smooth move, he went over the front seat and dropped the cuffs in front of Bennie, the short chain landing against his Adam's apple.

Bennie hollered as David gave a sharp yank. Gagging, sputtering, Bennie slammed on the brakes, throwing David forward. The car spun to the left, hit the guardrail, then went over the side of the mountain, trunk first.

David registered Summer's scream. An object slammed into his forehead, causing him to flinch. He almost lost his grip, but regained it with the next shift of the vehicle. Bennie fought for air as the car bounced down, ricocheting off trees and finally sliding to a stop at the bottom of the hill.

He grabbed at David's hands, bucking against the restraint. David held on, his ears ringing, muscles straining, ribs screaming. Fortunately, gravity worked with him.

Finally Bennie went limp and David slammed back against the seat. His head throbbed. Blood dripped into his eyes.

Summer groaned.

David shot her a glance, relieved she was conscious. "You okay?"

"Yeah. I married a crazy man who just wrecked the car and could have killed us, but yes, I think I'm okay."

Her spunkiness reassured him. He lifted a hand, swiped the blood from his eyes. "Good. Look for the weapons." He checked Bennie one more time. Felt his pulse. Faint. Breathing? Barely.

Summer held up his weapon.

He said, "Hang on to it, I've got to find the other one. Check back there."

He heard her start to rummage, noting she hadn't asked about Bennie. Probably thought he'd killed him and didn't want to know for sure. "I don't see it."

David shoved on the door. Jammed. He climbed over into the front seat and tried the passenger door. Also jammed. But the window was cracked. He told Summer, "Do you see the handcuffs back there?"

"Yes." He heard her scrambling. She shoved a pair into his hand. David swiped at the blood still trickling from the wound on his forehead. What had hit him? David maneuvered Bennie until he had both of the man's hands behind him. He cuffed him, then searched his pockets. When he found the key, he shoved it into his pocket. "Keep the gun on him in case he wakes up."

He waited until she had the weapon held against the man's temple, then leaning back against Bennie's still form, David rammed a foot against the window. Glass shattered. He continued to kick until he had a hole large enough to climb out of. "Climb over him. We need to get out of here. I don't know what communication he had with Raimondi, but we're not going to wait and find out."

She handed him the gun. "What about Marlee, David? You may have just gotten her killed."

David climbed out of the hole in the window then looked back to say, "No, the longer we're alive, the longer she's alive. I probably bought her a few more hours. Now come on."

"What do you mean?" she asked as she climbed over into the front seat.

195

"The minute Raimondi had us where he wanted us, Marlee was expendable. He still needs her to get to us."

Summer frowned, the tight lines on her forehead saying how worried she was. Frankly he was too, but decided to keep that to himself. She let him help her out of the vehicle and stood shivering next to him.

"Where's your coat?"

"In the car."

David didn't want to take the time to get it, but she would need the heavy down jacket if they didn't find shelter tonight. They both might. His leather jacket would do for now, but the temperatures would drop and the down coat would feel good. Especially if she'd let them share body heat.

"What are we going to do with him?" she asked when he handed her the coat and crawled back out of the window.

"Leave him here. Someone will find him. Bennie was talking a lot on the phone. Wouldn't surprise me if someone's right behind us."

Fear flashed in her eyes. "Then we need to hurry, don't we?"

"Yes."

"What are we going to do?"

"Start walking."

"I don't exactly have on walking shoes." She had worn her lawyer clothes—black slacks, a blazer, and black pumps. At least the shoes were comfortable, but she wasn't sure how well they'd hold up walking through the woods. "How far?"

"You can do it. I'll help you."

"In other words, I don't want to know how far, huh?"

He gave her a grim smile and held out a hand. She placed her cold fingers in his.

"How did you get the cuffs off?"

"I always keep a handcuff key in my wallet."

Of course he did. "Who does that?"

"Me." He smiled.

"Down there!"

The shout spurred him to action. Summer too. She didn't hesitate when he tugged her after him. "Where are we?" she gasped.

"In the state park."

"Is it open?"

"Yes. This is still tourist season. I'm hoping we can find a group to blend in with. If not, I grew up around here. I know a few places to hide."

She hurried after him. He looked back over his shoulder to see two men skidding down the side of the mountain toward the wrecked SUV.

"Hurry," he urged. Summer picked up her pace. "Head for the cliff just ahead."

"A cliff?"

He led her through a tangled copse of trees, found a trail, and kept going. She stumbled and caught herself with his help. A steadying hand on her upper arm kept her upright.

Shouts behind them spurred him on.

They came to the edge and David looked down. A steep drop off the side of the mountain. He knew he could use the rocks and ledges for hand and footholds, but wasn't sure about her. "How do you feel about going down?"

She stared at him, then behind him. Swallowed hard. "If it's the only way."

36

Alessandro was nearly apoplectic. "What do you mean they got away again?" He'd hired incompetent idiots. Unbelievable. He was glad his father wasn't alive to see this mess.

Hayes grunted, then cursed. "We're on their tail right now. Let me call you back as soon as we catch up to them."

"No. Let the others chase them. I need information. What happened to Bennie?"

Hayes told him and Raimondi wanted to punch something. He'd spent a lot of money on that man, and now David had ruined yet another good thing.

"Josh is with him," Hayes said. "Bennie's hurt pretty bad. The good thing is, Summer and David don't have a phone. At least as far as we can tell."

"How do you figure that?"

"Bennie said he'd tossed their phones back in the bushes of a parking lot. We picked them up to make sure no one found them right away, which is why he got so far ahead of us. When we got here, the car was wrecked and Bennie's unconscious. The only other phone we found in the vehicle was the one Bennie had on him."

"Tell Josh to finish Bennie off. I don't need him taken into custody. No telling what he might spill."

"I'll tell him."

"Where are you?"

"In the middle of a jungle."

Raimondi listened as Hayes explained where the car wrecked. "I have an idea. Now listen up."

Summer followed David, her senses tuned to sounds behind her. Right now, she heard nothing. "Have we lost them?"

"Let's hope so. I think they fell for it."

Much to Summer's relief, David had decided going down the cliff was too risky. It would be way too easy for one of them to get hurt. Then they'd be sitting ducks. He'd pushed a large boulder over the edge of the cliff and had Summer let out an ear-piercing scream.

Then they'd taken off down the trail, putting as much distance between them and the cliff as possible.

Right now, no one appeared to be following. If they were, she couldn't hear them.

The undergrowth pulled at her slacks. Her shoes sank into the mud and she had to pay attention to each step or she'd wind up with a twisted ankle. "Are they still behind us?"

"I don't think so, but we need to keep moving. I need to find a phone."

"Who are you going to call?" she panted as she let him help her over a fallen tree trunk.

"Chase and Adam and a few other people. Now that we know who was behind setting us up, we need reinforcements. And I know exactly who I can trust at this point."

"What about Marlee?"

"We're going to get to her shortly. First we have to make sure we're going to stay alive for a little while longer."

Summer wanted to protest. To insist they head straight for wherever Raimondi was holding Marlee. "How are we going to find her?"

"I know where she is."

His quiet admission took her by surprise. "You know? How would you know?"

David sighed and stopped walking. He turned and she nearly ran into him, but managed to stop before her nose smashed into his chest. He said, "I've been in Raimondi's house before. I recognized the room where Marlee was."

Summer gaped at him. "Been in his house? How? When? Why?"

A shot rang out. Bark flew off the tree nearest Summer and grazed her forehead. She dropped to the ground while David whirled, weapon pointed in the direction the bullet had come from. He squeezed off one shot, then leaned over to grab Summer's hand. "Time to move a little faster."

Summer leapt to her feet, heart in her throat, and let David lead her at a fast jog. She shoved the fear down deep and tried not to think how bad it would hurt to have a bullet land between her shoulders. "How did they find us so fast?"

"They've done this before."

"So how are we going to get away from them?" Fear for Marlee, fear for herself and David was almost a tangible thing. Something she could taste. A bitter thing she wanted to spit out.

"We're going to find a place to hide. Keep going."

"I'm trying, David, but I'm getting tired," she panted, "and these shoes aren't exactly hiking boots. I'm going to hold you back."

"You'll be fine."

They raced like the wind and her lungs burned, her legs ached, and she thought she might throw up.

When Summer decided she had reached her limit and it was time for her to simply lie down and wait on Hayes to come finish her off, David stopped and pulled her into the thick area.

"There," he whispered.

She looked, straining to see what he did. It wasn't until they were almost on it, she noticed he'd pointed to a makeshift cave.

The rock had formed against the side of the mountain leaving a crack that didn't look big enough for David to fit through.

He said, "Wait here one second and let me check to make sure there's nothing in here that's going to wake up and decide we're dinner. Keep watch through those trees. If you see movement, get in here." He turned sideways and, with a twist and a grunt, disappeared.

Sweat beaded her face and slid between her shoulder blades. She'd worked up a sweat running in the heavy down coat. She slid it off her shoulders and hung it over her arm. Standing still, she began to cool off. She looked back over her shoulder, watching for Raimondi's men. So far, they'd lost them. But she also knew they'd probably left a trail a blind man could follow.

David stuck his head out of the crack. "It's safe."

"No bears?"

"No. Can't promise you won't see a spider or two."

"Ick." But she didn't hesitate. "Better the eight-legged creepy crawlies than the two-legged."

"My sentiments too."

Summer slid through the crack. "How did you know this was here?"

David led her to a place where he'd cleared out a spot. He took her jacket and laid it on the ground. "I grew up roaming this area of the Blue Ridge Mountains." He gestured toward the coat. "Have a seat."

She did, grateful for the respite. Her stomach was still doing funny things and she was afraid if she didn't rest, it would rebel on her. She leaned her head back against the hard rock. The coolness felt good and she turned so she could press her cheek against it. The nausea faded. "Don't we need to watch for them?"

He slid down beside her and leaned his back against the wall. "Yeah. From here, I can see if anyone approaches. Let's keep our voices down, though."

Summer whispered, "So you grew up around here?"

"Just during the summertime. My parents traveled a lot with their jobs, and my brother, Les, and I were just in the way. So we were shipped off to my grandmother's house for the summer." Light filtered through the crack, illuminating the small area where they sat. She could see a small smile curve his lips. Pain grabbed her by the heart and wouldn't let go. She choked it down.

"So you have a brother named Les, not Jake."

He sighed. "Yes."

"Tell me more about your life before you met me. Before WIT-SEC."

David shifted beside her. The cold from the rock seeped through her blazer and she shivered. David wrapped his left arm around her and brought her against his chest. She leaned in, relishing his warmth. A part of her shouted that she had no business being close to him. Not after his lies, but she couldn't bring herself to move away from him.

When she didn't resist, his arm tightened. "Before we met, I wasn't the nicest guy around. My parents are wealthy, influential. Nice people. But weren't really interested in raising kids."

"Ouch."

"Yeah. So I learned to get my parents' attention by getting into trouble. By the time I went into the military, my parents were pretty much done with me."

"When did you go to college? That's where you met Sam, right?"

He sighed. "After high school, I went straight into the Army. Did a tour and came home and got out. It was at that point I decided to go to college and get a degree in business. Sam and I met the first day I stepped foot on the Berkeley campus in New York. We hit it off and were best friends almost instantly."

"So what happened?"

"I didn't finish. See, I have special skills the Army likes, so my old unit commander called me up and asked for my help. I agreed."

"Why?"

"Because when I decided to go to college—and Berkeley at that—I was suddenly acceptable to my parents again."

"And that was a bad thing?"

"No. And yes. They were constantly on my back about my major and what I was going to do with my life, so in the middle of my junior year, I ditched school and went back into the Army. At least they accepted me the way I was and weren't trying to change me into someone I didn't want to be."

Summer's heart clenched. She tried to harden it. It was difficult because she knew how he felt to a degree.

Rocks and wooded debris rained down over the small opening. David tensed. He stood and Summer immediately missed his warmth.

David walked over to the crack. His hand rested on the grip of the weapon at his lower back. His body blocked the light and the small cave darkened.

Voices reached her ears and she stood, heart thumping.

"They're around here somewhere. They didn't just disappear into the side of the mountain, now find them."

Corbin Hayes's cold voice sent her pulse into overdrive. A tremor spread through her, causing her to shake like a leaf on a windy day. The thought of being in his clutches stirred her stomach to nausea once again. She swallowed hard and tried to regulate her breathing.

David stood still as a rock, the weapon held tight in his hand.

Summer moved to stand next to him. When a shadow fell over the opening, Summer pressed against the rock wall. David held a finger to his lips. He knew she didn't need the reminder, but it made him feel better. Clamping her mouth tight, she stayed still.

Footsteps crunched close by. "They came this way."

"Well, they're not here now. You forget how to track?"

"Shut up, Nico. You think you can do better, do it."

No answer. Then one of the men said, "The trail stops here."

"Or does it?" Nico shot back. "Looks like a pretty clear path heading up the hill right there."

"Fine. You follow it. But I'm telling you, they're around here somewhere."

The men grumbled amongst themselves for a brief moment. Finally, he heard Nico say, "You do what you want. I'm going up the trail."

David shifted to get a better view and his foot scraped against some loose rock. The sound was quiet, muted, but his gut clenched at the slight noise.

"What was that?" Nico demanded.

David froze and heard Summer's soft indrawn breath.

"What was what?" Hayes asked.

"I heard something."

Hayes barked a laugh. "You're in the woods, moron. You're going to hear all kinds of things. Now let's get going." Hayes headed for the trail.

But David could now see Nico's face. The man paused, glanced right at the crack. David didn't move. And he didn't look directly at Nico. Eons passed before the man took off after the others.

David eased back against the wall and let out a breath. "That was close."

Summer moved back to sit on the coat. She pulled her knees up and wrapped her arms around her legs. He walked over and sat beside her, resuming his previous position.

"I'm scared, David," she whispered. "More scared than I've ever been in my life, I think."

David pulled her into his arms. His feelings for her were definitely all grown-up, but he knew he needed to tread carefully. He cradled her like a child. "I'm going to make this right, Summer. Or die trying."

She shuddered and buried her face against his neck. "I'm so mad at you, but I don't want you to die."

He swallowed at the feel of her warm breath brushing his throat. "I don't want to die either. I've got too much to live for." He paused. "Is that cliché?"

"No."

David looked down and nudged her face up so he could look into her eyes. Neither spoke. Words seemed unnecessary. Then he leaned down and covered her lips. Her sweet familiar taste sent longing shooting through him. Not just a physical desire, but a need to make things right with her. A desperation to see this through to the end and come out stronger. With Summer by his side. He let his lips linger, his arms tightened.

She groaned and pushed her way out of his arms, rolling to sit a foot away from him. "No. I can't do this. I can't love you anymore."

Her words pierced, sharper than any knife. "Summer, don't say anything. Wait until the danger is over, then we'll sit down and have a long talk."

"I can't," she whispered and stared at him, sorrow and grief etched on her face. "If I can't trust you, I can't love you."

David let the pain shatter through him, then shut it off. He stood, and before he could help her, Summer got to her feet, the words leaving a black hole between them.

He gathered her coat. "They're gone. It's time to move and get this over with."

Summer followed David from their temporary haven. She wrapped the coat tightly around her and couldn't help examining every nook and cranny her eyes landed on. Her heart ached with a sorrow that felt like a mortal wound. The flash of pain he hadn't been able to hide still stood out in detail in her memory. Waves of fatigue pulled at her as she pushed herself to keep up with David.

I want my life back, God. I hate this. I don't understand why you're doing this. I want you to make it all go away. Please make it go away. It's not fair and I'm just really, really tired.

Summer plodded on, nausea dogging her steps.

"You okay?"

"Peachy."

He stopped and turned. "You're pale. You sure you're all right?"

She dropped onto a rotting tree trunk. "I'm just whining."

He lifted a brow. "I haven't heard you complain about one thing."

"That's because I wasn't talking to you." She swallowed hard. "I need to sit for a minute. I feel really shaky."

He leaned over and cupped her chin. "If you can make it to the cabin, I'll be able to fix us a meal."

Her stomach growled in response. A smile curved his lips, but the pain of her words still lingered in his eyes. She sighed. "What cabin?"

"An old cabin my grandmother used to lease out during hunting season. It sits in the middle of twenty-two acres. It's got four deer stands, a lake with a canoe, and a pantry stocked with canned goods."

"Won't they know that's where we're going?"

He shook his head. "No one knows about this place."

"What about your parents? Your brother?"

"Well, they know about it. Technically. But they probably haven't thought about it in forever." He held a low-lying branch so she could scoot under. "And they don't know I own it."

"Why not?"

"Because it was put up for auction about six years ago after the man who bought it from my grandmother passed away. My parents didn't want anything to do with the place when my grandparents lived there. Sold it as soon as the ink was dry on the will."

She stopped and leaned against a tree to catch her breath. She studied him. "That made you mad, didn't it?"

He checked the trail behind them, checked his weapon. "Yeah." He shook his head and sighed. "It made me mad. My grandparents were there for me when I was growing up. It seemed . . . dishonorable . . . to just sell everything off. Like their lives didn't matter. Or like they just never existed."

"So you bought the place."

"Yep. It's my refuge."

She shoved away from the tree. "Then let's get going." Together, they made their way north. Sometimes they followed a trail. Sometimes they fought their way through the dense growth. Thirty minutes passed.

"Do you think we're safe?" she asked.

"For the moment."

"Until they figure out we didn't go that way?"

"Yeah. Something like that." He glanced at her. "You're looking a little better."

"I feel a little better."

He stopped and pointed. "There."

"What?"

"It's just about a mile that way."

"You knew exactly what you were doing, didn't you?" she asked.

"What do you mean?" He shot her a sidelong glance and took her hand to help her along.

"I mean, you brought us this far. You used Bennie as a taxi service to get us up here." She stumbled and he helped steady her. She rubbed a hand across her eyes. "At least all this exercise is keeping me warm."

"Yeah. I did. I knew where I could wreck the car and hopefully walk away from it."

"You took a big risk."

"It was even riskier to let Bennie stay in control."

"I'm still worried about Marlee."

He blew out a breath. "We'll check on her soon. She might be uncomfortable, but I'm willing to bet she's still alive. He won't kill her yet."

Summer prayed he was right.

But what if he wasn't?

They crested a hill and she looked down into a small valley nestled in the midst of the trees. Four small log cabins lay before her, divided by a rushing creek. Two cabins on one side, two on the other. "Which one is yours?"

"All of them."

"Why do you need four log cabins?"

He smiled. "After my grandfather died, my grandmother used to rent them out."

"To who?"

"Vacationers who wanted to escape civilization, hunters during hunting season." He shrugged. "She kept them booked year-round for the most part. The winter months were a little slow, but . . ." He shrugged.

"And now they're yours."

"Yep." He led her over to a tree. "Stay here for a minute."

"What are you going to do?"

"I just want to check the area."

Summer leaned against the tree and slid to the ground, pulling the coat tighter around her neck. When she quit moving, she cooled off fast. Shivering, she watched David skirt the trees and make his way down to the first cabin. He must have been satisfied with whatever it was he found, because he stepped out and waved her down.

Summer stood and took a deep breath. Thoughts swirled like a whirlpool. *Please God, just . . . please.*

She started down the hill to the cabin. The back of her head tingled as though she had a red-and-white bull's-eye stamped there with one of Raimondi's men looking through the scope.

She hurried to the door and stepped inside. Sparse, covered

furniture greeted her. Dust coated every surface. But at least they were out of the wind.

"Can you make a fire?" she asked.

"Not here. But the electricity's on and I have a couple of portable heaters we can use. Just don't turn on the lights. The windows are covered so we're good there." He walked down a small hall and came back with two small heaters. He plugged them in and said, "If you want to pull the covers off the furniture, I'll be right back."

He left and she peered through the small window over the couch. He crossed a small bridge over the creek to the other side. Curious, she continued to watch, wondering what he had planned when he entered the cabin directly across from her.

Ten minutes later, smoke curled from the chimney, and she frowned as she pulled the cover from the couch. Dust swirled and she coughed. Then sneezed. Expensive brown leather greeted her. Opposite that was a wooden rocker with a cushion.

David came back in and laid his gun on the small kitchen table. He walked over to the corner of the kitchen and knelt down. "There are some canned soups and things in the pantry by the refrigerator. The fridge is empty except for some water bottles, but that should do for a meal for now."

Summer, still feeling a bit shaky, examined the selection of soups. "Vegetable or chicken noodle?"

"I don't care. You don't even have to heat it if you don't want."

She wrinkled her nose at him. "Ew."

He ducked his head and she thought he might be trying to hide a smile. "There's a pot in that cabinet next to the sink."

She rummaged and found a pot. Next she scrounged up a hand-cranked can opener. Once she had the soup on the stove, she asked, "Why did you build a fire in the other cabin?"

He glanced at her. "Because if they track us down, I'm hoping they'll check that cabin first and we'll get advance warning that they're here."

"Oh. But what if they see the fire and come investigate?"

"In the dark, they won't see the smoke in this little valley. If they're close enough to see the smoke, they know we're here."

"Okay. How long do you think we have?"

"A couple of hours at the most. Maybe less." He grunted, then pulled at a piece of the flooring and it popped loose.

"So what are we going to do?"

He reached into the small hole in the floor and removed a metal box. He walked to the table and sat on one of the wooden kitchen chairs. "Think."

"About?"

"How to get out of this mess alive and keep Marlee alive in the process." He set the box on the table and opened it.

She sat across from him. "What's that?"

"My emergency stash." He reached in the box and pulled out two revolvers, a stack of cash, and a cell phone.

"That's why you wanted to come here."

"This and other reasons."

He stood and walked to the window. He pushed aside the dusty curtain to peek out. "So far so good."

"Are you going to call Chase or Adam?"

"Not yet."

She nodded to the phone he held. "What are you going to do with that?"

"Call for . . . more experienced . . . reinforcements."

37

David finished the calls and felt some of the tension ease from his shoulders. Now that he was the one calling the shots, his blood pressure eased even while his pulse quickened. Now was the time to end this. Now was the time to act. Making it to the trial had been his goal. Now, he just wanted them stopped. He'd given them almost two years of his life.

No more.

David readied the weapons and handed one to Summer. He had four guns. His Glock and the two from his stash. He also had the Smith & Wesson in his ankle holster he'd managed to retrieve from the wreck.

David knew he would be cutting it tight with the reinforcements on the way. He had no doubt Hayes was still out there hunting. And Raimondi was doing his best to dig up every last detail of David's life. He knew Raimondi finding out about this place was a long shot, but it wasn't impossible. If the man decided to search the public records, he'd find it. David hoped to be gone before that happened.

He wolfed down the equivalent of three cans of the soup. He finished chugging a bottle of water and looked up to find Summer watching him. "What is it?"

"Why me?" she asked.

He set aside the extra ammunition, buying time to develop an answer.

"Why me, David?" she asked again.

He sighed. "Summer, the moment I saw you, I knew there was something special about you. Not just your outward beauty, but an inner something that I've seen only on rare occasions and never had the opportunity to spend any time around. All my life I've only been around people who want to take. Or hurt. Or kill." He swallowed hard and met her gaze. "But when you looked up at me and laughed after spilling your purse everywhere in the bank, I was . . . captured." She didn't say anything. He said, "I wanted what you had."

Confusion creased her forehead. "What did I have?"

"I think—God."

She blinked. "God?"

"You have such a close relationship with him, you don't even realize how that comes through in just your everyday living."

A low laugh escaped her. He winced at the lack of humor. She said, "I don't know about that. I'm not really speaking to him much right now, although I suppose I should be."

He gave her a gentle smile. "Well, I am. And you're speaking to him or you wouldn't be listening to your praise and worship music every chance you get."

She nodded, acknowledging the truth of his words.

David said, "And while Ron was the one that led me to know who Christ is, you're the one who showed me what living for him day in and day out is all about."

Her mouth moved. She shut it. She couldn't seem to find the words needed to express whatever she was thinking, feeling. He waited.

She finally said, "Tell me about when you went to New York to get the laptop. And how does Ron fit into the picture? You said he saved your life and led you to Christ. How?"

"I gave the file with the video of the murder on it to the FBI. They were working with the local OCTF."

"The what?"

"Organized Crime Task Force."

"So that's when you went into the Witness Protection Program?"

"Yes. But I was also thinking."

"You're always thinking," she said softly.

"True." He couldn't deny it. His brain never shut off, not even to sleep. When he did manage to snag a few hours, when he woke, he was still chewing on a problem—or had a solution to one. "I was thinking about that laptop and the flash drive. And the more I thought about where I'd hidden it, the more I worried it wasn't secure enough."

"Where was it?"

"In a safe deposit box."

She blinked. "And that wasn't safe enough for you?"

He shrugged. "Stranger things have happened. I could see Raimondi staging a bank robbery or hacking into the computer system and discovering which box it was in or—" He grimaced. "I should have left it alone, but I went back." He gave her a soft smile. "And I wouldn't change the way everything played out for anything."

"Why?"

"Because it led me to Ron and to Christ, but hush, I'm telling this story my way. I'm getting to the good parts."

"And how is this information on the flash drive so important it was worth risking your life for? Risking our lives for now?"

"A lot of high-ranking government officials are in Raimondi's pocket. If that laptop comes to light, Raimondi is a dead man. He's committed murder for some of these people. And the proof is there. Pictures, dates, everything. All logged and documented. Sam had the flash drive hooked up that day I was copying the video. I saw a lot of that stuff that day."

"How did they know all that was on it?"

"Sam told them. He's using it for the same reason I am. He let them know that if he dies, the laptop will fall into the hands of the authorities."

"But how is that going to happen since you now have the laptop?"

He rubbed his eyes. "I suspect there's already a plan to have Sam killed."

"Oh."

"So you got the laptop and flash drive from New York and brought them here."

"In a roundabout way." He did another sweep of the windows and checked the guns again. "When I went back to New York after our honeymoon, I had one thing in mind. Get the laptop, hide it in a much better place, and get back to you without anyone being the wiser."

She grimaced. "Only it didn't quite work that way."

"No."

"Where does Ron fit in?"

"I made it to New York, got the laptop without any problem, and figured I was pretty good to go. I made it almost to Virginia when I came across this guy hitchhiking."

"So you picked him up?" She stared at him.

"I figured why not? Raimondi's men weren't looking for two guys, they were looking for one. I decided a hitchhiker would provide a nice little bit of cover."

She shook her head. "Did you use everyone you met?"

He winced and cleared his throat. "You have to understand, Summer, that's all I saw growing up. I thought that's what you did to be successful. I thought looking out for me was the smart thing to do, the only thing to do. So . . . yeah. Everyone who crossed my path was a 'potential.' I would size them up and ask myself, 'What can this person do for me?' or 'How can I use this person to further my own agenda?'"

"That's awful, David." She swallowed hard. "I'm having a hard time picturing you that way. I just know the man who sat with Mrs. Carlisle until the paramedics came and got her blood sugar stabilized. I see you helping the Smith kids build their tree house because their dad was serving overseas and they needed a male role model. I see you biting your tongue 99 percent of the time when Marlee is being selfish and demanding." She pulled in a deep breath. "I keep playing those scenes and more, over and over in my head, telling myself that you're not this other man." Tears welled in her eyes and his heart ached.

"I'm . . . both. Or I was." He knelt in front of her and gripped her hands. He'd effectively trapped her. Sitting in the chair, she had nowhere to go. Maybe she'd stay put and listen. "Summer, I've been forgiven. I've desperately tried—with God's help—to change my life." He leaned his forehead against hers. "Some days over the past year, for just a brief moment, I would forget everything else and just focus on the present, on us, our life. And I would thank God for it." He looked up. "It was dangerous to do that, but I wanted what we had to be real. To be true."

"I thought it was," she whispered.

"I know."

She pulled away and stood, forcing him to shuffle backwards on his knees. He rose and she smoothed her palms down her jean-clad thighs and stepped away from him, keeping her back to him. "What happened after you picked up Ron?" she asked.

David gave a snort and rubbed his eyes. "Summer, I was a gambler."

She swung around to look at him. "A what?"

"I gambled. A lot. And I lost. A lot." He held his hands up. "It was like therapy or something. When I was playing cards and betting large sums, I could forget the nightmares of war, what I saw in Afghanistan, what I had to do while I was there. I could forget each piece of evidence that I found that proved the FBI was right and my partner, my closest friend, was a crook." He shrugged. "I don't really know how to explain it. But gambling is just as addicting as any drug." The shock in her expression cut him, but he knew he had to keep going. "In the end, I owed a lot of money to a rather unscrupulous bookie. You see, I moved from cards to horses." He shot her a look. "I was a statistic. I had a lot of money, but it was tied up in my business. And I never wanted to do anything to hurt the business. I was a gambler, but I wasn't going to be stupid and hurt my livelihood. I did manage to keep from doing that."

"But?"

"Yeah, I thought I was so smart. I'd always been a winner. Borrowing from a loan shark was no big deal. I could pay it back from my next winnings. Only there weren't any winnings." He gave a rough laugh. "At least not enough to pay my debt. I was a fool." David paced, his story making him antsy. It was hard to revisit those days, but she deserved to know the truth. "You want to hear something crazy?"

"More crazy than what you're already telling me?"

She had a point. "Before I had Raimondi after me, I had a bookie who was ready to do some serious bodily damage to me."

"David," she whispered.

"I know. I know. But here's how it all ties together. The night I left New York with the laptop, the bookie's goons found me."

"How?"

"I still don't know. Dumb luck, chance, whatever." He paced a few more steps, then stopped. "I prefer to think of it as a divine appointment. God did it."

"God? God sent the bad guys after you?"

Her confusion made him grimace. "You'll understand in a minute. So, I'm driving down the highway and I pick up Ron. We make small talk for a while and then he pulls out his Bible and starts reading silently." He tapped his finger against the butt of his weapon. "I've never cared much for religion. It had never done anything for me, so why would I be interested in it? I let Ron know this in no uncertain terms."

Summer swallowed hard and stared. "But you went to church with me. You had all the right answers."

He sighed. "Yes, I knew all the right things to say to get you to fall in love with me. And I knew it would make you happy."

She flinched. "What about your grandmother? I remember you telling me about her one time. That she was a big influence in your life when it came to God."

"She was. Which is how I knew all the right things to say and do. But I ignored her for the most part. Until Ron started saying the same things she'd said. The same things I'd heard you say . . . and seen you live."

"Oh."

"About that time, I noticed a tail, but Ron had piqued my curiosity. I decided to keep an eye on the car behind me and keep Ron talking. But he noticed the tail too. He looked at me and asked what I'd done and wanted to know why we were being followed. For some reason, I spilled the story. We were followed for the next three hours. Ron talked the whole time, answering my questions. And then they ran us off the road and started shooting at us. Ron pulled out a gun and shot back. I was beat up and fading in and out of consciousness with a concussion. The next thing I remember is waking up in the hospital."

"That seems to happen to you on a regular basis."

He raised a brow and gave a chuckle. "I suppose twice in the span of a little over a year is a bit much, isn't it?"

"What happened to the computer?"

"That was my first thought when I opened my eyes and remembered what happened. Ron was sitting beside me. He handed me the laptop. He asked if he could pray with me, and I let him. Then he walked out of the hospital room. I left that night, sick with a concussion, but figured that was the least of my worries. I knew it wouldn't be long before either the bookie showed up or Raimondi's goons." He checked his watch, then the window. "All right, the sun's going down. I need you to keep watch."

"That's it?"

"What?"

"The story with Ron. That's it?"

"No." He shoved his weapon into the holster under his left arm. "There's more, but it'll have to wait."

"David—"

"Sorry, I'll finish it later. Right now, I have a job to do."

"What kind of job?"

"I'm going to set a trap."

38

Raimondi let the boa slither to the floor before he answered the phone. "You better have good news."

"We lost them."

Raimondi sighed.

His door opened and Georgina stepped into his office. Raimondi leaned back in surprise. She looked wonderful. He spoke into the phone. "Hold on a second." He looked at his daughter. "Are you going out?"

"I am."

"Do you need something?"

"I need to know the truth."

He lifted a brow.

"Are you looking for David for me or are you looking for him to kill him?"

Her blunt question left him speechless. He stared. Then found his tongue. "What kind of question is that?"

She walked toward him and placed both hands on the desk to lean in. "I know what you are. I know what this family does. I'm not an idiot." Her dark eyes blazed with a passion he hadn't seen in a long time. "Now obviously David has done something and you're tracking him, desperate to find him—and not for me to confront." She shrugged. "And I've gotten pretty good at eaves-dropping."

Raimondi felt an explosive rage building inside him. With effort he swallowed the first words that came to his tongue. He said, "That's not a good thing, Georgina."

"What? Are you going to kill me?" she taunted.

Raimondi stared at this girl he no longer knew. Her blatant disgust and disrespect caused his heart to pound and the blood to rush in his ears. "Surely it won't come to that."

The disgust and disrespect disappeared. She fell back against the chair behind her and slumped into it. "You're serious. You would actually kill me?"

Raimondi forced a small laugh. "Of course I'm not serious. You would never give me cause to do anything so drastic."

"Never give you—" She stared at him. "Stop looking for David. I don't want you to find him anymore."

"Stay out of things that aren't your business, Georgie." His child-hood nickname seemed to deflate her. "I love you. You're my flesh and blood. Everything I've worked for has been for you and this family. But you need to leave certain things alone. Am I clear?" He saw her swallow hard. And give a slow nod. He stood and picked up the boa that had made its way over to Georgina. She slid farther back in her chair and watched it with distaste.

He should have had a son. "Good. Now, where are you going?"

Georgina stood and walked toward the door. "I'm going shopping with a friend. I'll see you later."

The door shut behind her with a click.

Raimondi stared at it for a few more moments, wondering if she was going to be a problem. He'd have to deal with her later if she was. A trip to Europe might be in order. For now . . .

He picked up the phone. "You still there?" Hayes confirmed he was. "Where are you?"

When Hayes told him, Raimondi narrowed his eyes as he thought.

"Give me fifteen minutes and I might have something for you. In the meantime, we need some more insurance."

"We have the sister."

"We do. But Marlee and David have never gotten along. I don't know that he wouldn't sacrifice her to keep his secret."

"How did you know about the friction between David and his sister-in-law anyway?"

"I have sources everywhere. You should know that by now." Mike had kept in touch with Bennie, his boss, on a regular basis. Bennie had passed on bits of information that he thought Raimondi would find useful and people he thought could be used. Only it looked like Marlee had quickly outlived her usefulness. "I'm thinking of something a little more compelling."

"What's that? The mother and brother are out of town somewhere. They're not due back until next week, and frankly, we don't have the time to track them down."

"No. There's someone Summer cares about even more than her family, I think."

"Who?"

"Olivia Todd and her two little girls. Summer and David risked their lives to be in court and keep those children from their father. That tells me a lot."

"You want them?"

"I want them."

"Then you'll have them. I'll start making calls while the others keep searching for Hackett."

Summer snapped her mouth shut as David walked out into the darkness. She shivered and helped herself to another bowl of the canned vegetable soup, wishing she'd thought to ask David to grab her purse from the wreck when he'd gotten her coat. There wasn't anything in it that she particularly cared about except her iPod. She hadn't had any cash on her and she could cancel the credit cards. Even the pictures could be replaced.

She finished off the soup with a sigh. Not gourmet by any stretch of the imagination, but filling. Her nausea eased with the food and she felt much better, less shaky. She threw the paper bowl and plastic spoon in the trash and paced to the window.

Moving the curtain to the side, she peered out. Darkness hid David and covered his mission.

She kept the lights off. The sliver of the moon would have helped to light the small cabin if she'd felt comfortable opening the dusty curtain a little more. Her eyes adjusted and she finally caught sight of a shadow moving several feet to her left.

She stepped outside onto the porch and shut the door behind her. "David," she whispered.

"Over here," he called.

She moved toward him, guided by the dim light of the moon. He dug another scoop of dirt and tossed it on the growing pile behind him. At her approach, he stopped and leaned on the shovel for a short rest. Then his movements resumed and she watched him.

She swallowed hard. The initial flutters of attraction when they'd first met no longer attacked her midsection when she looked at him. And while she thought him the best-looking guy ever, the warm fuzzies had faded to leave a deep love and a respect she had thought was mutual.

Being betrayed by the one person she'd trusted implicitly had done some huge damage to her heart. Damage that might be beyond repair.

How had she come to this place? What was she going to do when this was all over? Was divorcing this man the right thing? The thought of it made her shudder. She'd married him for life. 'Til death do us part. But was she going to honor those vows she made when she'd been deceived? How did God feel about that? Would he still hold her responsible for them? Did she even care?

Yes. She did. She sighed. As mad as she wanted to be with God about the situation, she knew she needed to trust him, to continue to pray that he would keep them safe. And Marlee. Her heart thudded an extra beat. *Please keep Marlee safe, Lord.* Then she felt guilty for asking God for anything when she blamed him for letting everything happen.

But *not* praying for Marlee wasn't an option. She tried not to imagine her sister in the hands of men who didn't have any problem cutting off body parts or killing. Worry pounded inside her. But first, they had to do this, and she had to trust God would take care of Marlee. She *had* to. "Did you get it?"

"Not yet." He paused, glanced at his watch, and looked out into the distance.

"What are you looking for?"

"Reinforcements." He frowned. "You need to get back inside, okay?"

Summer sighed. "Look—"

A gunshot shattered the window behind her. Then the next window popped.

Summer gasped. David grabbed her arm and propelled her to the ground even as he reached for his weapon. He rolled close and whispered, "Don't move." And then he tensed.

She twisted beneath him to see Corbin Hayes standing above them, gun pressed to David's ear, black eyes glittering. "Well, well, Mr. Hackett. We finally meet again."

39

David froze. Summer did likewise.

"Get up," Hayes ordered. David helped Summer roll to her feet.

David stood, keeping Summer behind him. He could feel her trembling. His eyes scanned the area and his nerves twitched. "What now?" He kept his hands where Hayes could see them.

"Now, we get what I came for." He gestured to the ground. "Don't let me stop you from finishing what you started."

"How did you know we were here?"

"Raimondi usually finds out what he wants to know. You haven't figured that out yet?"

"But no one knew about this place." David never would have brought Summer here if he'd thought someone could connect him to it.

Hayes laughed. "Sam's always been a bit of a snoop—one of the reasons he's in such trouble. However, it seems he remembers seeing some papers in your office one afternoon. He said he thought it was interesting you were buying such an out-of-the-way place, because he never figured you for a mountain man."

David clenched his fist, desperate to plant it on Hayes's nose. He resisted and stepped back, keeping Summer with him. Hayes was joined by two more men dressed in black. Again Hayes motioned for David to continue digging. David picked up the shovel. Hayes lifted the gun higher. "Try anything stupid with that shovel and I'll shoot her."

David glanced again at the area across the creek. He could smell the smoke from the fire he'd started in the other cabin. The night air chilled his face and dried the sweat that had popped out onto his forehead as he'd dug the hole. He settled the shovel back into the ground and lifted a mound of dirt that he added to the growing pile. Summer stayed near him. One of Hayes's goons kept his weapon on her while he held a flashlight with his other hand. But David knew one wrong move and Summer was dead. His stomach clenched and he kept digging, the flashlight's beam making it easier to see.

Finally, he heard a loud clank.

Hayes drew in a satisfied breath. "Well, looks like we've hit pay dirt."

David didn't respond. He simply continued to remove the dirt. Finally, he said, "I'll need some help with this. The laptop's not the only thing in there and it's heavy."

Hayes studied him for a moment, then motioned one of his men forward.

David said, "You grab that end, I'll get this one." He looked at Summer. "Stay out of the way, will you?"

She crossed her arms and narrowed her eyes. However, she took several steps back. David reached in and wrapped his fingers around the handle. The other man did the same. Together they pulled the waterproof trunk from the ground.

Hayes grunted. "What do you have in there?"

"Nothing for you to be concerned about. The laptop is all you need."

Hayes shot him an annoyed look, and David set the trunk at Hayes's feet. "Just so you know, while the laptop is in there, you won't be able to access it without me."

225

Hayes smirked. "We have our guys for that kind of thing."

David kept his face expressionless. "And I know that. Which is why I programmed the security the way I did."

The smirk slid off Hayes's face. David figured he was remembering exactly what David did with the Rangers. And the fact that David would have the skills to make a computer practically hack proof.

"Move," Hayes snarled.

David slipped his gloved fingers around Summer's and gave her a tug. She glanced at him, her silent questions surfacing through her fear. He winked at her. She lifted a brow.

He took another subtle step back. Summer moved with him.

But Raimondi's men were well trained. The one to their left simply lifted his weapon. David stood still. Summer did the same.

"Diego, keep an eye on them. Don't kill them yet."

Diego's weapon stayed steady as Hayes leaned over the trunk. David leaned against the tree and gave a slight tug on Summer's hand. She shot him a questioning frown, but moved closer. He tucked her up under his shoulder and she stiffened, then leaned into him.

Hayes pulled at the lock, then turned to shoot David an impatient look. "The combination?"

David told him. Hayes spun the lock.

David tensed and whispered in her ear, "Get ready."

She glanced up at him again, but thankfully didn't say anything, just nodded.

Hayes and the unnamed assailant opened the trunk and leaned in to look. "What is this? Just a bunch of—"

David pulled Summer behind the large tree. Diego moved as the explosion rocked the air.

40

Summer swallowed the scream as the left side of her face mashed into the trunk of the tree. David covered her with his body for a brief moment, then he was gone. She whirled, ignoring the pain in her cheek.

Hayes and the other man who'd been helping him, lay on the ground, unconscious or dead, she wasn't sure which. David had his arms wrapped around Diego, wrestling the gun from him. Diego put up a good fight, but he was no match for her husband, who had him on the ground, weapon ripped from his grasp. Three good punches left the man unconscious.

Movement to her left caught her attention. Four black-clad figures came from behind the last cabin. Terror shot through her. David had managed to take out three of Raimondi's hired killers, but how would he be able to overpower these guys? "David?"

He looked up, saw the men coming.

And grinned.

Summer released the breath she'd been holding. She asked, "Your reinforcements?"

David wiped the grin from his face and the sweat from his upper lip. "Yeah." He waited until the men stepped into the middle of the calm, then snorted. "Papa Bear. Nice timing. Late as usual, but at least you showed up for the party."

The tallest man, dressed in dark cargo pants and a black sweat-shirt grinned through the black paint on his face. "Fashionably late is still in." David rolled his eyes and Papa Bear asked, "What was the hurry? Looks like you have it all under control. What do you need us for?"

David stood. "You can help me get these guys in the cabin and make sure they're tied tighter than your grandma's Thanksgiving turkey. I've got rope and duct tape. We'll use them both."

"So we're here for cleanup?"

"For now."

Papa Bear shrugged. "That works. Come on, guys."

The men moved, easily getting the three assailants into the cabin. Summer stared. "Who are they?"

"My old unit. Fortunately, they weren't deployed somewhere and were able to make us their 'official' business for the next few hours." He gave her a grim smile. "Now just pray they don't get called up to leave anytime soon." David shoved his weapon back into his holster and headed for the cabin. "I'll introduce you, then we'll go get Marlee."

"You said you knew where she is."

"Yes."

"How?"

He stepped into the cabin, then looked back. "I recognized the place in the video. Raimondi's got her at his house."

Summer followed him inside to find Hayes groggy, but awake. The left side of his face was charred and bleeding. He had to be in horrible pain, yet he stayed quiet. Still. Just watching.

Even in his injured state, he glared at them with a hate that made her shudder. Summer read the expression in his eyes with no trouble. If he got loose, they were dead, no matter what Raimondi's orders were.

The one who'd been helping Hayes with the trunk still had his eyes closed. Blood trickled from his nose and his left ear. Diego also lay unconscious. Hayes finally shut his eyes and leaned his head back with a hard swallow.

"He needs medical attention," she said. "He probably has a concussion."

David lifted a brow. "You want to take him to the hospital?"

She flushed. "I know it sounds ridiculous when he was trying to kill us, but," she bit her lip, "I don't want him to die. I want him to stand trial and go to jail."

David shook his head. "He'd be a lot less trouble if he were dead."

She looked at the man. "True, but . . ."

"Yeah." He looked at the other men who were now waiting for him to tell them what he wanted. "Guys, meet Summer." They nodded to her. David pointed to each one. "This is Brown Bagger or Doc B for short. He's our medic." To Doc B, he said, "Why don't you take a look at Hayes and see if he's going to die anytime soon or if he can wait a little for medical attention."

Doc B knelt by Hayes. Summer felt slightly better. David pointed to the next man. He wasn't as tall as the others, probably only around five feet eleven, but he was wiry with sharp green eyes. "This is Papa Bear, our combat engineer."

Summer shot him a smile and he nodded.

David motioned to the next man, who stood head and shoulders above the rest. Summer put him at around six feet five inches. "This is Little Lou, our weapons specialist." She noticed how he included himself in the unit. She wondered why he'd left. "And this is Blue, the communications specialist."

"Nice to meet you, ma'am," Blue said. "David left some big shoes to fill."

So, this was the man who'd taken David's place on the team.

"Let's take a minute to come up with a plan to get Marlee away from Raimondi without any of us ending up dead," David said.

Summer sat on the couch while the men huddled around, drew

on sheets of paper David produced from somewhere, and worked on a plan.

"What's my job?" she asked.

They went silent and turned to stare at her. Then looked at David.

He pursed his lips, then opened his mouth.

"And before you say 'nothing,'" Summer said, "I'm telling you now, I'm not sitting here doing nothing. I'll be safer going on a raid with you guys than sitting somewhere waiting for Raimondi to dig into his apparent never-ending supply of assassins to track me down and kill me." She crossed her arms. "No thank you. I'm going." She paused. "And besides, I'm probably the only one who can keep Marlee from wigging out. She doesn't even like David and might not cooperate with him." She eyed her husband. "You want to deal with her?"

He shuddered. His lips firmed. "I could deal with her, but neither of you would like it very much, I'm sure." He handed her one of the guns from the box he'd pulled from the kitchen floor. "Stay with me and do exactly what I tell you, understand?"

"Yes." Relief filled her. She was probably insane for insisting she be allowed to go, but Marlee was her sister. She'd protected the girl all her life. She wasn't about to stop now.

A thought hit her. She asked David, "Did you just blow up the laptop?"

He laughed, a low chuckle that meant he was very pleased with himself. "Of course not."

"Then where is it?"

"I have it. I've had it all along."

Summer whirled to find Ron standing in the doorway.

41

"You made good time," David said.

"You sounded like you needed me to."

Papa Bear smirked, as did the others, who made a few wisecracks. David almost smiled. All the ribbing meant they still considered him a part of the team. No hard feelings. He hadn't thought there would be, but still, it was good to know for sure. The fact that they showed up said a lot more than the ribbing. He introduced Ron, then got right to business. "All right. The cops should be here in a few minutes. They'll take care of these guys. FBI is coming too. The two agencies are in touch so we can go get Marlee."

"And Raimondi," Ron said.

"And Raimondi," David agreed. He hesitated. "Just one thing."

They looked at him. "Raimondi has a daughter. Georgina. She's . . . innocent of anything Raimondi's guilty of."

"And you know this how?" Summer asked.

David wanted to squirm. Georgina was the last part of his story that needed telling. "I spent a lot of time with her while trying to get evidence against Raimondi."

"I see."

He wondered if she did.

David nodded to the door. "These three aren't going anywhere and Marlee's waiting."

Summer stepped outside. David and the other men followed. She looked at David. "Transportation?"

"I've got a van about a mile up the road," Ron said. "No sense in us trying to fly since we're keeping everything under the radar. Word is going to get back to Raimondi that his men failed to take care of you and Summer. He's not going to be happy and he's going to have others looking for you."

David's jaw tightened. He made an effort to relax it. "It'll take a bit for word to get back to him. Then it will take a couple of hours to get his men in the air, headed this way." He narrowed his eyes. "Hopefully we'll arrive on his doorstep before he realizes we've left town."

Summer said, "What about Hayes? He was awake some while we were all in the cabin. Won't he come to the conclusion that we're headed for New York?"

Ron said, "I've got him taken care of. None of the three of them will be allowed near a phone for the next twenty-four hours. Now, let's move."

"We've got our SUV parked out of sight. Give me the address and we'll recon there," Papa Bear said.

David gave him the address.

Little Lou motioned to David and Summer. "I'll go with them in case there's trouble."

Summer, David, and Little Lou followed Ron to his van. While they hiked, David helped Summer, squeezing her fingers. "It's almost over."

"I guess we'll find out."

"Raimondi's gone over the deep end this time. He's made a mistake that he won't be able to recover from. There's a video out there with Marlee begging for her life in his office. It won't take much to find it. No jury in the country wouldn't find him guilty of at least a kidnapping charge. And with everything on that laptop to add to it, he's going away for a long, long time."

After the mile trek to the van, Summer was visibly worn. She was tired. He was too. "You okay?"

She lifted her chin. "I'll be fine."

They climbed into the van with Ron taking the wheel and Little Lou taking the front passenger seat. Ron said, "You two might as well get some sleep, it's going to be a long twelve-hour drive to New York."

David leaned the seat back, but Summer turned to him. "Finish telling me about you and Ron."

"You should rest, Summer."

"I can't rest right now. I've got adrenaline rushing through me. Help me wind down. Tell me more."

He caught Ron's glance in the rearview mirror. Ron gave a small nod.

David clicked his seat belt into place. "After Ron left, I lay there trying to get up the strength to walk out of the hospital. I laid there too long. Imagine my surprise when my bookie walked in."

"The one who wanted to hurt you?"

He clicked his tongue. "I only had one bookie, Summer. And yes, he was the one who wanted to hurt me."

"How did he find you?"

"It was a logical conclusion. I'd been hurt, not seriously, but bad enough that a visit to the hospital for some stitches was in order. Ron said he couldn't get the bleeding stopped so he took me in. By the time the ambulance got there, Ron had already covered the incident with the cops. Chalked it up to a simple attempted carjacking or mistaken identity."

"So, your bookie found you."

"When he walked in, I figured I was dead. Or he was going to add substantially to my current wounds." He cleared his throat. "And all I could think of was how mad you were going to be when Mike came to tell you the truth."

"Mad doesn't begin to cover it." She shot him a dark look.

He winced. "I know." When she didn't look away from him, he said, "My bookie's name was Henry. Henry came in and sat down

233

in the chair beside my bed. He handed me an envelope and said, 'You're one lucky man, Hackett.' Then got up and walked out."

"What was in the envelope?"

"A note from Ron."

She waited.

"It said, 'God just did something for you. Now go do something for God.'" The emotion of that day came back like it always did when he thought of what Ron did for him. What God did for him by sending Ron into his life. "Ron had paid off my quarter-of-a-million-dollar debt to Henry." Summer gasped and David let out a low laugh. "That was my reaction too. I thought for sure it was some sick joke, but Henry hadn't broken any bones and I wasn't on life support. He'd just left. That made me a believer—in more ways than one. I called Ron and he prayed over the phone with me. I couldn't wait to get home and start studying the Bible, start figuring out how God was going to fit into my life from that point on."

"Only God doesn't 'fit' into your life," Ron said. "He's not there for your convenience, to 'rescue' you when you get in trouble. It's a relationship thing."

"Right," David agreed. "But it took me awhile to get that." He drew in a deep breath. "However, watching Summer, I was finally able to understand it. Sort of."

"I noticed you seemed to ask more questions about God," Summer murmured. "And I didn't have to drag you to church anymore."

"The whole point of this conversation is to make you understand that it took something huge for God to get my attention." He leaned back. "Ron set me straight on a few things and one of those things was being honest with you. I knew deceiving you was wrong." His fingers curled into fists on his thighs. "But at that point, I couldn't tell you the truth either."

Summer stared at him a few more seconds before closing her eyes. "I'm tired. I think I'll try to sleep now."

David reached over and clasped her fingers in his. Hope sputtered and sparked when she didn't pull away.

42

Raimondi's phone rang once. Twice. He snatched it on the third ring. "What is it?"

"Hayes and the others are in custody."

Raimondi went still as fury ignited in his gut. "How?"

"Hackett had help. A regular army. Hayes and his men were simply outnumbered and overpowered."

"How do you know this?"

"You'd be surprised who I have at my beck and call around this country."

"So we still don't have the laptop."

"Affirmative. And my picture is still on there."

Raimondi closed his eyes and bit back curses. Could nothing be simple anymore? "I thought you had inside help there."

"I do. Right now, he's not able to provide me with any information." A pause. "Will Hayes talk?"

"No."

"What about the two he's with?"

"They don't know details." Raimondi stared at the red boa, encased snuggly behind the glass cage. His fingers twitched with the desire to stroke it. "But I'll figure out how to make sure they don't talk. I'll take care of it."

"Good, because I need that laptop found. Now."

"Your neck's not the only one on the chopping block," Raimondi muttered. "I'll call you back shortly."

Click.

Summer jerked awake and wondered what had awakened her.

The pressing need to go to the bathroom. She shifted on the seat and worked the crick out of her neck. She looked over to see David asleep. Or rather his eyes were shut.

They opened and she blinked. Could he feel her watching him?

"I need a rest stop," she said.

He glanced at his watch. "Can you wait fifteen minutes?"

"Yes."

He handed her a fast-food bag and a mostly melted chocolate shake. "You slept through the food run."

"Sorry."

"Don't be."

She opened the bag and pulled out a double cheeseburger. A weakness she didn't allow herself to indulge in very often. Tonight, she indulged. She took a bite and savored the explosion of juice and flavor on her tongue. "How long did I sleep?"

"About ten hours."

She stared at him. "What?"

"We're almost there."

"I can't believe I slept that long."

"You were tired."

"Must have been."

When the conversation became stilted, she took another bite of the cheeseburger. Her taste buds were the first to wake up, followed by the rest of her body. Slowly, her strength returned. She felt better at this moment than she had in days. How odd. Maybe she should eat cheeseburgers more often.

She finished it off, then the shake and even the cold fries David silently handed her with a slight smile on his face. She never ate like this. Embarrassed, she shrugged. "If I'm going to have a last meal, I might as well enjoy it."

Thunderclouds chased away his smile. "No negative talk—or thinking. We're going to be just fine."

Shame engulfed her. "I'm sorry. That was uncalled for."

"Aw, don't feel bad about that," Little Lou said. "You just sound like one of the unit now."

David frowned at Little Lou, then gave a shrug. "You're right, but I don't like it coming from her."

"You need to chill out, man."

Summer allowed herself a small smile. David returned it.

Ron pulled the van to a stop at a gas station. Summer took in her surroundings. The sun was up, shining bright in the sky. A promise for a good day. She could only pray.

"Here." David handed her a small bag.

She looked inside and found some toiletries, including a toothbrush and toothpaste. Again, he'd gone out of his way to ensure her comfort. A lump swelled in her throat and conflicting feelings gathered in the pit of her belly. She ignored them. "Thanks."

Summer quickly took care of business while David and the man he'd called Little Lou hovered outside the door. Ron filled the tank. When she was done, she opened the door and they all swept back to the van.

David said, "Next stop is Raimondi's. The others are already there."

She lifted a brow. "How'd they get there so fast?"

"Papa Bear is known for his lead foot. But it's a good thing. They're in the process of casing the place and will find the easiest route inside." He looked at Little Lou. "Raimondi's mine."

Summer shivered at the ice in his voice. She sat in silence the rest of the trip while David seemed to withdraw into himself more so than she'd ever seen him do, during the short year they'd been together. In their twelve months of marriage, he had often been moody and silent. She had just attributed it to his personality. And she was probably right, but the intensity radiating off of him now made her shudder. And feel almost . . . safe.

She turned her attention from David and stared out of the window. High-rises greeted her. Traffic jammed around them and they crept down the street. She finally looked at him and asked, "Where does he live?"

David snapped his gaze to her. "About three streets over."

Little Lou passed back a handful of technology. David shoved something into his ear, then clipped another item to his belt. Yet another piece, a thin wire, looped around his neck and under his shirt. "Almost ready. Papa Bear, you hear me?" He nodded so she supposed he got the response he wanted. At her questioning look, he said, "We're all wired for sound so we can talk to one another and listen to what's going on."

Ron pulled the van into a parking spot. "I'm not parking in the parking garage. Too easy to get trapped."

David nodded. "Papa Bear parked in the garage."

"Easier for him to get out. This van doesn't maneuver like his Navigator."

"They're working on the security cameras as we speak."

"Which apartment is his?" Summer asked. She looked up at the tall building and felt her heart start to pound. The man who wanted her dead lived there. It was hard to imagine.

"The penthouse. Five thousand square feet of the upper floor."

Ron pulled a weapon from the bag in his lap, checked it, then slid it into a shoulder holster. David opened the door and stepped outside. He looked at Summer and handed her a cell phone.

Chase and Adam stepped out of the café down the street and headed toward them.

Summer swung her gaze back to David. "You called them?"

"I texted Chase. We're going to need some more help."

"You trust them?"

"Bennie was the snitch, not them."

Adam reached the van first and glared at David. "I should arrest you."

"For what?"

"I'm not sure yet, but there's gotta be something I can charge you with."

"How about disturbing my sleep?" Chase muttered.

David gave a small smile. "I need at least one of you guys to stay with Summer."

"So you're insisting on going into the line of fire?" Adam asked.

"I have a feeling it's the only way this is going to be resolved." His gaze drilled into Chase. "I'm going."

"If you were anyone else, I'd knock you out and drag you to a safe house," Chase said.

David cocked his head. "Try it."

"I said if you were anyone else. You're not. Which is why I'm going with you. You're still under our protection. Well, I suppose we'd be excused if we let you go in there and get yourself killed, but I'd prefer not to see that happen."

David nodded. "Appreciate that. Now, who's going to stay with Summer?"

They exchanged glances. Adam shrugged. "I'll do it."

"What about Marlee?" Summer demanded.

"We'll see how she reacts," David said. "Stay close to the phone. If I can't keep her calm, I'll call."

Summer didn't like it but knew she had no choice. She could take care of herself pretty well in a one-on-one situation, but she wasn't trained to go in there and confront people who killed for a living, then went home, had dinner with their families, and tucked their children into bed.

Which made her worry. She grabbed David's hand and pulled him around to face her. "Kyle . . . David . . . I—"

He placed a finger over her lips. "Shh. It's going to be all right."

"There's no guarantee. I can't let you go in there without . . ." She bit her lip. "Just . . . please be careful."

Her husband leaned over and kissed her like his life depended on it. As mad and hurt as she was at his deception, she realized that beneath it all, he really did love her—and she'd never stopped loving him. And he was trying to do the right thing. Now. She wrapped her arms around his neck and returned his kiss with a passion that left them both surprised and breathless.

And their audience a bit embarrassed.

She laughed. She couldn't help it. With a glance at Chase and Adam, she ducked her head and murmured, "Sorry."

"No apologies necessary," Chase assured her. "I'm so stinking jealous, it's not funny, but don't apologize."

And then they were gone.

Summer climbed back into the van and wrapped a blanket around herself. Adam followed and settled in the seat beside her and locked the door.

She closed her eyes and began to pray.

43

"Jealous?" David asked.

Chase went red. "Not of you and Summer specifically, just the fact that you have someone you love and who loves you."

Surprised at the admission, David glanced at the man just before he grasped the door handle. "Well, things aren't perfect and they're never going to be the same, but I sure hope and pray Summer's willing to work with me on keeping our marriage together."

"Yeah."

"So, you're ready to find someone, settle down, and have a few kids?"

"Maybe. Yeah, I think I am." At David's raised brow. Chase shrugged. "Some days I have to admit the job's getting old." He paused. "And so am I."

David snorted. "You're what . . . thirty-four? You're not any older than I am."

Chase gave him a wicked grin. "Like I said. Getting old."

David rolled his eyes. He looked up the street and back down. The sidewalk teemed with people on their way to work. Everyone with a place to be and people to see.

On the drive to New York, David had been in constant contact with the governor of South Carolina. She'd made a quick call to some military higher-ups, then granted him and his unit law enforcement powers. She'd agreed to see if she could get the co-operation of the New York governor to allow them clearance for the operation. He wanted his team on it but didn't need the local cops getting in the way or asking questions. It had taken some finagling, but she'd managed to convince the governor to let them come in and do the assignment. "I owe him now, David," she'd warned him. "Don't mess this up or my head is on the chopping block and Operation Refuge is toast."

"If I mess this up, ma'am, I'll be dead."

"Well, yes. Let's not see that happen, okay?"

"I'm good with that."

"You have four hours."

Four hours? "Starting when?"

"Now."

That had been an hour ago. Local law enforcement had already cleared as much of the building as possible, going door-to door and telling residents there was a gas leak. They were under strict orders to go no higher than the twenty-first floor.

The gas truck pulled up as they entered the building. They'd be safe in the basement where David had reported the leakage. It had an outside entrance with no access to the main building except through a door that Papa Bear had already secured. By the time the gas people got that far, hopefully Raimondi and his goons would be wrapped up prettier than a Christmas present.

He hoped. Prayed.

Besides, Ron would keep them occupied, releasing them only when the mission was a success and David gave the all clear.

Papa Bear's voice came right into his ear. "Cameras are down. We've cleared the five floors directly under Raimondi's and NYPD is working on the rest."

"Of course Raimondi's on the top floor," Chase grunted and pushed his earpiece tighter into his canal. Having everyone wired and in contact with each other was priority.

"Naturally. Where else would a Mafia don live?" David asked.

"Wish he lived anywhere but an apartment building. Figured he would live on some big estate with lots of fence and a few guard dogs."

"He's got one of those too. The big estate in the country, I mean."

"Then how do we know he's here?"

David eyed Chase. "Trust me. He's here."

Chase shook his head. "He's already got one hostage, we don't need to give him the opportunity to terrorize someone else." He paused. "I'm really questioning whether or not we need to fill the NYPD in on the rest of the story. They know the gas leak is bogus. We might need them for backup," Chase said.

"I've got the Chief of Police on speed dial thanks to the governor. He knows the whole story. He's dispatching various teams to be on standby. They'll be there if we need them. Right now, the less people involved the better. We've got the training and we know who we're after. Coordinating with everyone would take time we just don't have."

"Your friends could still get in a lot of trouble for this."

"They know the risks." He knew he sounded cold. He didn't mean it that way, it just was what it was. He figured Chase would get that too, since he was risking his neck going into the situation with him. "This is above and beyond the call of duty for you too."

"I've got well over a year invested in this case. I'm seeing it through to the end."

"All right, then, let's go." They made their way to the elevator.

Through his earpiece, he heard Doc B say, "One elevator is working. As soon as you're at the top, give me the signal and Blue will jam that one too."

"So the only way down will be the stairs," he told Chase.

"Wonderful. Guess I didn't need to go for my early morning jog today."

"You'll be fine. It's only twenty-six floors." He checked his weapon once more. "At least we'll be coming down, not going up."

Chase gave a long-suffering sigh. David knew he didn't care, he was just letting off tension. "So how are we going to get in?"

David held up a key. "I'm hoping this still works."

Raimondi stared down at Marlee. "You have failed me too."

She sat on a wooden chair, arms bound behind her. Tears leaked down her bruised cheeks. "I did what you wanted. I let your guys beat me up and put me in the hospital. I wouldn't leave with the marshals, I made her and David come get me at the hospital to give you the chance to get them. I did everything! Everything!"

"Yes. You did. However, you failed to put Hackett and your sister into my hands. Therefore our deal is off."

She jerked against the ropes and glared through her fear. "It's not my fault you can't hire competent help."

With the speed of a mad snake, he struck, adding one more bruise to her face. She cried out. "Stop! Hayes said you just wanted David. He said you would get him away from her. He said he would be out of her life if I helped. Well, I did!"

"And you have one more chance to help me."

She stared at him, lips quivering, lower one bleeding. "What?"

"I'll let you know when I'm ready."

He shut her door and opened the one next to it.

The woman with her two children cowered together on the bed next to the wall. They'd arrived about an hour earlier. The children said nothing. They didn't speak or even cry, just huddled against their mother. For some reason, the older girl's eyes made him uneasy. "What are you staring at?"

She didn't answer and he walked over to her. Lifted his fist. She simply watched him. No cringing. No fear. The little one whimpered.

The mother said, "Leave them alone, please."

He ignored her and focused on the one who watched him with

no emotion or expression. "I asked you a question. What are you staring at?"

"Nothing," she whispered and dropped her head back against the wall with a thud and closed her eyes. "Absolutely nothing."

Raimondi waited a few seconds to see if she would look at him again. She didn't. And yet he still had the strangest feeling about her. Like he'd better not turn his back on her.

He couldn't remember the last time someone made him feel like that.

A few enemies, but certainly not a child.

Shrugging off the weird sensation, he grabbed the woman's purse and she shrieked. "No, please. I need that."

He eyed her suspiciously. "What's in it?"

"Sandy's inhaler. She's already used it twice. Take the purse, but please, leave her medicine."

Raimondi rummaged through it. His phone interrupted him, and he tossed the purse back to her as he pulled the device from his pocket. He left the room, walked down the hall, and shut the door at the end. He twisted the key and pressed the button to move the bookcase in front of the door. He smiled. He loved his home. So many hidden secrets behind his doors. The phone was insistent. He sighed and looked at the number.

Rosalinda. He ignored her.

He entered his office. The boa waited patiently, his head bobbing against the side of the tank. Raimondi reached in and lifted the reptile. The snake slithered through his fingers and Raimondi felt a rush at the thought of how easy it would be to crush the life right out of the boa. But he would never do that. The snakes were his friends. They brought him pleasure. In their presence he found a peace that seemed so elusive everywhere else in his life.

He dropped into his chair and looked at his monitor.

Blank.

He frowned. That was odd. He wiggled the mouse. Still blank.

He gave a disgusted sigh and pushed the mouse away. He picked up the phone and dialed security. "Trent, what's wrong with the cameras?"

"Just a slight malfunction, sir. We'll have them up and running in about five minutes."

Raimondi hung up. His brain whirled as he absently stroked the snake he'd yet to name.

A sound distracted him and he looked up from his boa to find Agostino in his office doorway, simply staring at him. "Something I can help you with?"

The snake wrapped itself around his wrist and turned its attention to the newcomer, weaving and bobbing, curious.

Agostino stepped farther inside, hands shoved into his back pockets. "I've been talking to Georgina, she seems to be doing better."

"Yes, I think she does. Maybe she has finally put that traitor behind her." He waved a hand. "But I don't want to talk about her. What have you got for me on Hackett?"

"We don't know where he is."

Raimondi wasn't surprised. Agostino moved forward and took a seat on the love seat to the right of Raimondi's desk.

Raimondi stroked the boa. "I just received word that Hayes and his two associates have been arrested by the FBI. They're under arrest for attempted murder and an assortment of charges."

Agostino closed his eyes and sighed, then tilted his head back to look at the ceiling. "Should we just drop this?"

Raimondi stared at his nephew. "Do you understand what is at stake?"

Agostino opened his eyes and leaned forward. "Yes. Of course. I'm sorry. It's just . . ."

"What is it?"

"Do you ever get tired of it all?"

"Tired? Of it all?" Raimondi stood, impatience making him rise fast. The chair slammed back into his bookcase. He walked to the tank on the far wall and placed the boa inside. "Agostino, we do what we do because this is our life."

"Yes. I know. Isn't it possible to have a different life?"

Raimondi felt his face grow red. He snorted. "Who has been filling your head with this nonsense?"

His nephew shook his head. "No one. Of course you're right. This is the life I was born to. Forget I said anything." He stood. "I'm going to tell Georgina goodbye and then head out to see if I can find anything else on Hackett."

"I need you to go to North Carolina and take care of Hayes and those two losers he was using."

"What do you want me to do?"

"I want you to take them to Disney World," he snapped. "What do you think I want you to do? Get rid of them. They're no longer of any use to me."

Agostino's eyes went wide. "Hayes too?"

Raimondi's jaw tightened to the point he thought it might snap. He pulled in a deep breath through his nose and forced himself to relax. "Yes. Especially him. He has utterly failed me this time."

Agostino rose, his eyes on his uncle. "He's been with the family for years, Uncle."

"Do you have a problem with what I'm asking you to do?"

Agostino hesitated. "No. I will take care of it."

Raimondi said, "Before you do, get rid of that woman."

"Marlee, the sister?"

"Yes."

A frown pulled his brows together. "I thought you still needed her."

"Not anymore. Kill her and make sure her body is never found. She has annoyed me to no end. I don't want to even breathe the same air as she does."

Agostino shoved his hands into his coat pockets and nodded. "Fine."

"Good." His phone rang as his nephew left. "What?"

"They're on the way there." He could barely hear the low voice.

Raimondi stood. "They are coming here?"

"Yes."

"How long do I have?"

"Not long." Click.

"Agostino!"

44

Blue nodded as they passed the security desk. Another man sat beside him, quiet and pale. Trent Porter. A hint of excitement lit his brown eyes, though. Blue would make sure he stayed safe and out of the way.

David punched the button for the floor just below Raimondi. Ron's voice came through his earpiece. "Gas leak is contained."

"Copy," David said. He understood that to mean the gas guys were busy looking for the nonexistent leak and were safe for now. He looked at Chase. "Like I told you guys at the cabin, Raimondi'll have guards on the doors. One on the entrance to his home and one on each of the halls at the stairwells."

"And you know this how?" Chase asked.

"Long story." They stepped onto the elevator and Chase gave a jaunty salute to Blue, who nodded again.

The elevator came to a smooth stop on the twenty-fifth floor. The doors whooshed open and David's adrenaline kicked in to high gear. "All right, boys, here we go."

Papa Bear and Doc B went left. David and Chase went right. They hit the stairwell and started up. David spoke, knowing the mic would carry his words to the others who were mimicking his movements. "Don't hit the door yet."

"Let us know when you're there."

At the last flight of stairs, they slowed, measuring their steps, keeping their upward progress silent. Finally, David stopped and lifted his hand. Chase handed him a small device with a mirror attached. David slid it in the crack under the door. Fortunately, the door wasn't well sealed and soon he had a picture. "Nothing to the right. Guard immediately to the left—and he's watching the door with his weapon ready." He knew Raimondi paid his help well. It had to be the most boring job on the face of the earth, but these guys lived like kings.

And the job was about to get a little more exciting.

He spoke low to Papa Bear and Doc B. "Your guy waiting for you?"

"Affirmative."

David frowned. "Can you go low?"

"On three."

"One," David counted.

"Two," Papa Bear said.

David dropped to his knees. Chase did the same. "Three," David said and nodded to Chase, who grasped the knob and gave it a twist even as he dropped lower and rolled to his back with his weapon up. The door flew open, the guard fired. A low *pop-pop* that told David he had a silencer on the end. The shots cleared his head and missed Chase by a nice margin. David clipped the shooter in the knees while Chase fired once. The man screamed and dropped, left hand clutching his right shoulder.

David kicked his weapon away and looked up. Papa Bear and Doc B had their guard taken care of as well. David patted his prisoner down, removing a pocketknife, a wallet, and two other guns, one hidden in the waistband, the other around the man's left ankle.

The guard stared, his eyes narrowed. Hate and pain spilled out. David ignored him and took the duct tape from Chase. He bound the man's hands behind him, ignoring the gasp of pain when he pulled on his wounded shoulder. He then slapped a piece of tape over the guard's mouth. Several layers of tape around his ankles and Chase rolled him into the stairwell. "Sit tight and we might get you some medical attention before too long."

David checked on the others. Identical measures were happening down the hall and no shots had been fired on their end. David figured he could count on Papa Bear rubbing that in when it was all over. He prayed the man had the chance to rib him.

When they were done, they slipped down the hall, David and Chase coming from the east, Papa Bear and Doc B from the west. David led, Papa Bear faced him. David's blood rushed, his senses sharp and in tune. He'd missed this. The action, the rush. Probably one of the reasons he'd turned to gambling. It gave him a similar emotional high he'd found in running missions.

Only he'd discovered that after marrying Summer and finding Christ, he didn't need that high. He'd found peace. A contentment for the first time in his life.

And there was no way he was going to give that up. After a quick prayer to the Almighty to end this madness, he was ready.

Summer couldn't take her eyes away from the front of the building. The glass doors had shut behind David and Chase only a short time ago. Ron had disappeared around the side to take care of the guys in the gas truck. Law enforcement was there, but not in huge numbers. Not enough to make her feel safe. But she hoped the uniforms would keep away the people after her.

"No one knows we're here, right?"

Adam sat beside her, keeping watch. He slanted her a glance. "Right." Then silence. A silence that stretched until he finally broke it. "David's a good guy."

She looked at him. "Tell me why you say that."

"I guess he told you the story about how he and Ron met."

"Yes. At least most of it anyway." She looked back toward the building. "He told you the story?"

"No. Mike did."

"Is Mike all right?"

"I don't know. We haven't heard from him." The grim tone said more than his words. He checked the street one more time. "According to Mike, David's personality did a one-eighty after he ended up in the hospital. After Ron got ahold of him."

"He said Ron paid off a huge gambling debt."

"I know. It's crazy, but apparently David's not the first person Ron's helped."

She nodded. "Who *is* Ron?"

Adam shrugged. "I'm not sure. I don't think David even knows the details about him. He just seems to show up when he's needed."

Summer watched the pedestrians passing and absently wondered who they were and where they were going. She felt a pang of jealousy at their outward confidence that no one was going to try to shoot them as they walked down the sidewalk.

She shifted, antsy and uneasy. "You think they're in there yet?"

"Yes. I'm listening to them." He pointed to his earpiece. "But right now they're only speaking when they have to." He paused. "Why were you so determined to be at court on Tuesday?"

She lifted a brow. "You mean you haven't read the dossier that contains every last detail of my life, including my past?"

He had the grace to flush. "Yes. I've read it."

"Then you know why."

"No, not really. It had the basics in there, but nothing about you, your personality."

Summer looked away. "It's not a pretty story."

"I know your father was killed in a bar fight."

She let out a bitter laugh. "That was a blessing."

Adam stayed silent and Summer shrugged. Why not? "My parents were a lot like Silas and Olivia Todd with one exception. My mother was . . . is . . . a very weak woman while Olivia grew a backbone and saved her kids."

"Your father was abusive."

A statement, not a question. She nodded anyway. "Very. Verbally, physically, you name it. Especially when he'd been drinking."

"But your mother got up the guts to leave him."

"She did. Finally. When I was almost ten years old. Marlee was around four and Nick was seven. My dad broke Nick's arm and his jaw one night, and I think that's when my mother had had enough. At least for that night. She packed us up and took us to my grandmother's house about an hour away."

"Then what?"

"He came after us the next day, of course, but my grandmother was a fighter. She'd been trying to get my mother to leave my dad for a couple of years at this point. Grams called the cops and told them what he'd done to Nick. My mom didn't want to press charges, but my grandmother did. It didn't matter anyway. You know how a domestic violence report works. It doesn't matter what the facts are, if someone makes a report, the cops make the arrest. So they arrested my dad, but of course he didn't stay there very long. When he got out, he was ready to draw blood. And the way to do that was to use us kids."

Adam snorted and she nodded. "Right," she said. "He moved out of the house and filed for divorce."

"He did?"

"Yeah. And he filed for full custody of us kids."

Adam winced. "And?"

"He got it. He had some dirt dug up on my mom that he used against her. And then my mother's lawyer didn't show up and his lawyer went for the jugular."

"Ouch, I'm sorry." He peered out the window, moved to the back, and looked out that window. Then the front. Then he settled back into the seat beside her. "Keep an eye on that side mirror. We don't want any surprises."

She nodded. "My mother's lawyer had been detained. She'd

253

passed out in the bathroom of the courthouse, and no one found her until after the judge ruled."

"But you would have had to have a lawyer, right? I mean the judge just wouldn't rule without hearing arguments."

"Oh we had a lawyer. They had someone come over from the firm. Someone totally unfamiliar with the case. He didn't care what happened to us. The judge ruled my mother unfit and gave us to my father."

"Didn't you protest?"

"All the way out the door." She bit her lip. "I actually had a choice. I could have gone to live with my mother, but my brother and sister were to live with my father. I wasn't going to leave them alone. And I paid for it for the next three years."

"Then he was stabbed to death in the bar fight."

"Yes. But—"

The van window exploded and Adam shouted. A gunshot cracked and Summer screamed as she saw Adam jerk. In horror, she realized the bullet had gone through his Kevlar vest. She reached for him. He stared at her and mouthed, "I'm sorry," before his eyes closed and he went limp. Her window shattered and glass flew in on her.

Another scream welled as a black-gloved hand reached in and flicked the lock button. Summer scrambled for the handle on her door, but she just couldn't move fast enough. Adam's door flew open and rough hands grabbed her. "Don't give me a hard time or I'll just kill you right here." He pulled her across Adam's still body and onto the sidewalk.

Pedestrians scattered, fleeing into open doors or hiding behind vehicles, terrified and screaming. What had only seconds before been a busy sidewalk now looked deserted and bare. Summer fought against the hold, kicking out, but he was too strong and her position too awkward for her to do anything.

She struggled wildly as he pulled her toward the building.

45

David flinched at the sound of gunfire coming through his earpiece and froze with his hand on the handle that would open the door to Raimondi's home. A woman screamed in his ear. One that sounded a lot like Summer. He looked at Chase. "You hear that?"

"Yeah." He frowned. "Where's it coming from?"

"Cover the door." David removed the key and trod on silent feet to the window at the end of the hallway.

"Adam," he hissed. David's blood scooted a bit faster in his veins. He had been listening to Summer tell Adam her story. He knew the others on the team had heard it too, but not one of them would let on. What was Adam thinking, getting her to talk about something so personal when he knew they were all online? Then he realized Summer knew they were all listening when she told her story. She didn't care who knew about her past. She'd risen above it and now helped others. Maybe she thought by telling the story, it would paint Adam a better picture of why she'd chosen to show up at the courthouse on Tuesday.

At the window, David peered down. "Looks like trouble on the street. We're so high up, it's hard to tell. Adam. You there?" Adam's continued silence sent cold chills up David's spine. "Adam? Answer me."

Blue came over the line. "They've got Summer. Heading for the door. Want me to stop them?"

Words he never wanted to hear. Dread centered itself in his gut, cold and hard. "No, let them come up. Make sure whoever has Summer has no reason to believe we know anything is wrong, then get help for Adam. We'll take care of the guy who has Summer."

"I'm at the desk. I watched the whole thing go down. Help for Adam's on the way." A pause. "And here they come. We're ducking behind the desk and gonna let them go up. I've got the elevators online right now."

David's heart slowed a little as scenarios flashed through his mind. Should he tell Blue to trap them on the elevator? No, getting to her would take too long and with such tight quarters, if a weapon went off . . . no, not the elevator.

In the hall? Should they wait on them? But again, if shots were fired, no telling how much help Raimondi had behind his closed door. He rushed back down to Chase. "You heard?"

"Yeah."

"Okay, they don't know about us yet. Let's keep it that way. We need to get things under control before they get up here and I'm guessing we don't have long."

"Not long enough," Chase said. "Cops'll be on the way too."

David hesitated, everything in him wanting to be waiting when the elevator opened. But he'd have a better chance of containing the situation inside the penthouse. As long as the rest of the plan went the way it was supposed to.

Please, God.

He slid the key into the lock once more and twisted. This time, he pressed on the handle and the door opened without a sound. Chase entered first, weapon ready, grip held close to his chest, prepared for any threat that should surface. David followed and scoped the place with quick, short glances, his pose similar to Chase's.

David let the door click shut behind him. The foyer was empty.

It led to a den area straight ahead. A formal dining area to the left and a hall that led to the bedrooms branched off to the right.

Papa Bear's voice came again. "Little Lou is rappeling down the side of the building. He'll be coming through the bedroom balcony door. If it's locked, it may take him a few seconds."

"It'll be locked," David murmured, remembering the man's obsession with security. Even on the twenty-sixth floor, Raimondi still locked everything that could be opened. The place looked empty, but with almost five thousand square feet, it wouldn't be hard to overlook someone.

He scooted farther into the room, keeping to the left. He knew the cameras had been disabled, but he still wanted to be careful. Where was Rosalinda? His gut clenched. Where was Georgina? And Marlee?

The apartment seemed eerily empty.

Communicating with hand gestures, David motioned for them to spread out. He nodded for Chase to follow him. Chase jerked his chin that he understood and they crept toward Raimondi's office.

Down the hall, around the corner, arms extended, guns ready.

Little Lou said, "On the balcony to the right. Should have entry within twenty seconds."

"Copy," David whispered.

They came to the door.

"Kitchen's clear," David said.

Papa Bear nodded. "Bedrooms are clear."

One by one the rooms were cleared. David frowned. Was anyone here? Blue's voice came through. "They're getting off the elevator."

Into his mic, David said, "Doc B, meet me at the front door." To Chase he said, "Wait here and keep an eye on that door right there."

"That's his office?"

"Yeah. Contain him if he comes out. I'm going to get Summer." Chase nodded.

Blood rushing, nerves humming, David made his way back to the front door. Doc B positioned himself on one side. David took the other. "Let them come in. Just like Afghanistan. Before he rings the bell."

Doc gave him a grim smile and a sharp nod.

David waited, glad they'd left the guards in the stairwells. He watched through the peephole. Saw a shadow, then Summer's scared and defiant face. No weapon he could see on the man who held her, but knew it was there. Possibly in her back. No, wait. He held it low. If he pulled the trigger, she'd get shot in the leg, not the back. He liked those odds a lot better. "I'll have to immobilize his arm."

"I got him covered on this end."

Please, Lord. David moved to the side. Grasped the door.

And pulled it in.

Doc rounded the doorjamb and placed his gun against the surprised captor's face. "Make a sound and you're dead."

Before Doc even started his sentence, David grabbed Summer's arm and yanked. It seemed to take forever. In reality, everything took place in less than a second. In one smooth move, Doc removed the man's weapon and forced him on his knees, hands in the air.

Summer's surprised shock faded to relief as David motioned for her to stand to the side. The shakes set in and she pressed a hand to her mouth. David duct taped the man's hands behind his back. "We'll be with you in a moment. Don't go anywhere." He looked at Summer. "You all right?" She nodded, her face pasty and slightly green. "Are you going to be sick?"

"Maybe." She swallowed hard and took a deep breath. The green faded, but the white remained. "He shot Adam. It went through his vest," she whispered.

"Unfortunately the vest doesn't stop all the bullets," David said. "He's getting help." He glanced toward Raimondi's office. "We're not done. Can you hold it together?"

She squared her shoulders and nodded. "I'll have to, won't I?"

David pulled an extra gun from its resting place against the small of his back and pressed it into her hands. "Shoot him if you have to. Help is only a holler away, okay?" He spoke into his mic. "Papa Bear. Need you up here." Within minutes, Papa Bear was in the room. He glanced at his former unit team member. "Papa Bear's going to stay with you, okay?"

"Okay."

Once he was sure Summer was all right and under Papa Bear's watchful eye, he motioned toward the office. Chase waited. "All's been quiet."

The door was closed. David positioned himself on the opposite side, then reached out and wrapped one hand around the knob.

Twisted.

And pushed.

Chase swung around the jamb, arms extended, weapon pointed. Shots blasted at him from a man behind the desk. Doc B grunted and went to his knees. Chase and David fired back. A scream echoed from the shooter and David dropped to the floor and rolled inside. Chase mimicked his movements on the opposite side. David came up shooting. Three shots from him. Three from Chase. The man dropped.

David raced to him and kicked his weapon. "Little Lou, need you to get in here and get Doc. He's hurt." David looked down at the dead man. "It's not Raimondi. I don't recognize this guy." He turned to Doc. "The bullet went through your vest." He grabbed the small bag on Doc's belt and pulled out medical supplies. "Watch my back, Doc."

Doc coughed. "These guys play dirty."

"They knew we'd have vests on, they were prepared," David murmured as he ripped the vest from Doc and tossed it aside. He pressed the gauze against the bleeding, then taped on a few more layers. It wasn't gushing. That was a good sign.

Little Lou came to the doorway and hefted Doc B to his shoulders. David said, "Get him out of here. He needs medical attention."

Doc protested. "It's just a little scratch. We can finish this."

"Not today, Doc. Thanks for the help." Their eyes met and David hoped he communicated his gratitude, but he wouldn't let Doc continue when he didn't know how bad the man was hurt.

Little Lou said, "I'll be back."

David nodded. "Take Ron with you if you need him." He looked up to see Papa Bear and Summer watching from their position next to the man who'd kidnapped Summer. They'd moved him to a more hidden location behind the wall off the foyer. A nice place to protect themselves should they need to. "Summer, go with them."

"No." Her low, quiet word hung in the air for a brief second. David knew she wasn't going anywhere, and he didn't have time to convince her. He looked at Little Lou. "Go."

And then they were gone.

David turned to stare at the empty room. Empty except for the dead body on the floor. And the row of snakes in their aquariums lining the far wall. All of the bullets had missed the glass cages.

"Clear in here, what about there?" Chase asked. He moved toward the black door and on the count of a silent three, pulled it open.

Together, they rounded the doorjamb. And found stairs that led down. Chase hit the light and went first while David watched behind. Within seconds Chase was back up. "No one's down there, but this guy is one sick dude."

"What is it?"

"Snakes. Lots and lots of slimy creatures."

David grimaced. "Yeah, they're his pets."

"Nasty."

They shut the door and scanned the office once again. "My gut is shouting at me," David said. "Stand ready."

"There's no one here."

David looked around the room. "He was warned we were coming."

"Definitely," Chase said. "Our shooter was waiting for us to come through the door. He didn't come running when the shots went off outside the office. We've got the guards but no family. Guards who were watching the stairwell. His wife, daughter, servants aren't here. No one's here. And yet, someone went to the trouble of getting Summer and bringing her up here. So I'll admit that's a good indication that he's still here."

Adrenaline surged. "He may have been warned, but it wasn't soon enough. He didn't have enough time to do anything, but—"

"—hide," Chase finished for him.

"He's definitely still here." David turned in a full circle.

"I'm pretty sure I said that first. But where?"

"I don't know. Here. The shooter was here. What was he guarding?" David nodded. "He's here. Somewhere close." David looked at the black door behind Raimondi's desk. "Okay, he wouldn't be down there, not with his family."

Chase shook his head.

Papa Bear reported in. "All still clear out here. Little Lou got down the elevator with Doc. Ron's helping them sneak out of the building, then he'll be back if they don't run into any trouble."

"Thought he was entertaining the gas guys," David said.

"Police made 'em leave when they couldn't find any gas issues."

"Right. Keep me updated."

"Will do."

David looked back at Chase. "Raimondi's got to have some sort of emergency plan," David said. "A place he could go if he felt threatened or . . . whatever." He nodded and looked around with new eyes. "It'd be just like him."

"Where?"

David did another three-sixty. "I don't know. We're on the twenty-sixth floor." He studied the desk. Looked at the floor. "Tap the floor, the walls. Move the furniture."

Papa Bear reported in. "All still clear."

Adam was in the back of David's mind. Near the window, he

261

looked out and down. "Put us back online, Blue. I need eyes." David jiggled the mouse on Raimondi's desk. The monitor flashed blank for a few seconds then six black-and-white pictures popped up. All pictures from different cameras.

The front door of the building, the street view with law enforcement pulling up, the elevators. He clicked and he gaped at the next screen that showed up. Georgina sat on a bed with her hands clasped in her lap. Her mother sat next to her, looking older and more frail since the last time he'd seen her.

Chase said, "I think I have something."

"What?" His mind still on the images on the screen, he barely registered Chase's comment.

"Scrapes on the floor. Slight and not really noticeable if I wasn't looking for something."

David waved him over. "Look at this."

Chase joined him and leaned over to examine the monitor. "Whoa." He backed up and tripped over one of Raimondi's smaller aquariums. It tilted, tipped, and crashed to its side.

Footsteps.

David stood and pointed his weapon at the door.

Summer, followed by Papa Bear, stopped in the doorway. David lowered his weapon.

"What's going on?" Summer asked. "What happened?"

David glared at Papa Bear, who shrugged. "She bolted."

She held her weapon at her side.

"Chase tripped," David said. "Where's the guy who snatched Summer?"

"I knocked him out," Papa Bear grunted. He rubbed his knuckles against his lips and blew on them. "Got tired of his trashy mouth."

David said, "We've got to move faster." Into his mic, he said, "Stall the cops. I don't want them up here yet." Raimondi was his to deal with. "Did Ron go with Doc and Little Lou?"

"Copy that," Blue said. "And no. Ron's down here stalling. He's singing 'The Star-Spangled Banner' and acting crazy. Cops have to deal with him before they can come your way. And when they do, they'll be taking the stairs, it seems like the elevators aren't working for some reason."

"You've got to be kidding me. Don't let them hurt Ron, please."

"I'll intervene if it comes to that. Looks like Ron's pretty capable of taking care of himself."

"He is." David went to the bookcase and asked Chase, "Where are those scratches?"

"There. Where you're standing."

David examined the floor, then the bookcase, running his fingers over the shelves, the books, the sides.

46

Laura Todd shook against her mother and eyed Raimondi with a stare full of hate. The little one had tuned out and shut her eyes. At least they were quiet kids.

It was Marlee who had nearly sent his nerves over the edge. He ground his molars together and raged at his stupidity. He should have left the mother and daughters alone, but he'd given in to his desire to hit Summer and David hard. He should have just had them killed. The husband would have been the perfect patsy.

Now he was trapped.

If he had been smart, he would have built a secret passage out of the hallway. But he'd deliberately closed this part of his home off. So that if one of his prisoners escaped one of the four rooms lining the hall, he or she would have nowhere to escape *to*.

And now the time had come for Raimondi to use his secret as a hiding place. For him and his family. He'd tucked Rosalinda and Georgina away in the farthest room on the left. They'd been shocked to see his secret area but had followed him at his urging when he'd explained they were being attacked by a competing organized crime family.

Agostino hadn't had time to get rid of Marlee, and the woman had screamed at Raimondi as soon as he'd entered the room. A punch to her face shut her up, and he wondered why he hadn't just shot her with the gun he now clutched in his right hand. He wrapped his fingers in her hair and yanked. She screamed and he pulled her to the next room and shoved her toward a chair. With one last yell that was a cross between a screech and an angry roar, she sank into it, burying her face in her hands. Raimondi grabbed her by the back of the neck and placed the gun against her temple. "Shut. Up."

Her lips clamped together and she kept her eyes squeezed tight. She shook so hard, he vaguely wondered if she'd be able to stay in the chair. Waving the gun at the kids' mother, he said, "Any of you makes another sound, and you're all dead."

She simply pulled them closer to her and turned away from him.

Agostino had soundproofed everything back here. Raimondi wasn't worried about anyone hearing anything past the bookcase in his office, but he didn't want to be annoyed by their cries. He had some thinking to do. He left them and shut the door, clicking the dead bolt behind him.

Agostino stood in the middle of the hallway and Raimondi clutched his chest. "Are you trying to give me a heart attack? I thought you were watching Georgina and your aunt?"

"What's going on, Uncle? You may fool Auntie and Georgie, but I know there's no attack. Why do you need them out of the way?"

"Well, it's an attack all right, but by David Hackett, not another family."

His brow shot up. "Hackett's here?"

"Indeed."

"He bring the cops with him?"

"If not, they'll be here soon enough, but they can search all they want, they'll never find us."

Agostino looked a little doubtful but Raimondi didn't care. He'd see soon enough. They just had to wait them out. David and his little band of wannabe heroes would search and find nothing and be gone.

And Raimondi would move his family out to his estate and put this place on the market.

Either that or he'd just burn the building down.

That thought made him smile for the first time that day.

David motioned Summer back and down. She dropped behind the desk, confused, but knowing this was not the time to ask questions. She still shook from her encounter with the man on the street and worry for Adam pierced her.

David looked at Papa Bear. "You got her?"

"We're good." He leveled his weapon at the bookcase. "Can watch your back too."

David nodded to Chase and sent him a grim smile. "You ready?"

Chase nodded.

When the bookcase began to move, Summer sucked in a deep breath. From her position behind the desk, she peeked around the corner and could see a door revealed by the moving bookcase.

David reached out and twisted the knob. It opened inward and now Summer could see down a long hallway.

"Alessandro! I know you're back there! Show yourself!" David pointed his weapon down the hall.

Silence echoed.

A cry sounded and Summer tensed. That was the cry of a child. She saw David and Chase exchange a concerned look. "Raimondi!"

Chase shook his head. "We're sitting ducks if we walk down that hall. All he has to do is pop out of one of those rooms and we're done."

"Be careful. Hold your fire. If he pops out, he'll have a hostage in front of him."

Chase nodded. "I've done this a few times."

"Alessandro! You're not getting out of this one. Come on out."

47

Raimondi knew they'd found his hiding place.

Hackett.

He'd learned too much about Raimondi during his short time as a part of the family. Because anyone who dated Georgina was immediately welcomed—that is, put under a microscope.

Of course Raimondi had done a full background check and David's past had panned out. Gambled a little too much, but his finances said he had self-control. And he was Sam's friend and co-owner.

Sam had been a loyal partner too. His enthusiasm and his love of money had made him an easy man to manipulate into doing whatever Raimondi wanted.

David had killed that profitable business too.

But before all that, Georgina had been crazy about him.

So Raimondi welcomed him. At some point he even figured he might be his future son-in-law.

And David hadn't been put off by the organized crime ties. He'd seemed to relish it. Only Raimondi had soon learned David had been playing a role. "The man should have been nominated for an Oscar."

"What?" Agostino looked at him. Looked at Marlee. Gazed at the mother and her two girls.

"David. I believed him just like Georgina did."

"Focus, Uncle. How are we going to get out of this?"

Raimondi heard David yelling at him. The oldest girl, Laura, had let out a holler that left no doubt that someone was back here. He considered shooting her, but that would lead them to the exact room where his hostages were, where Raimondi and Agostino were, and he wasn't ready for that yet.

Think. Think.

A plan formed and he turned to Agostino. "Here's what we're going to do."

David waited and got no response. He said, "We're going to have to go after him. He could sit back there forever."

"You need us in there?" Ron asked.

"No. Not yet."

Blue's voice. "Cops are here. Staking out the building. Snipers are on the roof across the street. Stay away from the windows, they don't know where you are."

Indecision warred within him. Summer was up here. If shooting started . . .

"Even with vests," Chase reminded him, "he starts shooting and we're toast."

David pursed his lips and considered their options. And what he'd do in Raimondi's shoes.

"He's got hostages. He'll use them to his advantage. If he shoots us, there's more where we came from. Right now, he probably just wants out. He wants to bargain."

"You willing to bet your life on that?"

David winced at Chase's choice of words. Bet. Another gamble. He glanced back at Summer. Then back down the hall. "Yeah."

"Okay, let me put it this way. Are you willing to bet *my* life on it? Because I'm not so sure I am."

David considered everything he knew about Raimondi. "Stay behind me."

Chase stared. "Back to back. You take care of what comes from the front and I'll cover anything that comes from the rear."

"And I've got a good line of sight where I'm positioned," Papa Bear answered.

"Little Lou, you back on the bedroom balcony?"

"Yep. Delivered Doc to the paramedics and managed to sneak back up here. Ron's still doing what he can to delay the cops from getting up here, but they're not going to let him get away with his stunts for much longer. They'll probably tase him." A slight pause. "Next time the bad guy better live on the first floor."

"Keep us informed with what's happening on the street."

"Cops are on the ground, casing the place and forming a plan before they move right now. But it won't be long before they'll be in the building."

David raised his voice as Chase positioned himself at his back. "Raimondi, I'm coming to get Marlee. You shoot me and there's a whole police department who'll be coming up here."

A door opened and Marlee stepped out. David winced. She'd been beaten and looked like she might fall over at any moment. Raimondi followed close behind her, using her as a shield.

Raimondi stopped and stared.

"Let her go," David said.

"Not a chance. Now back up."

"I'm not letting you out of here, you should know that."

"You'll let me out if you don't want to be responsible for four people's deaths."

Four? David raised a brow in silent question.

Raimondi nodded to someone still in the room.

David's heart hit the floor when Laura Todd stepped into the hall, her face white and pinched. Sandy followed, clutching her big sister's hand. Their mother brought up the rear. She held

Sandy's other hand and Agostino pressed a gun to the woman's head.

So, two captors and four hostages.

Not good. "So what do we do now, Raimondi?"

"You back up into my office."

"And if I don't?"

"I start shooting until you do. I can spare three hostages, I really only need one."

True enough. "But I'll take you out after you kill the first one."

"And Agostino will kill another. One of the children. Now are we finished arguing about who is going to kill whom? Back. Up."

David nudged Chase and obeyed, knowing his team was listening, planning on how to help. He hoped they planned fast.

"Take out your earpiece. You too." He nodded at Chase. "Throw them on the floor and step on them."

David hesitated. Raimondi dug his gun harder into Marlee's ear and she cried out. A tear slipped down Sandy's cheek, but she never took her eyes off of him, the trust and pleading there, making him swallow hard.

Lord, please . . .

The knowledge that Sandy was counting on him to get her away from another evil man nearly strangled him. But he kept his cool and made sure his face showed nothing of his emotions. He pulled the earpiece from his ear and tossed it to the hardwood floor. Then settled his boot heel over it and stepped down.

Chase did the same. Raimondi smiled and motioned for them to keep moving.

David could only pray that Papa Bear had hidden Summer.

48

Hidden behind the desk, Summer peered around the edge to watch Chase walk down the hall toward her. David faced the opposite direction. Raimondi held Marlee at gunpoint and another man brought up the rear, with Olivia and her children. Summer's heart shuddered within her.

A tug on her arm brought her head around. Papa Bear placed a finger against his lips and motioned her toward the door. She nodded and slipped from behind the desk. They were heading back this way, and Papa Bear needed to get her out of the room so he could help David and the others. She understood that. They moved toward the door, Papa Bear motioning Summer to stay behind him. He stopped at the edge of the door and peered around it. Then snapped his head back inside.

"What is it?" she whispered.

"The man who attacked you and shot Adam is loose."

"Loose?" Summer swallowed hard. "So what does that mean?"

He shut the door and locked it. "It means we're trapped and we're going to have to fight it out."

And David was backing through the door that had been hidden by the bookcase. Chase saw them and his eyes widened.

Papa Bear pulled Summer to the edge of the door and raised his weapon.

David said, "All right, we're in your office. Now what?"

"Move back against the far wall. Stay where I can see you." He paused. "Is anyone else in the room?"

David snorted. "Of course not."

"Because if there is, somebody's going to die."

Summer felt her stomach rumble, the nagging queasiness she'd felt all day making her want to gag. She hated being afraid. Hated what it did to her.

Raimondi said, "I'm coming out. If there's anyone else in the room, he'd better show himself now. Otherwise Agostino will kill the woman, do you understand?"

Summer pulled in a swift breath. David hesitated and Chase said, "There's someone here."

Raimondi said, "I thought so."

"What are you doing, Papi?" A husky female voice demanded. A pause. "David? David?"

A sob? Summer wondered. Was the girl crying?

"What's going on, David?" Summer heard her whisper.

"Don't hurt Olivia or the kids," David said.

He shot a look at Papa Bear and the closed door behind him.

Papa Bear mouthed to David, "We're trapped."

Summer's gaze swung to David. His jaw went tight.

Papa Bear whispered, "Little Lou? Now would be a good time for a little help."

Summer heard his words, but didn't think anyone else could.

Papa Bear leaned close, his voice low, "Little Lou is on the balcony. He doesn't have a clean shot. Too many people in the way."

Summer moved closer to David, shifting to see Raimondi holding a gun on her sister's head. Behind him Olivia and the girls were held in a similar manner by another man. Marlee spotted her and her eyes went wide.

David said, "Back up, Summer."

But she couldn't. Not when Marlee was so obviously terrified. Not when a madman could end her life with the twitch of a finger. "Take me," she blurted.

Raimondi paused. The entire area went silent. Then David roared, "Get back, Summer." He glared at Papa Bear, who grabbed her arm. She resisted and stared Raimondi in the eye. "It's me you've wanted all along. Me and David. Well, here I am. Come get me, you coward. Or do you have to hide behind innocent children? Does that make you feel like a man?"

Raimondi's face went blood red.

Papa Bear got a good hold on her arm this time and gave her a hard yank.

"Are you insane?" he whispered.

"Not yet." She paused. "Getting close, though." She shook like a leaf in the wind. Fear turned her stomach to acid and she swallowed hard. Now was not the time to start throwing up. Several deep breaths helped her blood pressure, but the terror for those she loved hung on like a barnacle.

49

Adam clutched his bloody shoulder and rolled off the gurney, ignoring the protesting EMT. He stumbled toward the front door of the building. Authorities blocked him, of course, as he knew they would, but he could see Blue inside with Trent. Blue pointed to something on the monitor and the officer standing next to him nodded.

The entire block was one big command post. NYPD, SWAT, and every other available branch of law enforcement had turned out once they learned the address and who was involved. The report of shots fired and Raimondi's address brought out the big guns. Raimondi was on a lot of wanted lists.

"Sir?" An officer stopped him. "You need to get back in the ambulance."

"No, I don't." He probably did. His shoulder felt like someone held a blowtorch to it. He'd passed out at the initial jolt of pain. When he'd come to, Summer was gone and he was surrounded by witnesses and paramedics. "I'm a Deputy US Marshal." With his good arm, he fished his badge out of his back pocket and flashed it. "I'm going in there."

"Sorry, Deputy Marshal, I can't let you do that."

"You don't have a choice. I'm responsible for a man's life. I'm

going to do my job or die trying. Now get out of my way. Please."
He shoved past the officer and breathed a sigh of relief when the
man didn't stop him. Once inside the lobby, he told Blue. "Get
me up there."

"You don't look so good, man." Blue clicked a few keys on the
computer, then leaned in to whisper, "Cops are taking the stairs.
You can use elevator one."

Adam swallowed hard against the nausea threatening to overtake
him. The pain was incredible. He'd never been shot, and if he lived
through this one, he didn't plan on it happening again.

He stepped into the elevator and leaned his head against the
mirrored side. The coolness helped. He was so thirsty. He felt like
he could guzzle a gallon of water.

Darkness threatened again and he slid to the floor, the weakness
almost impossible to fight.

As he rode, he prayed. "I messed up, God, please let me fix this.
I've got to fix it."

50

Heart pounding at Summer's deliberate provoking of Raimondi, David moved to the side. He positioned himself so that Raimondi could still see him. And David had a clear view of Agostino, whose weapon never wavered from Olivia's head. Georgina had come from a room behind Raimondi. She'd spotted David immediately and her eyes widened.

He gave a silent groan. "Georgina, get back in the room and stay with your mother." He didn't need her getting shot.

She ignored him. "What are you doing, Papi? Put the gun down. I told you I didn't want him hurt. And who are these people?" She gestured toward Olivia and the girls. "And who was yelling at you?" Her eyes slammed back into his. "David? What's going on?"

He pulled his gaze from her and looked to his left. Right now, he couldn't answer the many questions spinning in her eyes.

Summer clutched her stomach.

David said, "Step where he can see you, Papa Bear."

For the life of him—and everyone around him—David couldn't think of a plan that wouldn't result in at least one person dead. It was a roll of the dice for him. A gamble. He could play it one way and Olivia would die, another way and Marlee might get the bullet. He couldn't take the risk.

They all now stood in Raimondi's office.

Raimondi glared at Summer while Agostino moved Olivia to the side. Georgina stepped to the side and her head swiveled from one person to the next. Laura and Sandy tried to stay as close to their mother as possible, however when Laura saw Summer, she gasped and ran to throw her arms around her waist. Summer took one step back but didn't let go of her weapon.

Raimondi gestured with his gun. "All of you. Place your weapons on my desk where I can see them."

"Do it," David said. "He's not bluffing. He'll kill her."

David gave a mental calculation. Blue and Little Lou could hear what was going on in the office now. He knew help was on the way. "The cops are all over this place, Alessandro."

Raimondi smiled and it was the cruel one David remembered seeing upon occasion. "I don't intend to shoot you. I have a much better plan for you."

Agostino hung back, his weapon still trained on Olivia. Papa Bear glowered. Summer clasped her arms around Laura after she placed her gun on the desk.

Once everyone laid their weapons on the desk, Raimondi motioned to the black door behind the desk. "Open the door and go in. All of you. Down the steps."

Georgina gasped, "No!"

Raimondi looked at the girl for a moment. "Shut up or go back to the room. This doesn't concern you."

"Doesn't concern me? You're trying to kill the man I love and you say it doesn't concern me?"

Summer gaped, but kept quiet.

"I don't have time for this," Raimondi screamed. He pulled in a measured breath and looked at Agostino for a brief moment. "Shut her up." Back to his hostages, he said, "Go. Through the door."

Chase raised a brow and looked at David.

"Now!" Raimondi's patience had obviously worn thin. His

breathing came in pants and perspiration dotted his forehead. "Now, I said!"

David moved toward the door and opened it. Georgina hovered near Agostino, who still held his gun on Olivia. He looked back at Raimondi, at the weapon held so tight against Marlee's head. It wouldn't take much for him to pull the trigger. Just a slight twitch and Marlee would be no more.

A part of him whispered, "Do it. You can beat him. You can stop all of this, end it now." His hands twitched, his leg muscles bunched. Chase laid a hand on his shoulder and David gritted his teeth. He couldn't risk it. As long as they were alive, there was hope. If he made a wrong move and someone got killed, he wouldn't be able to live with it.

Chase motioned for Summer to bring Laura. "I'll go first. Stay behind me." To David he said, "You got the rear?"

"I got it."

"Papi, you can't do this!"

"Shut up or I'll kill you when I'm done."

Georgina flinched as though he'd struck her. But it wasn't Georgina that concerned David. His heart clenched at the look in Summer's eyes. Fear mingled with hope that they would get out of this after all, that once they were away from Raimondi and his guns, they would find a way out. Only she didn't know what was down there.

But the snakes were in cages. As long as they stayed in the cages, all would be well. Right? And he had his ankle gun. It would do no good to reach for it now, but it was five chances of escape once they were down the steps. Raimondi knew the cops were on the way. He'd leave soon enough, and David and the others would find a way out.

He hoped.

With a prayer on his lips, he watched Chase disappear. Summer caught his eye as she passed him and he gave her a reassuring nod. She swallowed hard and descended, followed by Sandy and

Olivia. Agostino transferred his weapon to David. Raimondi shoved Marlee through the open door, and she would have fallen down the steps had David not reached out and grabbed her. An act that Raimondi had been counting on. The man moved back, his gun never wavering. "Goodbye once and for all, David Hackett. I am thrilled beyond belief that I get to choose the way you die."

David gave him a grim smile. "It's not over yet."

Raimondi laughed. "Oh, it's over." He looked at Marlee. "And thank you for all your help, my dear. So sorry things didn't turn out like you'd planned."

A tremor ran through the young woman's body, and David kept his grip on her upper arms to keep her from launching herself at the man. "Pig," she spat.

"Easy, Marlee."

Raimondi gave them an amused smile. "She wanted to get rid of you, you know. She was quite accommodating in letting us know where you were at all times." He nodded. "Very sneaky, that one."

Something he'd ask Marlee about should they get out alive.

Raimondi aimed the weapon at Marlee. "Now, I'm in a bit of a hurry. If you're not behind that door within two seconds, I will shoot her."

Georgina screamed at her father as David pulled Marlee with him over the threshold and shut the door. A gunshot sounded and Georgina's screams came to an abrupt end.

Adam stepped off the elevator, his weapon ready, his heart pounding. His vision blurred and pain nearly swallowed him, but he had to do all he could to help. He had to get in that apartment before the cops made it up here. He couldn't let David and Summer and the others die. "How much time do I have before the cops get up here?"

Blue said, "About two minutes. I've got the stairwell cameras

279

on to keep an eye on them and most are having to stop and rest along the way. A couple are getting close."

The empty hallway yawned before him. He moved to the door and twisted the knob. Shocked that it wasn't locked, he stood to the side and pushed the door open.

Gunshots greeted him with a fast *pop, pop, pop*. Adam dropped to his knees and took another quick peek around the doorjamb. Got a glimpse of the shooter.

He jerked back, ignoring the pain, his weakness, everything. He narrowed his focus to one thing. Get to Summer and David. Adam spun into the open doorway and popped off three shots, then ducked back. A scream sent satisfaction through him. At least one bullet had found its mark.

Adam scooted army style around the edge of the door once again to survey the damage. His ears rang but no more shots came his way. He'd have to go slow, use caution. He had no idea who was in the next room, who had heard the shooting and might be waiting for him to show himself. "Little Lou," he whispered. "You there?"

"Yeah, but I'm a little tied up at the moment. Got caught by surprise, but don't worry about me. As soon as this joker makes a mistake, I'll be in to help."

"Blue? You there?"

"Affirmative, but I've got to flush out some of Raimondi's leftover goons to get to you."

Looked like he was on his own.

———

As gunshots echoed through his home, Raimondi glanced at Agostino. "The cops are here. Make sure the office door is locked."

Agostino paced to the door and did as bid. "It's locked."

Raimondi sat at the computer and turned on the camera for the snake room. He would miss his friends. He would miss watching them do their worst. "Get your aunt and let's go."

"You shot Georgina, Uncle. How can you shoot your own child?"

Raimondi ignored his nephew's whining. And his daughter's whimpering. "She'll live."

Agostino's stare made him a tad uncomfortable. Maybe he had gone a little too far in shooting her, but at least she wasn't yelling at him anymore and trying to get to the door. At least Rosalinda had known her place and stayed back in the room like he told her to.

"Be ready to go as soon as I say when."

"Go where?"

"I'll show you in a minute." Raimondi pressed the button to release his friends. "Now, we just have to wait. The floor will get colder and colder and my friends will start looking for heat. If everyone stays quiet and doesn't panic, no one will get bit. If they panic," he shrugged and lifted his hands, "well, things will get interesting."

"Those kids don't deserve to die like that, Uncle."

"Those kids? Bah." He waved a hand. "Their mama should have picked a different lawyer. No more questions. Go get ready. Now."

Agostino turned and entered the passageway while Raimondi settled back in his chair to watch the monitor. He clasped his hands across his chest and smiled at the men's efforts to keep the snakes at bay. Useless.

Three shots sounded and his office door slammed open.

Raimondi jumped to his feet and grabbed the nearest weapon. Only he was too late. A bloody man had his weapon trained on Raimondi. "Where are David and Summer?"

51

Summer blinked and let her eyes adjust to the dim light, then jerked as three gunshots came from the office they'd just vacated.

David and Chase exchanged a look. "Wonder who got shot?"

Summer pounded on the door. "Let us out!" The girls joined her. Marlee added her screeching and pounding.

After a minute passed with no answer, Summer dropped her hands and crossed her arms. She looked at her prison. They were in a room about the size of her bedroom. Maybe fifteen feet by eighteen feet. Concrete walls and a tile ceiling. They'd only walked down about four steps from the door, so they weren't on a lower floor. It was warm in the room. Almost too warm. She pulled off her blazer and dropped it on the floor.

Laura huddled against her and she could make out Sandy and Olivia. She moved closer to the woman. "I'm so sorry about this."

"I thought it was Silas," she whispered. "I thought somehow he'd hired someone to kill us. To get revenge."

"No. This has to do with David."

Confusion flickered. "I thought his name was Kyle."

"It's a long story." She looked around and prayed she'd have the chance to tell it.

David came to her and drew her close. He looked at Olivia and her two girls. "We're going to get out of here, okay?"

"Why are we even here?" Laura asked. "Why did he come after us?"

David sighed. "Because he knew that if he hurt you, he would hurt Summer and me. And that was very important to him."

"He's evil."

"Exactly."

"Just like my father."

Sandy looked up. "Can we sing that song about hope? 'Cuz I'm hoping real bad that we get out of here."

Summer swallowed hard and David nodded. "That's a good idea. Why don't you guys do that while I work on finding a way out?"

Sandy started and Summer caught David's eye. He nodded toward the children. She caught his message. Keep them calm.

Papa Bear had been examining the room. "David? You know what's back here?"

"I do. But they're all behind glass, right?"

"Yeah. For the next few seconds. The glass is lifting."

David spun to see. As he turned, the lights brightened.

He squinted as his eyes adjusted but had no trouble making out the scene before him.

David estimated there had to be over a hundred of the writhing creatures. And if the ones in Raimondi's office were any indication, they were all venomous. He might be able to identify a few of them but decided to keep his distance and assume they were all deadly.

Chase shuddered beside him. "This place is locked down tight. Our only hope might be the small air vent in the ceiling." He gave a grim glance to the slithering snakes.

Sandy whimpered and began to cry. "I don't like snakes. I don't want them to bite me."

"Hey," Papa Bear had backed slowly away from the waking

mass. "They're not going to bite you. We're going to figure a way out of here, okay?"

David noticed that the temperature was dropping. He saw the snakes start to move almost as one.

Straight toward them.

The temperature continued to drop.

Was that on purpose? Part of an evil man's twisted thinking? Lower the temperature in the room so the snakes would seek out warmth? Like human body warmth?

"Mama?" Laura's low voice caught David's attention. She turned her head one way, then the other. "I hear something in the ceiling."

Summer looked up and moved closer to him. He pulled her toward the stairs they'd just come down. She shivered and he rubbed her arms. "Hang tight." David heard it now too. The snakes were not just in front of them, but above them. The drop ceiling looked innocent enough, but apparently Raimondi kept some of his pets between the insulation and the ceiling. He looked at Chase. "Guess that air vent is out."

"Looks like. If we start pulling that ceiling down, it's going to scare them. Make them mad." A muscle jumped in the man's jaw and he backed toward the stairs. "Snakes don't attack unless provoked or frightened. If we don't panic, the snakes will have no reason to strike."

Marlee whimpered and sat on the bottom step. "Just let them bite me. I'm so tired of everything." She began to sob and Summer went to her to wrap her arms around her sister. But Marlee pushed her away. "I don't deserve your comfort," she whispered. "I did this. I led them to you. I let them beat me up and put me in the hospital so you would take me with you, and I could let them know where we were. I kept my phone with me and on so they could track you. Even at the warehouse when we showered and changed clothes, I managed to keep the phone on." Tears tracked her cheeks and dripped off her chin. "I'm no better than that man who put us in here. I'm evil." She dropped her chin to her chest and continued to weep.

"Oh, Marlee." Summer closed her eyes, and David knew she was hurting at yet another betrayal. The snakes wiggled toward them. David shivered. It was now cold in the room. He knelt and felt the floor. Warm. Hence the snakes were traveling toward them. He'd bet the floor where they'd been sleeping was now cold.

Laura ran up the steps and started banging on the door. "Let us out! Please let us out!"

Summer jumped up and wrapped her arms around the girl. Sandy practically climbed up her mother, who dropped her purse to clasp her child to her.

David looked around. Grabbed a broom from its resting place against the wall. He snapped it in half over his knee. He shoved one of the pieces at Chase. "Take it. We may have to see if we can beat them back until rescue comes."

"And while you're doing that, I'll see if I can find a way up into the ceiling," Papa Bear muttered.

"There are snakes up there too."

"Well, I'll just have to move them out of the way."

"Too bad we can't make a fire," David murmured.

Papa Bear walked to the steps where Summer still held Laura.

Olivia walked Sandy up to Summer, then turned and grabbed her purse. She opened it and rummaged. David absently wondered what she was looking for while he jabbed at a snake that was getting a little too close for his comfort.

"Here," Olivia said. "Use this."

He glanced at her and saw what she held.

A lighter.

David spun. "Summer, give me your blazer."

She frowned but picked it up and tossed it to him. Her eyes widened. "Look out!"

He turned to see one of the reptiles nudging up against his shoe.

His heart beat a little faster. He wasn't afraid of snakes, but he didn't want to do anything to cause one to strike either. With the end of the broom handle, he gently lifted the snake off his shoe and gave him a toss back into the too-close pile.

David wrapped Summer's blazer around the end of the stick.

"You still got your ankle gun?" Chase asked.

"Yeah."

"Let me have it. This lock looks like a cheap one. One or two bullets ought to do it."

In the back corner, Chase had located a cabinet with a combination lock. David handed him the gun, then flicked the lighter against Summer's blazer. It caught, then snuffed out.

He tried again. And again. And yet again. Finally it caught and held. Started to burn, but was slow.

Still, he shoved the small flame at the snakes and they backed off. He turned in a circle, waving the makeshift torch.

Chase warned everyone to hold their ears. Then a gunshot echoed throughout the room followed by a clunk as the lock hit the floor.

52

Adam winced, his vision blurred. Soon he'd pass out and drop his weapon. "Open the door."

"You'd better hurry. They won't last long," the girl on the floor answered. She pressed a hand to her bloody side and grimaced. "He set his snakes on them. They're poisonous. If one of them panics and starts fighting, the snakes will bite. You've got to get them out."

"Shut up," Raimondi growled. "You've been nothing but trouble bringing that traitor into my home. You don't deserve to breathe." He raised his weapon like he was going to shoot the girl again.

Three gunshots echoed and Adam ducked, spun to face this new threat. Only to see a woman in her late fifties standing in the doorway by the bookcase. She lowered the weapon and Adam turned back to see Alessandro Raimondi clutching his chest, eyes wide.

"Rosalinda?" he whispered as he dropped into his leather chair, then slid to the floor.

"You will hurt no one else in this family, you dreadful, evil man." She dropped the gun and raced to the young woman's side. "Georgina, oh my baby, are you all right?"

"I will be," Georgina gasped.

The man Adam recognized as Agostino went to the women's side and helped them up. He looked at Adam. "Go help your friends. The police are here. I'll let them in."

Adam nodded. His legs felt rubbery, weak. The door looked very far away. He went to his knees.

The door. He had to get to the door.

The gunshots echoed through the small room, freezing them all for a fraction of a second. Even the snakes seemed to startle.

"They're coming," Summer warned him in a tight voice.

Papa Bear looked at him. "I can't find a way up there, there're too many of them." He held up a hand. "One of the buggers got me. I didn't move fast enough."

David clenched his teeth and willed the blazer to burn faster. "Great."

"Guess we'll see if it kills me or not." With his other hand, Papa Bear caught one of the snakes behind its head, a viper, David thought, and tossed it aside.

They backed up and David waved the now-burning blazer at the mass. "If we don't get out of here real soon, you won't have to worry about one measly little bite." He was more concerned than he let on. "How do you feel?"

"It's swelling and it hurts, but other than that, nothing."

"David, what else can we do?" Summer asked him.

"Nothing. Unfortunately." He glanced at Chase, who'd moved from the cabinet back to the door. "Anything?"

"Snake food. Nothing that can be used as a weapon. Our only hope is to get through the door we came in." He turned his attention back to it.

David continued waving the torch to slow the snakes' advance. "You having any luck with it?"

"No. I think it's dead bolted from the outside. Hinges are on the other side too."

Pounding on the door startled him. "David? Summer?"

Summer yelled, "Adam! We're here! Open the door."

"Back up, I've got to shoot the lock off."

They moved down the steps, but no farther as the snakes now surrounded the area. Papa Bear held Sandy on his shoulders. Laura, Olivia, and Marlee crowded together. Sandy pointed and squealed. "They're coming closer."

David placed the makeshift torch at the bottom of the steps. "Shoot it!"

The shot came and the door shuddered.

53

The door flew open and Summer rushed into the office. She froze at the scene before her. Cops everywhere. Adam on the verge of passing out and Raimondi on the floor, his chest covered in blood.

Laura and Sandy followed her, Olivia and Marlee bringing up the rear with Papa Bear and Chase. The last one through the door, David turned and pushed it shut. The bullet had shattered the lock as well as part of the doorjamb so it didn't close well, but as long as it kept the snakes down below, that was all Summer cared about.

Chase muttered, "We need some serious pest control down there."

Officers swarmed them and, as soon as they realized they weren't the bad guys, started firing questions.

David ignored them and pointed to Papa Bear who had come into the office and leaned against the wall. "He's been bitten by a snake and needs immediate medical attention." He looked at Adam. "Looks like you do too."

The officer got on his radio and requested EMTs on the scene.

Olivia and her girls huddled next to an officer who began questioning them. Marlee sat on the love seat with yet another law enforcement official.

"David?"

Summer turned to the one who'd called her husband's name. But David wasn't looking at her. He gripped Summer by the upper arms. "Are you all right?"

She nodded. "Are you?"

"Yes." And Summer saw he was. There was an excited air around him, a glint in his eye that said he saw the end was really near. He finally turned to the girl who'd professed to be in love with him and dropped beside her. "Georgina, are you okay?"

She shrugged. Her gaze bounced between him and Summer. David took her hand and squeezed her fingers. The gesture squeezed something in the pit of Summer's stomach. Who was this woman to him? What else had he lied about? Just when she was hopeful things might somehow work out for them after all of this was over, the doubts crept back in.

"I'm sorry," she heard him whisper.

"I don't understand."

"I know." He looked up and Summer refused to look away from the two of them. Regret flashed in his eyes. He turned back and said, "I owe you an explanation, but not now. We need to get you to a hospital."

David stood and Summer sat on the couch next to Marlee. Her sister mumbled answers to the officer's questions, and he finally gave up.

Papa Bear sidled up to David and said, "Blue's got the elevators working. I told him to fade out of the picture as soon as possible."

"What about you?"

"I'll get checked out, get some antivenin, grab Doc B from the hospital, and disappear."

"How are you feeling?"

"Not so great."

EMTs and paramedics entered the room. They hauled Papa Bear off and then Georgina with her mother following, holding her hand. While they examined Adam, Summer walked over to him and she knelt beside him. "Thank you."

He gave her a wan smile. "I owe you a huge apology."

"You saved our lives. You're a hero." She took his hand. "You got here just in time."

"No. I—"

"Ma'am, he's lost a lot of blood, we need to get him to the hospital."

Summer moved out of the way and let the paramedics work.

Raimondi's body was photographed. The medical examiner finally arrived about two hours later, and Summer was ready to lie down on the floor and go to sleep. But she needed to have a conversation with her sister.

Marlee sat staring. At nothing. She'd been separated from the group and questioned by the officers as had everyone else. Now Summer could see she was lost in her thoughts, her betrayal. A battle raged within Summer. Everyone she'd loved and trusted had betrayed her. Lied to her.

David and Chase were still talking to the authorities. Things were finally starting to calm down and Summer had hopes that they would be able to leave soon. Ron stepped inside and Summer wondered about the badge that he flashed. Whatever it was, it granted him instant access to the room.

Marlee looked up and caught her eye. Shame darkened the woman's face and she glanced away again.

Summer dropped to her knees in front of her sister. "Why?" she whispered.

Marlee scrubbed her tears. "I'm sorry."

"But why? Do you hate me that much?"

"No." The swift answer told Summer at least it was honest. Marlee's gaze flicked to David. "They came to me about two weeks ago. Somehow, they'd tracked David to Charleston. I think he called his brother to wish him happy birthday or something."

Summer closed her eyes. Oh David. He would beat himself up over that one. A weakness. A momentary lapse in judgment and it had almost cost them all their lives. He'd taken a gamble and lost—and yet he'd won.

She opened her eyes and watched as they wheeled Raimondi's body from his office. "Why'd you refuse to go to the hospital?"

Marlee shook her head. "I don't deserve help. I wish Raimondi had killed me."

Summer's gut clenched. While she was angry with Marlee, absolutely furious with her, she didn't want her dead. "Tell me the rest of it."

"I don't know how they connected me. I guess they have their ways. Anyway, they came to me and asked me if I wanted to make some money. They told me who David was and that he was a con man. That he was wanted by the police and they needed my help to get him. I thought they were cops at first."

"And you jumped at the chance to help."

She shrugged and sighed. "I wanted the money, true, I'll admit it." A pause. "But more than that, I had wanted David out of your life before those guys showed up. When they arrived on my doorstep all official like and I thought he was using you for some reason, it made me angry."

"Surely it didn't take you long to figure out they weren't the cops."

"No, it didn't, but by then, I didn't care. I just wanted David gone and you back to the way you were before you met him."

"A spineless jellyfish?" Summer muttered.

Marlee blanched and looked away. "Of course not."

"They beat you up, Marlee."

She flushed and glanced back up. "I told you, that was my idea. The first time. I didn't know they were going to break my arm or that it would hurt so bad. That Corbin Hayes guy enjoyed it way too much. But it was the only way I could think to get you to come to me. If I landed in the hospital, as long as you found out, I knew you'd come."

A rap on the door caught their attention. Two uniformed pest control workers entered. The officer covering the door asked, "Are we about finished? They're here to get the snakes."

Summer looked at David. He gave a slight nod. She stood and held a hand out to Marlee. "Let's go. You need to get checked out at the hospital whether you want to or not."

Marlee stared at her. "Why do you care, Summer? Why would you offer to take my place when Raimondi had the gun on me? I don't understand."

Summer let her hand fall to her side and simply stared. "I love you, Marlee."

"But I betrayed you! I don't deserve your love!" Her shout brought all eyes to them.

Summer ignored them and gave her sister a gentle smile. "Doesn't matter whether you deserve it or not, you still have it."

54

David placed a hand on Summer's shoulder as her words sank in. Words that gave him hope that she could forgive him like she had just forgiven Marlee. A restlessness invaded him. He wasn't sure he wanted Summer to forgive Marlee. The woman had essentially done her best to have him killed. He wondered if she even realized that. Marlee was definitely petulant, selfish, and self-centered. But she was also, in some ways, incredibly naive, easy to manipulate, and foolish. Sort of like Georgina had been.

He winced at the thought. Could he hold a grudge against Marlee when his own sins were stacked to the ceiling?

Summer had no problem forgiving Marlee.

But that was her sister, she was blood. He was a guy who'd used her as a means to an end. He'd never imagined falling head over heels in love with her.

Summer held out her hand again to her sister. Marlee stared at it for a full thirty seconds before reaching up to grasp it like a lifeline. She swallowed hard and looked up at David. "I'm sorry."

The sincerity in her eyes held him. He nodded. "We'll all talk later. Summer's right. We need to get you to a doctor so you can get checked out."

Chase said, "The FBI's Evidence Response Team is going to

be here for a while. CSU might help, but this is FBI territory now. They've got a lot to process. Agostino's been arrested. He's cooperating and answering questions as fast as they can throw them at him. I have a feeling he might be our next assignment."

"What about Georgina and Rosalinda?" David asked.

"Rosalinda is being hailed as a heroine." He shook his head. "I still can't believe she shot him."

David nodded. "He went after her child. I guess motherly instincts can overrule fear."

"Where did Olivia and the girls go?" Summer asked.

"They're at the hospital also. I don't think there's anything physically wrong with them, but we just wanted to make sure."

Summer frowned. "They're going to need a counselor more than a physician."

"We'll see they get the help they need," David said.

Summer helped Marlee to her feet, and Marlee kept a tight grip on her hand. Summer steadied her as she wobbled, and David placed a hand under Marlee's left elbow. She glanced at him, unsure. But she didn't pull away. Summer wasn't sure whether it was because she was truly sorry for her part in the ordeal or whether it was because she might fall over if not for the support. They began walking toward the door.

Summer glanced at David. "Did you give them the laptop?"

He nodded. "Yes—or I will. Ron's retrieving it as we speak."

Summer bit her lip. "We still don't know who the man with the snake tattoo is. Raimondi had one on his wrist. The man in the picture on the laptop had one on his arm. What does it mean?"

"It's the symbol for Raimondi's family and those loyal to him. A Mafia symbol."

She shuddered and stepped into the elevator. Marlee began to shake and Summer tightened her grip. David pressed the button to go down.

Marlee finally agreed to be seen at the hospital but wanted Summer to stay with her. After two hours of pacing and flipping through magazines she wasn't interested in, Summer told David, "I know you're worried about Adam and Doc—" She planted her hands on her hips. "What's his name anyway? I feel weird calling him Doc B."

"Jesse Gonzales."

"Okay, well, why don't you check on him and Adam while I stay with Marlee?"

Doc had had surgery to remove the bullet that had blitzed him in the left side. Fortunately, the bullet had done minimal damage and now, according to Chase, he was awake and surly.

David hesitated, then nodded. "That should be all right. You've got a police officer outside the door."

She thought the precaution overkill. "We'll be fine. Raimondi's dead."

He thought about it a minute more, then with a long look that said they had a lot to talk about, started down the hall to the elevator.

Summer stepped back into the room and pulled the curtain closed. She turned to her sister who sat on the bed. "You're going to be all right."

"Maybe."

Marlee's answer concerned her. "What is it?"

"I just don't understand how you can forgive me."

Summer sighed. "I'm not sure how to explain it."

Marlee kept her head lowered but looked up through her lashes. "God?"

"Yeah. I suppose he is the only explanation."

"You always did get more out of church than I did."

Summer couldn't explain how she and her sister had turned out to be almost polar opposites, but maybe this experience would force Marlee to grow up a little. And possibly look toward the God she'd pushed aside all these years.

The minutes ticked by while they waited for transport to whisk Marlee away for X-rays. She'd been given some pain medication and Summer watched it kick in.

Finally, a young man pushing a wheelchair knocked and entered the room. "She ready for her X-rays?"

Summer shook Marlee's shoulder and she groaned, but took a deep breath and swung her legs over the side of the bed. "I'm dizzy."

Together, she and the tech managed to get Marlee into the wheelchair. "I'm going to check on Adam, okay? I need to thank him for everything."

"Okay. Tell him I'm grateful too."

Summer left her sister and walked toward the elevator, the police officer shadowing her. She was relieved the threat was finally over. Then thought about the unidentified man on the laptop and wondered if her relief was premature. She shivered, glanced over her shoulder to make sure the cop was still there, and stepped onto the elevator.

55

David knew there were several other marshals en route to the hospital. While Raimondi was dead, the trial was still set to go ahead. He'd be placed back into protective custody should he agree. He thought he might because of Summer. That was one gamble he wasn't willing to take.

Pushing a wheelchair, Chase followed him into Doc's room and tucked his phone into his pocket. The lines on his face and tense jaw didn't bode well. "What is it?"

"They found Mike."

David's heart clenched. "Dead?"

"Yeah. Shot in the head, execution style."

David nodded and swallowed hard. Mike had been gruff and a little rough around the edges, but he'd been a friend and he'd been willing to die for David. Sorrow pierced him. Just one more reason to make sure he made it to the trial. Determination filled him. Mike's death wouldn't be in vain. Not if he could help it.

Doc watched them. "Sorry to hear that."

David shook his head. He'd have to grieve later. And visit Mike's family. "You ready to get out of here?" he asked Doc.

"I'm past ready. I'm not used to being on this side of the knife and I can tell you right now, I don't like it."

"Yeah. Adam didn't either."

Together David and Chase got Doc to his feet and into the wheelchair. Sweat dotted the man's dark face and David could hear him breathing a little heavier. "What's your cover story?"

"Wife shot me," Doc said as he pulled the blanket over the scrubs he'd gotten from somewhere. Probably sweet-talked a nurse into them.

Chase laughed and David snorted. "You don't have a wife."

"I know, and as soon as the cops get to that fake address I gave them, they're going to find that out."

"Too bad you won't be here for them to get all mad at."

"I'm going to get that when the colonel finds out I'm down for the count for the next week or so."

David winced at the thought but knew Doc would handle it. He checked the door and motioned they had the all clear. As soon as Papa Bear and Doc were gone, he and Chase would get back to Summer and stick like glue until it was safe to come out of hiding.

Summer knocked on the door to Adam's room and waited for his call to enter. She stepped inside expecting to see David. Instead Adam lay in the bed, his shoulder bandaged and the sole occupant of the room. He had a towel slung over the other shoulder and his damp hair curled around his forehead. "How are you feeling?"

"Like I've been shot." He gave her a twisted smile. The blinds of the window were open and she could see the sun beginning its descent. "I'm so sorry."

"I should have been paying better attention." His eyes slid from hers, and if she hadn't known better, she would have thought she saw guilt flash across his face.

Summer frowned and ignored whatever her subconscious was trying to tell her. This man had saved her life. "Did David come up to see you?"

"Briefly. He said he and Chase were going to help Doc slip out of the hospital."

"Oh." Shadows filtered through the blinds. "You want me to turn on a light? It's getting kind of dark."

"No. I almost prefer the dark right now." He swallowed hard and shifted, glanced toward the door. He took a deep breath. "I'm resigning from the marshals."

Summer felt as though a bolt of lightning shot up her spine. "What? Why?"

"I . . ." He shook his head. "I made some stupid mistakes and I—"

A knock on the door drew her attention from his struggle to say whatever it was he was trying to tell her. A tall man slipped in the room, well dressed in a heavy leather coat and a fedora. When he saw Summer, he jerked. Looked like he might leave, then removed his hat and stepped forward. "Hello, I'm Parker Holland."

Summer shook his hand. Something about him struck her as familiar, but she knew she'd never seen him before. "I'm Summer Abernathy." She studied his face in the dim light. A lighter forelock gave him a distinguished look, but his bearing was almost haughty.

Adam narrowed his eyes. "Uncle Parker, what are you doing here?"

The tension in the room increased tenfold. Summer backed toward the door as Adam's uncle moved toward him, shedding his coat and draping it over his arm.

Summer said, "I'll, um . . . just be outside." She let her gaze bounce between the two men. "David should be back anytime and . . ."

Parker reached over and flipped on the light. When he did, his shirtsleeve rose, revealing a tattoo on his left bicep. The head of a snake.

Summer froze as awareness hit her. The shock of white hair combined with the tattoo left her with no doubt who'd just entered the room.

A deep fear invaded her as she realized who was in the room with her and Adam.

56

David didn't bother to watch his former unit members drive away. He hurried back into the hospital and headed straight for Marlee's room. He rapped his knuckles on the door and waited.

When no one answered, he pushed the door open to find the room empty.

Puzzled, he walked to the nurse's station. "Do you know where Marlee Chastain is—and her sister?"

The nurse consulted her computer, looked up, and smiled. "Yes, they've taken Ms. Chastain to X-ray. I'm not sure where her sister went. Maybe with her?"

"Probably. Do you know how long they're going to be?"

"I'm sorry, I don't have any way of knowing. I could call or you could go down and find out." She told him how to get to X-ray.

"Thanks. I'll walk down."

David headed for the elevator wishing he'd left a cell phone with Summer.

"Summer? Summer?"

Adam's voice penetrated her stunned revelation. Parker Holland was the man on the computer.

He was the one, along with Raimondi, who'd been trying to kill her and David. And now he stood between her and the door.

She moved to brush past him. "I've got to go, Adam. I'll see you later."

The man placed a hand on her upper arm. "Don't be so quick to leave, Mrs. Abernathy. I'm always interested in Adam's friends."

Summer froze and pulled away from him.

"Uncle Parker." Adam's stern voice cut into her rising fear. "Leave her alone and let her leave. You and I need to talk in private anyway."

Summer backed away toward the door, never taking her eyes from Parker Holland's.

He pulled a weapon out of his jacket pocket and aimed it at her.

Adam sat up and swung his legs over the side of the bed with a grunt. "Put that away! Are you kidding me?"

The silencer on the end said he wasn't. He was dead serious. Parker said, "Get back in the bed, Adam. Summer, you go stand beside him."

Summer curled her hands into fists. Adam hadn't had a guard on his door, although the policeman who'd escorted her to the room should still be outside.

"What are you going to do?" she asked. It could be thirty minutes before anyone came to check on Adam. His heart monitor flared for a moment when his heart rate escalated, but he was so focused on his uncle, he probably didn't realize it. He was also used to controlling himself in stressful situations, so his heart rate didn't do drastic things. Like alert the nurses that something was wrong in room 512.

Parker Holland's eyes flashed as Adam placed himself in front of Summer.

"Get out," Adam said.

"You betrayed me."

Adam gave a bitter laugh. "You're a criminal. I betrayed myself and everything I believe in by even agreeing to help you." He paused. "Not that I really knew what I was agreeing to."

Summer's breath left her lungs in a whoosh. "You called Raimondi and told him David and the others were on the way up."

Adam stiffened. "No. I called my uncle and told him the deal was off and that we were going to get Raimondi." He paused and pressed his fingers to the bridge of his nose. "I was trying to give him a chance to run if he wanted to."

"But he didn't."

"My uncle came to me not too long ago and told me about a trial that was coming up, that he had a key witness who refused to hand over crucial evidence." Adam drew in a deep breath. "He said he was worried about how admissible it would be. He needed the laptop way before the trial because that would be the only way to ensure the right people were locked up. He asked me to find the location of the laptop. After all, family helped family, right?"

Adam raised his fist at his uncle, then dropped it when the gun didn't waver. "David described you to me. The man in the pictures on the coveted laptop. I didn't realize who it was at first. Until he told me about the tattoo." He glanced at Summer. "I couldn't believe my uncle would be involved with the Raimondis, so I kept quiet." He swung an angry look back at Parker. "But when you kept hounding me about the laptop, I knew it had to be you. I was stunned—"

"Shut up, Adam, and let's go."

Summer moved so she could bounce her gaze between the two men. But Adam wasn't finished. "I ingratiated myself with Mike and caught a lucky break when he needed extra help to guard you and David."

Summer stared at the weapon. She stayed close to Adam, praying his uncle wouldn't shoot him. Unfortunately, she had a feeling the man would do whatever it took to protect his name. "Raimondi's dead," she said.

"And I still need that laptop," Parker said. "I can't let the authorities get their hands on it. I'm sure my contact information is in there somewhere. Along with those pictures."

"How did you know about the pictures?" Summer asked.

"Sam sent them to me. Said he could just as easily leave the face in them. The only reason he's still breathing is because I held out a faint hope that he might tell me where he hid the laptop. Then I got word that David had it."

"Bennie told you, didn't he?" Summer asked Parker.

"Yes. Bennie was very helpful in a lot of ways. Divorce is a costly venture and he went through two of them. He also went through all of his money."

Summer's mind raced. She shifted and looked at Adam. "Did you tell them how to find us at the cabin?"

"No. I didn't know where you were at that point. And I never told anyone where we were."

"Except when we got to Raimondi's."

"Yeah." He looked at his uncle. "You tried to have me killed." Bitterness spewed from him.

"You wouldn't do the job. And you knew too much." A faint frown pulled his brows together. "I hated to do it." He glanced at the bandaged wound on Adam's shoulder. "Apparently my guy didn't know the difference between a head shot and a body shot." He shook his head in disgust.

Summer looked at the weapon in the man's hand. "So you're going to kill him—us—in the hospital? How do you think you'll get away with that?"

"I won't. We're leaving." He waved the gun toward the door. "It's not like I came here planning to do this now, I just wanted to talk to Adam. But you recognized me and it is what it is. So, let's go."

"And yet you have a gun."

"I always carry a gun. Never know when you're going to need it." He sneered. "Looks like I made a wise decision. Now move."

Summer asked, "How far do you think he'll get with the heart monitor and no shirt."

Parker Holland wasn't quite as cool and in control as he would like them to think. He was thinking on his feet, trying to come up with a plan that would allow him to commit murder and get away with it.

"Get a shirt on and let's go," the man growled.

"Forget it."

Holland moved fast and jammed the gun in Summer's face. She flinched and backed up. "Then I can shoot her right here. No one will hear the shot and she'll be dead. Then it will be your turn. The story of what happened will be a little harder to come up with, but I'll think of something. It's up to you, Adam."

Adam moved slowly, wincing with every movement.

"He's lost a lot of blood," Summer said, noting that his uncle had lowered his weapon. She helped Adam pull his shirt down over his injured arm.

An idea occurred and she wrapped her fingers around the wires on the patches of the heart monitor. "Don't scream," she whispered. And yanked.

57

David, trailed by Chase, hunted down Marlee, who told him Summer had decided to go visit Adam. Now back on the elevator, he tapped his fingers against his thigh and told Chase, "I can't relax."

"You've been living on adrenaline for so long your body doesn't remember how to feel without the rush."

David nodded. "Yeah, but I just keep thinking it's not quite over yet."

"The guy on the computer."

They stepped off the elevator to find chaos. Chase pointed. "That's Adam's room."

David bolted for the door only to come to a screeching halt when staff backed up. Adam walked out first and caught David's eye. A bad feeling grew in David's gut. Then Summer appeared in the doorway and he breathed a sigh of relief only to feel his blood start to pound when he saw the weapon held against her temple.

She walked slowly from the room to the hall. At the sight of the gun, the medical staff gaped and ran for cover. David stood in front of Summer and the man behind her. "Who are you? What are you doing?"

"I'm getting out of here. Just back up and let us get to the elevator. As soon as I get in the car, I'm gone."

Adam's eyes met David's. He gave a slight shake of his head. Meaning, if they got out of the hospital Summer was dead.

David had no doubt hospital personnel had already dialed 911. Help was on the way. He also figured the man with the gun knew that too.

Summer kept her eyes locked on his. Fear mingled with fury stared back at him. She said, "He's the man on the laptop."

"He's also my uncle," Adam said in a low voice. "David Hatchett, meet Judge Parker Holland, my mother's brother and a traitor to his robe, his family, and everything else you can think of."

"Shut up, Adam. If you'd done as I told you, we wouldn't be in this situation."

David processed the words even as his brain tried to figure out how to get the man to release Summer. "You won't get out of here. You can't even go home now. Let Summer go and take your chances with the court."

"I'll take my chances on running at this point." His jaw tightened and his eyes darted. "If only you had given up the laptop, none of this would have been necessary."

"Raimondi was willing to go to great lengths to get that laptop. He didn't want anyone to know you were in his pocket, did he?"

"Raimondi and I go way back."

"Well, he's dead now and you're on your way to prison."

The gun pressed tighter against Summer's temple and she winced.

"The cops are on the way, security is probably on the elevator and in the stairwells as we speak."

Parker pushed Summer toward the elevator. "Which is why it's time for me to say goodbye." To Summer he said, "Press the button to go down."

"They'll just shut down the elevators, Uncle Parker, please don't do this. Or take me." He stepped forward. "Let Summer go. I'll go with you."

"No." The man pushed Summer toward the stairs. "Tell them if they block the stairwell, I'll shoot my way out. They shoot back, they'll hit her, I guarantee it."

David's blood rushed through his veins and his heart pounded in his chest. How could he stop this? Summer pushed open the stairwell door and Parker let it close behind him. David followed, Adam close on his heels.

Adam was on his phone with Chase.

Chase headed for the bottom floor via another stairwell. Hospital security would also be waiting.

David could hear Summer and Parker rushing down the steps. The thought of Summer getting caught between a shootout terrified him. He grabbed the gun from his ankle holster.

A loud thud, a rattle, and a startled scream reached his ears. He continued his hurried descent, his small Smith & Wesson in his right hand.

Summer refused to give in without a fight. As the man behind her pushed her faster and faster down the stairs, she knew she had to act. She could hear David behind her. *Give me a plan, Lord.*

As her feet touched the bottom step of the second floor, she let herself go limp. Her move took her captor by surprise. She let herself fall, bracing for the pain she knew was coming.

With a yell, he grabbed for her, lost his balance, and crashed to the landing beside her with a hard thud. Summer's hip hit hard and pain sliced up her side. She couldn't help the cry that flew from her lips. Parker's gun skittered from his fingers, and ignoring the pain, Summer dove for it.

His left hand wrapped around her right ankle and jerked her to a stop. She rolled to her right and her left foot shot out. Her solid kick caught him under the chin. He gave a strangled cry and his grip loosened.

She scrambled toward the weapon that lay on the first step of the next landing.

A hard grip wrapped itself in her hair and yanked. She screamed and fell back.

Away from the weapon.

With her peripheral vision, she saw his hand reach for the weapon, grasp it, and swing it around to point it in her face.

The look in his eye said she was dead. He would shoot her and run. She closed her eyes.

Three shots that sounded almost like one rang out. A cry, a grunt, a slight gurgle, and then all she could hear was the ringing in her ears.

58

David pulled Summer away from Parker Holland's still form. Blood pooled beneath the man and all he could do was thank God over and over that she was all right. Summer clung to him, then pushed him away and sat hard on the steps as though her legs would no longer hold her.

"I'm going to be sick," she whispered. "And I can't get up."

"Lean against me and take deep breaths."

She turned her face into his chest and inhaled. Once. Twice.

David looked up to see Adam staring down at his uncle. Sorrow etched deep lines on his face, and he looked like he'd aged a few years in the last few minutes. He shook his head and looked at David. "I'm sorry."

"Yeah. I am too."

Adam held his weapon in a loose grip between his knees. He stared at it. "I pulled it from my nightstand when he was introducing himself to Summer. I don't know why, I just . . ." He shrugged.

"You saved her."

"I had to." Adam's gaze met David's as footsteps and yells reached their ears. "I had to make it right."

David nodded. "You did."

The door opened and law enforcement swarmed them.

As Parker Holland's body was removed from the stairwell, Adam simply sat and watched. David held Summer and decided he didn't like being betrayed. Betrayal. There was no way to pretty it up.

No matter what label you wanted to put on it—family loyalty to the point of selling out your soul or using others to bring down the head of a Mafia family. Either way, it was still betrayal. David stared at the man he'd only known for a short time. A man who'd taken an oath to protect those he was entrusted with. A man who'd betrayed him. Betrayed Summer.

Adam dropped his head. Rubbing his eyes, he sighed. "He called me up and told me he needed a favor. He got me on your protection detail when you turned up in the hospital." He gave a smirk. "Bennie was the one who really pushed it. I had to get the laptop and I had to do it fast. They had to have that evidence for the trial. When my uncle couldn't stay out of it, I wondered what the deal was. Then he had someone shoot me. With Kevlar-penetrating bullets." Grief flashed and he blew out a harsh breath.

"You could have gotten us killed."

"I never told them where we were. I never used my phone so that they could trace it. I was as confused as everyone else when Raimondi's men kept tracking us down." He gave a short laugh. "All I wanted to do was get the location of the laptop from you and give it to my uncle or Bennie. That's it." He swallowed hard. "I never imagined he was involved with Raimondi. Not until you described the pictures that night in the safe house."

"You didn't know why he wanted the laptop?"

"No, I was trying to work it all out in my mind." He shrugged. "I just knew he needed my help, and he was family so I was going to help."

"And when you found out he was linked with Raimondi?"

Adam's jaw worked. "I called my uncle and told him to forget it, that we were going to get Raimondi and that I couldn't get to the laptop, that I wasn't trashing my career for him."

"And your uncle called Raimondi and told him we were there to get him."

Adam nodded. "He must have." He glanced at Summer. "I figured if I stayed behind with Summer, I could protect her. Keep them away from her."

David stared. "He put a hit out on you. That's why they didn't hesitate to shoot you to get to Summer."

Adam's jaw tightened. "Yeah. He figured if I would back out of helping him, I might even go so far as to turn him in, laptop or not. I was a loose end he needed to tie up."

"And yet he came to the hospital himself."

Adam shook his head. "He wasn't here to hurt me today. I believe he simply wanted to see where I stood, what my intentions were. But when Summer recognized him, he had to do something, act fast." Adam gave a sad smirk. "That's never been his strong point. He's never been impulsive. Everything he's ever done has been fully analyzed before being acted upon. Today, he just didn't know what to do when he had to improvise."

"And he made a costly mistake."

David tightened his grip around Summer's shoulders and shook his head, amazed he and Summer were still alive. Marlee, Bennie, and now Adam. Unbelievable.

Chase motioned for David. "We need Summer to give a statement, then you."

David nodded and Summer said, "They have to come to me. I'm not moving for the next few minutes."

Chase gave a small smile and sat on the step beside her.

Summer stayed on the step for a long time. So long, she lost track of time. She did notice that David kept coming to check on her before fading away again to talk to various people in law enforcement. The ME hadn't had far to travel, and in no time, Parker Holland was transported down to the morgue. His blood stained the floor and she couldn't seem to look away from it.

It was just hard to fathom that someone was willing to kill so his dirty deeds wouldn't come to light. But it happened every day and she knew it. She'd just never been this close to it before.

She didn't turn as the footsteps sounded behind her. She'd stayed in the stairwell for privacy. And to get her ears to stop ringing, her mind to stop spinning.

David sat beside her. "Hey."

"You used me," she blurted. Then snapped her mouth shut. Was she really going to rehash this? "You used Georgina." She sighed. "I'm not liking the pattern."

Yep, she was going there again. She needed to in order to let it go. At least that's what she thought.

David dropped his head and nodded. "I'll admit, I didn't think twice about doing it, either. Not then."

She clasped her hands between her knees. "So what happens now that my usefulness is over?" Summer wondered at her detachment. She figured she should be feeling something. But a numbness had settled over her heart.

"I know you think I used you at first, Summer, but that's not entirely true."

"What do you mean?"

"You were different. From the moment we met, I knew there was something about you that was different."

"So you've said."

"I don't want to lose you. That's the difference." She saw his throat work. "I didn't care if I lost Georgina because it wasn't really losing her. I never considered her mine, just a means to an end. I wanted to bring down Raimondi and she was my way to do it."

"But you consider me yours."

"Yes. And I'm yours. It would break my heart if you walked away from me. Which was one of the reasons I married you." She lifted a brow. He shrugged. "I guess I figured if we were married, it would make it harder for you to leave."

"You should have told me."

"I wanted to. Almost more than I wanted to live to go to trial, I desperately wanted to tell you everything. And I was going to do it too. Friday. Our day off."

She took a deep breath and shook her head. "I want to forgive you. I need to. When I thought you might die, I didn't want you to die with me mad at you."

"And now that I'm going to live?"

"I don't want you to live with me mad at you." She gave him a small smile.

Hope flared in his eyes. "Summer, I promise, I'll never lie to you about anything ever again."

"Anything?"

He thought about it. "If you ask me if a certain dress makes you look fat and it does, then yes, I'll probably lie about that, but—"

A surprised laugh burst from her and she smacked his arm. "Now I won't know!"

He laughed and caught her fingers. "You'll just have to ask one of your girlfriends." He sobered. "Why was it so easy for you to forgive Marlee? She betrayed us both. Wanted me dead for all intents and purposes and yet you forgave her on the spot. No anger, no bitterness."

"Oh, I was angry, but I don't think she thought about what would actually happen to you if you fell into Raimondi's hands. She just wanted you out of my life." She frowned. "I didn't know she was so dependent upon me. I really didn't." She looked him in the eye. "You saw it, didn't you?"

He nodded. "My brother was a lot like that. I finally had to sever all ties with him to force him to grow up. It didn't end pretty."

"Where is he now?"

"He's still on his farm, eking out a living and refusing to speak to me."

"I'm sorry."

"You didn't answer my question."

She sighed. "I don't know why I could forgive her like that. Part of it's because I know that's what Jesus did for me. Not just on the cross, but every day of my life. Part of it's probably because that's so Marlee. She's always looked out for number one. I don't really have high expectations of her."

"But you do for me."

"Of course." Sadness invaded her. "You're the man I love. The man I expected to spend the rest of my life with, grow old with. Share my deepest secrets with." She looked at him. "I suppose I've forgiven you. After all we've been through the last few days, I understand why you did what you did." She licked her lips. "It's just the trust factor I'm having trouble with."

"I know it's hard to believe anything I say right now, but I'm a changed man, Summer. I don't want to give up on our marriage. I don't want you to give up on me. On us. I want us to get through this and be stronger than we ever were before." He gave her a gentle smile. "Think about what we'll tell our kids when they ask us how we met?" The smile slid. "I know I don't deserve it, but I'm praying you'll give me a second chance."

Summer drew in a deep breath. She nodded. As crazy as it was, she believed him. Mostly because of the way he'd risked his life to save her while they were on the run. And the small ways he'd proven his love over the last few days. The last year really. "Well, I've figured out why I've been so sick the last few weeks."

"Stress?"

"Yes, that probably had something to do with some of it, but no." She looked him in the eye. "You know those kids you mentioned a few seconds ago?"

A frown creased his brow for one split, confused second before it cleared and his eyes went wide. "Are you saying—"

"I'm pregnant."

For a moment he didn't move, then in reverent awe, his gaze dropped to her stomach. "You're sure?"

"Pretty sure." She pulled the test stick from her back pocket. The pink plus sign stared back at them.

David took it. Stared at it. Then at her. "Where'd you get this? When did you have time—?"

"When we got to the hospital. I've suspected for a while now and was going to take the test Friday morning. The day we were supposed to spend together," she murmured. "I've had it with me all this time." She shrugged. "Right before I went to see Adam, I ducked into the restroom."

Moisture pooled in his eyes. He cleared his throat. "I'm going to be a dad?"

"Yes."

In one smooth move, he grabbed her and pulled her to his chest, squeezing and kissing her face.

"David," she gasped. "You're squooshing us."

He let her go, then kissed her. Once. Twice. Three times. Each kiss longer and deeper than the last.

She laughed when he finally let her catch her breath. "I take it you're okay with this?"

"I'm beyond okay. I'm thrilled. I don't even have the words to express what I'm feeling right now."

"I think," Summer said, "I think maybe you're looking for the word 'blessed.'"

"Blessed." He seemed to try the word out. Then nodded. "Yeah. Blessed." He leaned forward to touch his forehead to hers. "So are you going to forgive me?"

She sighed. "Yeah. I have to. I believe you're sincere. You did everything you could to protect me during the last few days of craziness. I saw your love in action." She paused. "You know, if you had told me and all this running for our lives stuff had never happened, I might not have been able to forgive you as fast."

"Why is that?"

She shrugged. "Because I probably would have let my anger simmer. I would have pouted and wanted to make you suffer."

"Ouch."

She smiled. "No, I don't know. I hope I would have been able to work through it pretty fast, but being together like this 24/7 has enabled me to get to know the real you in a very short amount of time. I never would have willingly spent this much time with you if I hadn't been forced to."

"So you're saying now that's it over, you're glad it happened?"

Summer gave a short laugh. "I don't know that I'd go that far, but . . ." She raised his hand to her lips and kissed his knuckles. "But I'm glad that God can take something so awful like murder and betrayal and bring something beautiful from it."

"Like us?"

"Yeah. Like us."

He went quiet for a moment. "After the trial, I won't have a job anymore."

"Actually you won't even have to go to trial now," Chase said.

Summer and David turned as one. Chase stood at the top of the stairs. He walked toward them.

"What do you mean?" Summer asked.

"Sam was killed last night by another inmate. Broke his neck on the basketball court."

Summer took a moment to let that settle in. A flash of grief sparked in David's eyes and he ran a hand down his face. "So there's no trial."

"Can't try a dead man." Chase squeezed his shoulder. "I know he was your friend. He made some rotten choices, but you guys were tight at one time. I'm sorry."

"Yeah, me too." David blew out a breath and looked at her. "Guess that means I'm unemployed as of now then."

Chase said, "You could always apply to the marshals."

David grinned. "Right."

Summer said, "I think you've found your niche, though."

"What's that?"

"Helping people. Working incognito to ferret out information to be used to put the bad guys away."

He nodded. "Yeah. I liked that part. I didn't like the info I uncovered, but yes, it felt good to see justice done."

"Then I think you need to look for a career along those lines."

"All right." He paused. "But I don't want to work for someone else. I think I want to be my own boss."

She lifted a brow. "I can see that."

"I'll think about it."

"And if you need an employee, I'd like to apply," Adam said as he rounded the corner and joined them on the stairs.

"You're really going to quit the marshals?" Summer asked.

"Yeah. I messed up. I should have told what I knew immediately." He shook his head. "If I don't wind up with jail time, I'll need a job."

Summer felt her throat tighten at the thought of Adam going to jail. So he'd made a mistake by calling his uncle. One that could have cost them all their lives, but he'd also done his best to rectify it.

David gave a slow nod. "We'll talk."

Adam nodded and winced as he moved to go back upstairs. Summer hoped he healed fast.

Chase clapped David on the back. "You two ready to go home? Need a ride?"

Summer glanced at David. "Not yet. We're still talking and I need to check on Marlee."

"All right." He gave them a salute. "I'll be in touch."

"Thanks for everything."

Chase gave a small smile. "Oh, here. One of the guys who investigated Bennie and the wreck thought you might want this back." He held up her purse and she took it with a smile.

"Thanks."

"No problem." Chase turned and disappeared up the stairs.

Summer captured David's lips with hers. "I love you, David Kyle Abernathy Hatchett."

He laughed and kissed her again. "And I love you, Mrs. David Kyle Abernathy Hatchett."

"So . . . after I check on Marlee, what do you want to do?"

He gave her a wicked grin. "Go home and take a nap."

Summer gave him a shove and his laughter was the best thing she'd heard in a long time.

"I have a better idea," he said.

"What's that?"

"I hear Jupiter Wind is going to be playing in concert tomorrow night. I know where I can score a couple of tickets. You interested?"

She pretended to think about it. "Sounds kind of boring after our recent excitement." His face fell and she hugged him. "I'm just kidding, silly. That sounds lovely."

He kissed her. "I love you. And I'm glad you're not running from me anymore."

She slapped his arm and smiled. "You were getting tired of the chase?"

"Not tired." He turned serious. "Scared. Very, very scared I wasn't going to 'catch' you." He wiggled his fingers at the word, then snagged her hands. "So will you be my date tomorrow night?"

She squeezed his fingers. "Tomorrow night and every night."

He grinned. "Deal."

ACKNOWLEDGMENTS

Many, many, many thanks to my friend, Drucilla Wells, retired FBI agent, for her priceless input into the story. If anything isn't accurate, it's the fault of this author.

Another huge thanks goes out to my buddy, Police Officer Jim Hall. Thank you so much for taking the time out of your schedule to critique my police procedure. AGAIN, if anything isn't accurate, it's my fault.

Both of these great people have taught me so much about law enforcement, and I appreciate it to the moon and back.

A huge thanks to my friend and critique partner, DiAnn Mills. Loved brainstorming this story with you. You rock, lady.

Thank you to Ginny Aiken for reading the story and giving me your spot-on comments. I appreciate you!

Thanks to my family, of course, for their willingness to allow me to do what I do.

Thanks to Barb Barnes! This book wouldn't read nearly so well without your keen eye and skillful tweaks.

Thank you, readers who visit me on Facebook. Your encouragement and love are powerful motivators to write the best stories I can for you and the Lord. Thank you for stopping by and making me laugh. Thank you also for sharing your trials and concerns and allowing me to pray for you. And thank you for allowing me to write the books I write. I love you all. ☺ If you've just found me for the first time, feel free to stop by at www.facebook.com/lynette.eason.

Thank you, sweet Jesus, for giving me the love of words and the gift for writing them. May they always make you smile. I give you all the credit and all the glory. Amen.

Coming This Fall

NOWHERE TO TURN

Book 2 in the
HIDDEN IDENTITY series

1

Danielle Harding pressed the ice pack to her bruised cheek and watched her husband back out of the driveway. No time for tears or for the hatred she felt for the man.

Instead, she turned from the window and rushed up the stairs to the master bedroom. From the closet, she pulled out her midsize suitcase and tossed it onto the king-size bed. She bolted into the large walk-in closet and grabbed the clothes she'd already planned to take. Next, the toiletries.

At the slam of the door she froze. Terror thrummed through her veins.

"Dani?"

He'd come back. No, no, no. Light-headed with the rush of terror, Dani grabbed the suitcase and shut it, zipped it.

Heard his footsteps on the stairs.

"Dani!"

A cold sweat broke out all over her body. She pulled the suitcase into the closet and shoved it toward the back.

Breathless, she called, "I'm up here, Kurt." What was he doing back? She should have waited.

Icy fear slugged her in the gut. She backed out of the closet and pulled the door shut. She made a beeline for the bathroom and grabbed the brush from the sink seconds before he stepped into the room.

"What are you doing?"

"Brushing my hair. It needed it." She dragged the bristles through the tangles he'd left when he'd grabbed her by the back of the head. Her hand trembled. She set the brush on the counter and turned to face him, hoping no emotions showed. "What are you doing back? Did you forget something?"

"Yeah. My wallet. Have you seen it?"

"You put it in your coat pocket."

"You sure?"

"I'm sure."

He stared at her. Before she could stop herself, she raised a hand to cover the forming bruise beneath her right eye.

"I'm sorry," he said, his dark eyes reflecting a remorse she'd seen too many times in their twelve years of marriage. A remorse that would vanish as soon as he perceived she'd done something wrong again.

"It's okay," she soothed. "You didn't mean it. It was my fault anyway. I shouldn't have pushed the issue."

She wanted to have a birthday party for their son, Simon. Kurt had said no. She'd begged him to reconsider and he'd punched her in the face.

He reached toward her now and she couldn't help the small flinch. His jaw tightened and his eyes narrowed.

Quickly, she stepped forward and placed a kiss on his lips. "I'll see you when you get back."

His features softened and he nodded. He glanced at the clock. "I gotta get out of here. You're sure it's in my coat pocket?"

"Positive."

"Right. Bye."

"Bye," she whispered.

He loped back down the stairs. She watched him from the balcony overlooking the foyer. He turned back and she caught her breath.

"I'll be home day after tomorrow."

"I know. Be safe." She tried not to choke on the words.

He gave her a two-fingered salute and slipped out the door.

Dani sank to the floor, her legs no longer able to support her. "Oh Lord, I don't think I can do this."

Jenny Cartee had assured her she could. Jenny. Dear, sweet Jenny, who'd recognized an abused wife and confronted her about it. Jenny, who'd showed Dani that she had worth, didn't deserve to be a punching bag, and helped her find the courage to leave before her husband killed her. Or Simon.

Just thinking about her son gave her the strength to rise to her feet.

Eleven-year-old Simon. If she couldn't do this for herself, she had to do it for her son. And her mother who wanted to see her and her grandson one more time before she died.

Dani waited fifteen minutes to make sure Kurt was really gone this time. Then she moved fast. She dragged the suitcase from the closet and finished packing it with her things, added Simon's, and then carried the luggage down the stairs and into the garage.

The black SUV sat in the far spot, just waiting. Only she didn't have the keys. Kurt hid them from her, said she didn't have anywhere she needed to go. Simon rode to and from school with a friend, and he was due home in an hour. As soon as he walked in the door, they would leave, thanks to a YouTube video that showed her how to start a car without the keys.

Dani went back into the house and up the stairs to the guest bedroom. She moved the nightstand and pulled up the swatch of carpet covering the small hole she'd cut into the plywood. The small box beckoned to her from its resting place on the two-by-four. She grabbed it, covered the hole with the carpet, and moved the nightstand back into place. She had managed to gather a few hundred dollars and stash the money along with some other items in the little box. But she needed more.

She hurried back into the master bedroom and set the box on the bed. Then looked at the picture on the wall. Before she had a chance to talk herself out of it, she removed the picture and looked at the dial on the safe. She'd played with the combination a few times, when the thought of leaving had consumed her. Always before she had come up empty. If this time was the same, she'd just have to take what she had and go.

Again, she tried birthdays, anniversaries, the time Simon was born. His brother's birthday, his mother's. Nothing. Frustration clawed at her.

Then it hit her. Kurt was a narcissist. It wouldn't be about his family. It would be about him. His pride. What did he cherish the most?

His job. His status. She tried his birthday, his graduation day from the academy. Her fingers stilled.

His badge number.

4892.

But she only needed three numbers for the combination.

She shot a glance at the clock. Time ticked away. Maybe she should just give up.

But not yet.

Something pushed her to get into the safe. She spun the dial. 4-8-9.

Nothing.

She ran her sweaty palms down her jean-clad thighs. Heart pounding faster than usual, she went back to the combination. 8-9-2.

Nothing.

48-9-2. She pulled the handle.

Click.

The door opened with a quiet whoosh.

A thrill shot through her. She'd done it. The door to the safe stood open. She wasted a precious ten seconds just staring at the piles of cash in front of her. Then raced to grab a bag from her closet. Almost weeping with gratitude, she swept the money into the bag and, after only a moment's hesitation, emptied the entire safe.

Which included a Glock 17 and other items she didn't have time to identify.

Her blood hummed as she saw the stacks of twenty-dollar bills. Elation flowed. She would be able to take care of Simon without worrying about money until she found a job. A new name, a new place, a new life. The thought nearly made her giddy.

She shut the safe and replaced the picture.

And the clock continued to tick away its minutes. Minutes to freedom. Her heart beat hard and she heard herself panting.

Taking a moment to compose herself, she breathed in through her nose and out through her mouth. "You're almost there, Dani. You're almost there."

She raced back down the stairs and out into the garage once more. She hid the bag with the money under the backseat. She returned to the house to fix a cooler of food when the phone rang. She jumped. Froze.

Then glanced at the caller ID. Kurt. Her hand hovered over the handset. What would he do if she ignored it?

Turn around and come back.

She snatched it up. "Hello?"

"Stuart's coming by in about five minutes," Kurt said by way of greeting.

"What? Why?" Her stomach cramped. That would ruin everything.

"He's coming to get something I left in the safe. He should almost be there."

The safe? Really? Today? Stuart came by occasionally to get something from the safe, but today? Fear screamed through her. She spun to look at the clock. "Couldn't he get it tomorrow?"

"Why? You got plans?" The low threat in his voice warned her not to push him. Not when she was this close.

Dani swallowed hard. "Of course not. Tell him that's fine, I'll be here."

"That's what I thought you meant." He hung up.

She ran to the window and glanced out toward the driveway. No sign of Stuart. Did she have time to get the bag out of the car and put the contents back in the safe?

Movement at the end of the street caught her eye.

Stuart.

No time.

Her mind spun and the only plan she could come up with was to play it cool. But what could she say when he saw the empty safe?

Just thinking about being alone in the house with him made her shudder. Three years Kurt's senior, the man that made her skin crawl. Blessed with outrageous good looks, he had the personality of a viper. And the reflexes. Striking when one least expected it. Silent and sneaky with cold eyes she couldn't read and avoided looking at.

Her fingers shook, her blood raced. *Oh dear Lord, what do I do?*

Tears surfaced. How had she ever thought she could get away with this?

Stuart pulled into the drive.

Anxiety made her nauseous.

"You can do this. Don't stop to think, just do it."

She watched Stuart climb out of the car and walk up the steps to the front porch.

The doorbell rang.

Lynette Eason is the award-winning, bestselling author of several romantic suspense novels, including *Too Close to Home*, *Don't Look Back*, and *A Killer Among Us*. She is a member of American Christian Fiction Writers and Romance Writers of America. Lynette graduated from the University of South Carolina and went on to earn her master's degree in education from Converse College. She lives in South Carolina with her husband and two children.

Come meet
Lynette Eason at
www.LynetteEason.com

Follow her on

 Lynette Barker Eason

 LynetteEason

Also from Lynette Eason:
The WOMEN OF JUSTICE series